Bourbon & THE Best Man

JESSICA COSTELLO

This is for anyone out there burning themselves out trying to prove their worth. Those who matter already see it, and those who don't never will. Live for you today, no one else.

Note to the Reader

Thank you so much for picking up *Bourbon & the Best Man*. I never want to catch anyone off-guard with the content of my books so I just want to preface this story to let you know this book does contain adult content, and discussions of child abandonment, child death, alcoholism, and portrayals of emotional abuse, anxiety, and pregnancy (side character).

Happy Reading,
Jessica

Chapter One

HANNAH

How can our siblings make us feel aggravation and adoration toward them, simultaneously? It's something I contemplate after reading my brother's last text message.

HOLT

> Hey, meet me at the pub tonight around five, please? It's extremely important!!

Not only has he assumed I didn't have plans tonight (I didn't), but he's disregarded the fact that I'm avoiding all contact with his best friend, AKA the owner of said pub (he doesn't know). Come on, Holt. How dare you?

I throw my phone at the couch across the room and it bounces off onto the floor, but I don't care. If I avoid the offending device long enough, maybe I can pretend I didn't see his message. He's known for his dramatics, so his insistence that it's important is surely another over-exaggeration. I re-tuck the sides of my blanket under my legs, with my laptop teetering on my knobby knees, and an episode of Gilmore Girls playing quietly in the background.

I usually edit at the comfort of my desk and the expensive

desk chair I bought when I moved in with my best friend Val about a year ago. It's May, so my photography schedule is picking back up after my post-holiday lull that sneaks up every year between mid-December to early April. In fact, I shot an engagement session for one of my summer wedding couples the other day. I was trying to edit said session when I finally moved out to the living room.

Val almost moved across the country, but decided to stay right before her college graduation. We moved in together in the house she grew up in a week later. She lost both her parents when we were still in high school. It took her years to come back to the place. I think we've done a great job of making it our own, if I say so myself.

Instead of the few clicks I usually make in my editing software for each photo, I exhausted my usual tricks to make it pop, and still hated every photo I'd taken. It had nothing to do with the subjects themselves. They're gorgeous—I'm not sure I could have gotten better models if I'd tried.

No, it's everything to do with me.

I'm a complete fraud. I've made a name for myself in the local wedding world with the work I've done in the past few years. That recent success is thanks to finding an occupation I love.

I fell in love with photography from my first shutter click when I was a child, where I got my first camera from—coincidentally—my brother's best friend, Miles. A vintage 1976 Canon AE-1 35mm camera that I still use from time to time.

I lean back with a groan, my chair reclining with the pressure. I take a deep breath and slam my laptop closed.

Being a full-time business owner is such an interesting thing to get used to. I've still got eight days before I'm contractually required to have these photos in my customers' inbox. Despite that fact, I like to work through each gallery as soon as possible. It's just the way my brain works, and how I remember my intentions behind each photo I took.

Then there's the other thing to worry about. If I let myself be lazy, I'll get stuck there, and never accomplish my goals. But there's too much pressure on my shoulders to feel comfortable doing that. My business is my life now. I'm in charge of my future, and that thought is as scary as it is freeing.

The warning sound I'd set as my brother's ringtone as a joke years ago goes off from its place on the floor. I sit up, realizing maybe he meant it when he said it's important.

I set my laptop on the side table and click the footrest down, crawling on the floor for my phone.

"Hello?" I ask breathlessly on the last ring.

"I was beginning to believe you might be dead."

See? *Dramatic.*

"That would be better than reality, but nope. My pulse is still knocking as hard as ever. What's up?"

"Did you get my text message?"

"Nope," I say, just to tease him, but regret it as soon as he goes off on a tangent.

"This damn phone. I swear, I buy the newest, overpriced model available, and it's still not working."

"Holt, I'm kidding. I got your text. I was too busy working to text back. But while I've got you on the phone—do we have to go to the bar? Why not just meet at Mom and Dad's?"

"Hannah, I can't stress this enough—if Mom finds out what I'm about to tell you, half the town will know my news by dusk."

True.

"Okay, so come over here and tell me. Or better yet, we're on the phone. What's wrong with telling me right now?"

"Trust me, I have to do this in person. It's something you'll want to see. And I'm not just going to the pub for a place to meet. I need you both there."

I pull the phone from my ear and groan, rolling onto my

back on the plush rug Val and I went halfsies on when we moved in together.

"I'll meet you at your house quick, then you can meet Miles at his bar for a drink to talk about whatever has you bursting at the seams. You don't always need both of us there with you."

"Why do you keep avoiding him? Did something happen?"

"What?" My voice reaches new heights as I squeak out the word. "No!"

"Seriously, Hannah. If something happened, you can tell me."

Oh, okay. Well, once when you, Mom, and Dad were all out of town, I called Miles to pick me up out of the ditch when I ended up there after a photo session. I was terrified—and cold—by the time he found me. Between the heightened feelings and the urgency, I almost *kissed* him. I've been trying to avoid him ever since.

Nope, definitely not telling him all of that.

"There's no reason, Holt. I'm just busy with work, but I'll be there at 5. It better be worth walking away from editing for."

"Thanks, Hannah. I promise it's worth it."

Chapter Two

HANNAH

I arrive at the bar a few minutes late on purpose. I only live two blocks away and could have walked, but I needed a getaway car just in case things went haywire. As I unfold from the front seat of my trusty Toyota RAV4, I search the loaded parking spaces on both sides of the street in search of Holt's car, but don't find it.

Miles lives in an apartment above the bar with a stair entry that leads to it. Holt usually parks back there, anyway. And since he's punctual to a fault, I shouldn't have to face Miles alone.

When I walk in, I'm surprised by how different the space looks. I'd heard through the grapevine, AKA my family, that Miles has been putting his heart and soul into the place now that it's officially his, and it shows.

The fresh white paint on the walls really brightened things up in the dining area, making them pop against the exposed brick along with modern signage. There are metal accents all over the place, giving it an industrial vibe.

I'm so busy taking in all the newness of the place, including the large sign painted on the wall boasting *O'Har-*

row's Irish Pub on my way up to the bar, I don't even realize that Holt isn't sitting in his usual spot.

"Shit," I say under my breath, looking back at the door, wondering if it's too late to turn around and hightail it back to my car to wait there for Holt's arrival. Then my mind immediately flicks to the possibility that he's dead in a ditch somewhere because it's so unlike him to show up late—especially to a meet up he scheduled.

I take a deep breath to calm my nerves. I'm sure he's fine. He probably hit traffic on his way back into town. Besides, it appears Miles isn't even here because he'd usually be behind the bar, and that is occupied by a middle-aged woman with light brown skin. I'm trying to remember her name—I know it resembles a town or a place. Georgia? Savannah? Those don't sound right.

I reluctantly take a seat as the woman in question meets my gaze and nods as she fulfills an order. "What can I get you, Hannah?"

Oh, so she knows my name. Now I feel like an asshole for not reciprocating.

"I'll take a mug of your seasonal beer, please."

I admire the new metal and glass shelves that take up the entire back side of the bar while I wait. It really accentuates the brick wall off to the side with a huge metal door that used to be home to the safe when this place was still a bank back when the town was first founded. From the many nights I've spent here with Miles as he closes the place down, I know it's where the extra liquor is stored.

My traitorous chest sings with pride for Miles, taking it all in.

"I've never seen you around here before," a deep voice says over my shoulder. I welcome the interruption from thinking of Miles, although getting hit on by a stranger in your hometown bar is the worst.

I take a calming breath and turn around to find a guy in a

button-down shirt and striped, multi-color blue tie and a smarmy smile to match his stiff hair.

"Oh yeah? Then you haven't been around long enough. I've been here a million times."

"Good, now I know where to find you," he says, propping his forearm on the bartop close enough that the movement wafts his expensive cologne right into my nose.

Oh, Holt, where the hell are you?

"Do you care to back up, maybe?"

Instead, he scoots closer. "You really gonna act like this doesn't do it for you?"

Before I can respond with my fist to his face, I sense someone at my back and pray it's Holt.

"Hey, babe. Sorry I'm late. Have you been here long?" *Nope, definitely not Holt.* In a possessive move, one arm snakes around the front of me, a large hand grasping my shoulder in a half-hug. The other hand moves the hair away from the side of my face.

I'd be using what little self-defense moves I know to wrangle myself free, but I'm wrapped in a scent I've known for ages.

I turn to look back at him the same moment he leans in to kiss my cheek. I freeze as his lips land on the corner of my mouth. With the way we both pull back with wide eyes, there's no way this guy is buying we're a couple.

"Babe?" He asks, brushing my hair behind my ear.

I lean into the touch until I realize he's staring expectantly. Right, he asked a question. "Oh," I say, jumping to attention. "Uh, I just got here. Then this guy showed up."

The guy whose name I still don't know takes a step closer to Miles. "And I was about to ask her what she's drinking."

"Your beer, hun," the bartender says, right on cue, and she knows it by the look on her face when I turn to hand her my money.

She smiles as she takes it, then her knowing gaze finds Miles over my shoulder.

"Well, I've got my drink now, so you can head back over to your bros. Thanks, though."

"Whoa. Now hold on a sec—" he says, moving closer, but Miles halts his advances with a hand to his chest.

"She's been more than clear with you," he says with authority, and I feel a tingle down my spine at the sound of it.

To my surprise, it's all that needs to be said. The guy walks away in a huff, Miles staring after him the entire way. I hate that I find his possessiveness so attractive.

"What the hell was that?" I ask, the words coming out far more frantic than I gave them permission to be.

The man of few words shrugs and says, "It looked like you needed a hand."

"And you thought you'd give me your lips instead?"

A barely-there smirk lifts the corners of his mouth. "Seemed like you didn't hate it."

"It was chaste, as far as kisses go, Miles."

He leans in to whisper, "If you wanted me to kiss you for real, it's all you had to say, Hannah."

I'm not proud of the way his words cause a dip low in my belly. Or the way my hand clenches around a fistful of his shirt at the thought of one minute of uninterrupted attention from Miles and those lips I've spent far too much of my life imagining brushing against my own.

"Miles!" a voice says from behind me, but it feels like two hands at my shoulders, shaking me out of my inappropriate thoughts.

Miles bites his lip, still looking at me—touching me— before his voice rumbles in the back of his throat. "I'll be right back," he says, then reluctantly removes his hands from my hips and walks away.

I take a deep breath and trying to regain my sanity. But when I don't find it, I take a few gulps of my beer instead.

When my heart rate finally returns to its normal rhythm, I remember why I'm here.

Holt.

Where the hell is he?

I swear if he bails after what just happened between Miles and I, I'll give him a charley horse on his bad leg he's always whining about.

When I turn to the back door, hoping to find Holt, my gaze snags on Miles, who is already looking my way. He's standing next to one of his employees, leaning sideways to hear him, but he's facing me. I watch him nod, then smile from behind his beard. I look away before I do something stupid, like smile back.

"Carolina, do you need anything here?" He asks a moment later when he appears behind the bar.

Carolina, I knew her name had something to do with a place. I was way off.

She points to the cooler, and he's off, retrieving, then uncapping a beer before delivering it to its new owner. Then he sets his sights on me.

I take a deep breath, settling my nerves as he approaches, but I regret it as I inhale his cedarwood scent. At least there's the bar between us this time.

"Hey," he smirks.

"Hey," I say, feeling my cheeks flush with his full attention. "You're so important now. It's weird."

"Well, it's been so long since you stepped foot in my bar, a lot has changed."

My playful smile drops. "Right, it has been a while."

His expression is unreadable when his gaze finds mine. "Went from seeing you almost daily to—what has it been? Five, six months?"

"We saw each other at New Year's," I answer lamely.

"Not sure five minutes counts, Hannah," he says pointedly, referring to the fact that I left as soon as he walked through the door at my parents' place. This is the first time I've stopped to consider that maybe this friendship hiatus has been hard for him as well. But like they always do with me, the hard lines of his face soften as he takes on a teasing tone, "Started thinking maybe you've been avoiding me."

Shit.

"No, just been busy with work."

His brow furrows. "Really? I didn't know the winter months were a busy time for photographers."

They're not.

"Oh yeah, it's when I do a lot of my admin work."

Lies.

He smirks and shakes his head like he doesn't believe me for a second. I expect him to press me on it, but he lets it go. "Next time you're going to go home and pour yourself a glass of wine, stop and say, wouldn't Miles prefer to pour me a drink? And come here instead—your drink's on me."

"And if you're not the one behind the bar?"

"I'm either in my office, or up in my apartment. Just come find me."

"I don't want to interrupt. What if you have a girl up there with you?"

He scratches at his beard, smiling at his boots. "Yeah, no need to worry your pretty little head about that, Hannah."

"Noted. And I am proud of you, Miles. You've already done great things with the place. I can't wait to see it thrive."

His brows jump so quickly, I begin to think I imagined it. "That feels so far away."

"What do you mean?"

He waves off my worry, something he's good at. Miles is the type of guy who will stand up for his people at the drop of a hat, but the minute you try to reciprocate, he shuts it down. "Ah, nothing. Just growing pains."

"I'm glad you finally decided to make an appearance," he says, doing just that.

I smile at him, but before I can reply, a familiar voice comes from behind us. "Sorry I'm late, guys. Crazy afternoon at the office."

Miles and I give each other a prolonged look before turning to Holt, who sits at the barstool next to mine.

"Holt, you're never late for anything. You think I'm really going to believe you asked us to get here at five when you knew you'd have a meeting run long?"

"I've been spacing everything lately. I apologize." He accepts the beer Miles sets in front of him, and he knew what he'd be drinking because if my brother is anything, it's predictable. Except for today, apparently.

"Could the thing that's been making you spacey also be the reason you forced us to meet you today?" Miles asks, and I try not to watch him as he shoves the sleeves of his charcoal gray henley up his forearms. I fail miserably.

"It's definitely the reason, yes."

"Okay, so tell us," I demand, pulling my attention from the most glorious forearms I've ever laid eyes on.

Holt looks around at all the people near us. "Can we go somewhere a little more private for this?"

My face drops and I'm immediately thinking the worst. "Are you sick?"

"I have had a runny nose the past few days," Holt says, swiping a finger along the tip of his nose like it's second nature.

I smack his arm. "That's not what I meant, but thank goodness."

"Oh," he says, his eyes widening. "Oh, no, Han, I'm not sick. We're here for a happy reason, I promise."

"Okay, well get on with it then!"

"There's no one in the back room," Miles says, already rounding the bar. "Let's go there."

After a swig of my beer, I follow the guys into the room that doesn't get used as often as it did in the past when Miles' grandpa owned the place. I write myself a mental note to ask Miles what he plans to do with the it.

Miles leads us to a high top table in the secluded back corner of the room.

I stand there with my arms crossed, waiting for this so-called important news, but Holt pulls out a chair and looks at me expectantly.

I furrow my brow, thoroughly annoyed by my brother's enraging ability to draw things out, but take a seat.

Miles sits down in the seat next to me, his knee knocking against mine as we get settled, raising goosebumps on my skin.

I glance over at Miles, to find he's already watching me. Did that affect him too? I mentally shake away the thought and turn to Holt.

Before I can say anything, Miles speaks up. "So you going to tell us why you're rallying the troops, or is this some type of social experiment to see which one of us turns on you first?"

I'm just about to admit it will be me when Holt pats his pockets. Finally, in one of the internal pockets of his jacket, he retrieves something.

He's got his hand closed around it, so at first I can't see what it is, but in one swift motion, he pops open a black velvet box.

Working in the wedding industry, it shouldn't take me as long as it does for my brain to compute what I'm looking at. But when I take in the rose gold ring with an oval center stone and two circular side diamonds, glittering against the black backdrop of the box, I gasp.

"Holt, what are you doing with a wedding ring?" I ask, vibrating with excitement as I wiggle in my seat.

His smile is infectious as his gaze bounces between Miles and me. "I'm gonna ask Serena to marry me."

I nearly knock the table over as I throw myself at him, wrapping my arms around his shoulders, squealing as he holds me.

Miles is right there behind me when I pull away. I back up and push Miles forward, helping him make the decision to go in for a hug. "Congrats, man. She's your person, and I couldn't be happier for you," he says, and they smack each other on the back the way guys do.

Meanwhile, I'm trying to hold myself together, tears of joy in my eyes, thinking about Serena becoming my sister for real.

Serena grew up with a really hard home life. She was in and out of of the foster care system, thanks to her dad's inability to stay out of jail, and her mother's drug addiction. She hasn't gone into detail about what she's been through in front of me, but I know that she's removed them from her life for good. My brother has vowed to give her a better life than she had in her first twenty years, but that didn't help with the trust issues she learned early in life.

She couldn't have found a more patient partner than she did with Holt.

When the guys separate, Holt sees the tears trailing down my cheeks and crosses the space between us to pull me back into his chest. That's one thing about my brother. He gives the best hugs.

"Love you, Holt. I'm so happy for you."

"Thanks, baby sister. I hope you know I want you hiding in the bushes for the engagement."

I pull away to look at him. "Consider me there. Oh, she's going to be so excited."

"You think so?"

"Holt, she's been in love with you since you met in college, even when you had a girlfriend," Miles adds. "Of course she'll be excited when you ask her to spend the rest of her life with you. She loves you."

Ever the affectionate person, Holt lets go of me and tosses an arm around his best friend. "I can't wait until you find this kind of love for yourself, man. You deserve it."

A flash of pain flares in my chest, thinking of Miles

finding his happiness with someone who isn't me down the road. It feels like a dagger to the chest.

"Can I see the ring again?" I ask, inadvertently ruining their moment with my own insecurities.

Holt removes the box from his pocket again, plucking the beautiful piece of jewelry from its place and thrusting it toward me. I take it with care, inspecting it from every angle as it sparkles back at me in the minuscule light of the room. It has a vintage feel, and it's absolutely stunning.

"It's gorgeous, Holt. She's gonna love it." I say, bringing my hand to my cheek as I hand it back to him. "Gosh, she's going to be the best sister-in-law. Do you think she suspects anything?"

He chuckles, putting the ring back in the safety of his pocket. "I would have married her back on day one, and she knows it. But I respect her for taking her time and making me earn her trust. I know she's finally on board with the whole idea, and I think she has an inkling, but I think she'll be surprised."

"You two were meant to be. I knew it the moment I saw you together that first time. I'm so glad you found each other."

Now if I could only find that for myself.

Chapter Three

MILES

Why the fuck did I do that?

This is the question I'm still asking myself long after Hannah and Holt have left the pub.

I've been in my office trying to crunch numbers for the better part of an hour, and all I can think about is Hannah's mouth. And how the kiss meant for her cheek nearly landed there when she turned. The cheek kiss that had been a terrible plan in the first place. Now I'm here, replaying it in my mind.

The pencil I'd been holding in my grip snaps. I throw it in the trash.

Dammit.

I grab another one from the stash that was left behind with the sale of the bar, along with a mountain of hidden debt that my uncle Stuart was secretive about for years. I've wanted to own O'Harrow's Irish Pub ever since my grandpa Lyle left it to my uncle.

When it was still under Grandpa's management, the place was crawling with patrons. The building was well-loved back then, but in the fifteen years my uncle owned it, it was border-line run-down.

I started working here as soon as Stu would let me. At fifteen, I was bussing tables on the weekend. By the time I turned eighteen, my uncle refused to pay the head cook what he was worth, and he walked. Lunch and dinner were no longer something the pub offered, so Holt and I ran our own lawn care business that summer after high school graduation. I went off to college, then came back to bartend at twenty-two. I've been climbing the ranks here ever since.

That year I returned from college and moved in upstairs because I had nowhere else to go. Uncle Stu charged me a steep price for rent on a loft I ended up fixing up out of pocket.

People told me I was crazy for staying as long as I did, but owning this bar was always the endgame for me. I knew I owed it to Grandpa Lyle to turn it back around. When I was young, we used to talk about the day he'd give the bar to me. But that was back when we thought we had more time.

I swivel toward the bookshelves behind me, where a framed photo of us sits.

I'm trying, I think, as if I'm actually talking to the man in the photo. He's got an arm around me in the picture, which we took in his backyard when I was eight. I hope he'd be proud if he could see me now.

I rub a hand down my beard and sigh. I need to go for a walk. I stand, shoving my phone in my pocket and head for the back door.

But before I can reach the stairs that lead to my apartment, I remember the mental note I'd made this morning before Holt's news changed the trajectory of my day.

I need groceries.

I reroute to my truck parked in a little alcove hidden from the rear parking lot of the pub. It's an old thing. The two-tone white and red paint no longer shines, and it's got hail damage from a bad storm we got four summers ago, but Grandpa and

I fixed it up together after he retired. For that reason, I'll drive it until it falls apart completely.

I jump in and reach for the key in the ignition and turn. I don't even remember the last time I took them out of there after parking it. No one locks anything in a small town.

Speaking of small towns, it's a short drive to the store from my place on Main Street. It's a short drive anywhere in town, for that matter. Perks of life in Wellford.

A few minutes later, I park in the small lot outside of Hodge's Grocery and head inside. There are plenty of cars here, despite the fact that the place closes in about a half hour. When I'm through the door, I bypass the carts and settle for a basket stacked off to the side.

I'm tossing a block of havarti in my basket when I hear my name from across the store.

"Miles!" a voice I know all too well yells.

I turn, a practiced look of exasperation already plastered across my face.

"Edie."

She's shuffling hurried feet in my direction, completely abandoning her full cart in the bread aisle.

"Oh, Miles. I heard the news!"

How on earth did Edie manage to find out Holt bought a ring? Is the first thought that pops in my head.

"You kissed that Hawkins girl!" She yells so loud my ears are ringing in the aftermath.

I look around and find at least three people attempting to appear like they didn't hear our not-so-private conversation. Dammit.

"I did not kiss her," I say, damn well knowing it's not completely true.

"That's not what Carolina said."

"You two need to stop talking to each other outside the workplace," I grumble.

"Oh, come on. You really expect your employees not to

talk to each other? What kind of pub are you trying to run, kid?"

I bite my tongue against the urge to tell her for the thousandth time to stop calling me that.

"Fine, you two can talk to each other, just not about my love life, got it?"

"Ahh, so you're in love?" She waggles her brows. "How sweet."

"No," I say, raking a hand through my unkempt beard.

Edith Massey is my sixty-eight-year-old employee, and she knows how to push every one of my buttons. Unfortunately for me, she does so with pride.

"That little blush rising above your beard is telling me differently, boss."

"Whatever you say, Edie. I'll see you tomorrow afternoon, okay? I've got to grab my groceries before Hodge's closes."

I walk away, but make the mistake of doing so in the direction of Edie's abandoned cart, and she follows.

"It's okay, we can pick up this conversation tomorrow then."

"There's nothing left to talk about."

I hear the *clack, clack, clack* of her house shoes as she runs to keep up with my large stride. "You know, you could take the night off tomorrow and ask that girl on a date."

"No."

"I'm sure she'd say yes."

"No."

"But Miles, you don't need to spend all your time inside the confines of that pub. You have to get out and live a little sometimes."

There's no way she'd know, but her words slap me right across the face.

I've been spending too much time at the pub. My therapist says so, so do Holt and Serena. And now it's coming from my own employees?

But I just can't see a way out of it. I'm so overwhelmed with all these new responsibilities, I can hardly function in the outside world without feeling this bone-deep need to get back to the office.

Even now, doing a mundane things like buying food in order to survive, I feel like I should be there instead.

"I will once I feel like I have things under control."

She lightly smacks my arm with the back of her hand. "That's the thing though, boss. Things will never be perfectly under control. You can't control everything that happens within those doors, and you shouldn't dare try. It'll send you into madness."

There's truth in her words. I'm aware of that. But I can't bring myself to relinquish control. Yet.

"I'm already mad," I joke, rather than taking her seriously.

"With that attitude, I guess you deserve it. Oh well. At least I can say I tried."

I pause in the aftermath of her words, my hand in mid-air on its way to a bag of cavatappi, and watch her walk away. Her blonde-grey curls are especially out of control this evening, but I think the style matches her personality best. She grabs her cart and shuffles out of sight. But her words linger long after I've unpacked my groceries and uncapped a beer on my sofa. My meal-for-one's steam rising toward my face as I find a Cubs game on the TV.

Dammit, maybe Edie's right.

I head back to the bar bright and early the next morning. I mean, ten is early for a bar, right?

One thing about living above my own business is if I'm bored upstairs, I don't see the point in waiting to come down to get some work done. So as much as I'd like to pretend I've had a social life these past several months, it's really not the case.

After I unlock the back door, I walk through and flip on all the lights in the back room and my office. My eyes catch on that photo of my grandpa and me, but I look away.

This is one of the rooms that was left untouched after I bought the place from my uncle.

The first thing I did as owner was close for a few weeks to make some much-needed updates. Thankfully, my grandpa had a friend in the next town over who knew all the tricks of his trade. His fair pricing helped keep things at least somewhat affordable, not that it made a difference for my bank account. Once I finally put away the power tools and started figuring out the dusty, unkempt books in the office, I realized just how bad in the red we were—and still are.

So not only am I trying like hell to figure out how to run this place after years of being an employee, but I've also got the dark rain cloud of debt casting a shadow on my life, and I'm just waiting for it to pour. I've been in a perpetual state of anxiety the past few months, and when Holt caught me balled up on my living room floor, barely able to take a deep breath, he explained I was having a panic attack.

I come from a family of men who don't talk about their feelings, so I never would have expected that to be my problem. It took weeks, but I finally made an appointment to find out more about the state of my mental health and am proud to say I've been spending the past several weeks unloading years of suppressed emotions on an amazing therapist I found, thanks to Holt and Serena.

And although it helps, there's still that voice in the back of my head telling me I can't do this. That I'm not good enough —again.

My phone rings from beside me, breaking me away from my wayward thoughts.

It's Holt's name on the screen, so I pick it up.

"Holt, did you miss me already?" I ask by way of greeting.

"Miles, I have to make this quick," he whispers, ignoring my ribbing.

"Why are we whispering?" I ask at my normal volume, refusing to play along.

"Because Serena almost found the ring in my pocket this morning. I don't know what to do with it. Would you mind holding onto it for me until I'm ready to propose?"

"I don't know, man. That seems like something a best man would do."

"Yeah, yeah. You already know that's you. So will you do it or not?" he asks.

"I'll be your best man."

"No, I mean the ring. Will you take it?"

"Of course. Bring it over and I'll put it in the safe at the pub."

"Okay, I'll meet you there in ten minutes," he whispers, then hangs up before I can answer in the affirmative.

The back door has its own distinct, metallic thud that announces a newcomer, and it's that noise that has me piling my papers neatly on my desk to make it look like I haven't been here for an hour already. But when I turn toward the doorway, attempting to look innocent, Holt is already squinting at me with suspicion.

"How long have you been in this office already this morning?" He asks.

"Asks the guy who puts in about fifty hours at his high rise office every week," I volley.

"Yeah, but I have a boss who tells me to go home when he knows what's good for me. I'm that for you. Unless you've got a girl I don't know about who can help."

"I think you know the answer to that."

He shrugs. "You've always been pretty quiet in that regard, so it really wouldn't surprise me."

"It's easy to be quiet about things that don't exist."

Auburn hair, green eyes, and a smile that will most likely be the death of me flash in my mind.

Stop. You're a terrible friend.

"Well, I think I might have just the person for you, if you're interested?"

I wipe a hand through my beard and I pick up my coffee cup. I hold it out in front of me as I stare my best friend down. "Absolutely not."

We both know what I'm thinking of right now. The last time he tried to set me up, it was with a woman he worked with. And not only that, but he invited me to dinner with him and Serena, but failed to mention it was a double date.

I tried my hardest to be a gentleman, despite my best friend's faux pas, but I didn't feel sorry enough to invite the idea of date number two. That's been over a year ago now, and I've been hiding from the dating scene ever since.

"Alright, well," Holt says, digging into the breast pocket of his crisp blue suit. "If you happen to change your mind. Please let me know and I'll make arrangements."

I shake my head as he holds out the black velvet box he introduced last night, my arm tingling with the realization of how important a task my best friend is giving me.

"Thanks for trying, but no."

He's still staring at me, his hand gripped tightly around the ring box.

"You can let go now, man," I say.

"Guard this with your life."

I furrow my brow. "I plan to. I can't believe you're even questioning that."

"Promise?" He raises one bushy, dark brown eyebrow.

"Of course." His other brow lifts as if that phrase wasn't confirmation enough for him. "I promise, Holt. Now let it go. I'll let you watch me put it in the vault if it'll make you feel better."

"It would," he says, finally letting his shoulders drop away from his ears.

I stare him down as I walk around him, a little put out that he doesn't seem to trust me, although I'd never say as much. "Follow me."

"It's not necessarily that I don't trust you, Miles," Holt says as he follows me down the hallway to an unsuspecting door, which I unlock. It leads to a room where I keep the pub's money hidden away. This building was a bank many moons ago, so it's an old safe deposit box room and I know it's secure.

I swing one of the bigger doors open and pull my keys from my pocket. After setting the ring inside it, I turn back to Holt, holding out my hand and giving him a look that says, *there, is that good enough for you?*

He nods and I lock it. When we exit the room, I lock that door, too.

"There, now it's safe, and Serena can't find it either," I say as we walk out into the main area of the bar. I lean against the countertop as Holt jumps up into a chair.

"Any idea when you're going to pop the question?" I ask.

"Soon. I can't hold a secret this big from Serena for long. Just need to solidify a plan with Hannah, since she'll be taking photos."

The mention of Hannah is like tossing an ice cold cup of water over my head and letting it trickle down from there.

I missed seeing her the past several months, but I guess I hadn't realized just how much until I saw her. Now it's like my body is buzzing in anticipation of that next hit of her and that scent that reminds me of a tropical vacation that's always radiating from her, all sunshine and ocean breeze.

"Alright, well, I'd better get to work. And you've still got several hours before your workday starts. Go enjoy the nice spring day before you start hunching over that damn P & L worksheet you didn't think I saw earlier."

I give him a noncommittal sound on his way out the door. But when I sit back down in my chair, my mind is nowhere near the lack of accounting records that were kept before taking over.

No, it's on those lips I almost mistakenly kissed last night. That clever mind that always keeps me on my toes. Thoughts of Hannah have taken over my brain again, and unlike any other instance, this time, I let my thoughts roam.

Hannah may be my best friend's younger sister, but she's my friend too. I don't have many childhood memories she isn't in. And we've bonded over the years for different reasons.

Where Holt is the analytical one, Hannah and I have always been creative. Her, far more than me, with her thriving photography business, but it's one reason we get along so well. When Holt and Val, Hannah's best friend, Val, were obsessing over life plans and problem solving, Hannah and I were off in La La Land, dreaming up fictional worlds and creating things we thought were beautiful.

I'd consider Hannah one of my closest friends, if it weren't for the hazy past several months where I've seen little of her. For the life of me, I can't put my finger on the exact reason, but we've grown distant, and I've spent an embarrassing amount of time wracking my brain for the reason why. It's not that she's found out about the feelings I've harbored for her the past few years. I've done too well hiding them.

At least, I *think* I have.

It was like one day I went from being her biggest protector, and seeing her as family to lingering looks, and surprising feelings that I'm still not sure I know how to navigate.

I'm afraid to bring this up in therapy because I don't want to hear what I already know—that I'm a bad friend for having feelings for my best friend's sister.

Chapter Four

Miles

On Sunday morning, I wake with a start when there's a commotion at my front door. I spring from bed in nothing but boxers, looking for something to use as a weapon. I settle on a nearly seven hundred page book that I'm not sure I'm awake enough to use to defend myself.

But it doesn't matter, because when I round the corner into my living room, I find none other than…

"Hannah?" I say, the enormous book falling from my grasp with a thwack that could wake the dead.

She jumps about a foot in the air. "Holy shit, Miles. What are you doing here?" Then, as soon as she looks at me, she covers her eyes and adds, "And where are your pants?"

"Hannah, I live here—and I closed down the pub last night, so your ruckus you made opening my front door woke me out of my slumber." I wipe a hand down my face. "Wait, am I dreaming right now?"

She peeks at me, and when her gaze lands on my torso, I can't stop the smile that reaches my lips.

"You're not dreaming, Miles. I was told you had an extra tripod I could borrow. And that you weren't home. Holt gave me a key and told me to walk right in and it would be on the counter waiting for me, but I'm not seeing it."

"What? Why wouldn't I be here?" Am I only tired? Or does this surprise visit make absolutely no sense?

"Holt said you were camping this weekend."

I scoff. "I haven't been camping for the weekend since I bought the pub."

She throws her hands up. "That's what I was told. I'm as confused as you are right now. Do you have a tripod or not? Holt is getting engaged today, and he wants footage from every angle. I told him I could put both cameras out, but I'm down to one tripod because my backup broke last fall."

That adds some urgency to the situation. He picked up the ring yesterday afternoon, but still wasn't sure when it was happening.

"Uh," I scratch the back of my head, trying to get my sleepy mind to work. "It's around here somewhere. You mind if I put some pants on first?"

Her gaze jumps below my waist and away again so quickly, I question whether it actually happened. "Yeah, do your thing. I'll just hang out—" she looks around. "On the couch," she says with finality, walking across the room.

I step through the first pair of athletic shorts I find on my bedroom floor, and make a pit stop in the bathroom to pee and brush my teeth. *Christ, I look terrible*, I think, checking my appearance in the mirror. A glance at the clock says it's only eight in the morning, which means I was asleep for about five hours. No wonder.

I grab a sweatshirt and am still tossing it over my head when I walk out to the living area, where Hannah's pointedly staring at her phone.

"Give me one second to find that tripod for you," I say, padding across the room to the one closet I have in this tiny apartment, besides the one in my bedroom.

"Thanks, Miles."

When I open the door, at least five things fall out at me. It's a pretty good sign of how this will go. "How soon do you need this?" I ask.

When I turn, Hannah's looking at the closet like I just opened a portal to hell, which isn't far off. I've been wanting a house for a while. Then I went and sunk my savings into a bar.

"I've got time," she lifts to standing, "but not much. Let me help."

With her this close, all my nerve endings buzz like they're begging for her touch. When she grabs boxes and random articles of clothing from me, our fingers brush each time.

Bring up the accidental kiss! My heart screams in my chest.

Hell no! My head demands.

It's been a long time since I've been in Hannah's presence without a clue what to say. But these past several days, I've been thinking about her so much. I'm half worried I'll bring up something embarrassing or inappropriate, like *I've been thinking about you non-stop since I kissed the corner of your mouth. My lips can still feel exactly where the contact happened.*

How ridiculous does that sound?

"You have a lot of stuff packed into this tiny little closet."

I huff out a laugh, thankful Hannah brought up something neutral. "Yeah, unfortunately, this tiny little apartment doesn't have much storage. Hopefully I won't be stuck her too much longer."

"You mean you don't enjoy living right above the business you own?" she jokes.

"Surprising, I know."

When I pull at an old throw pillow I'd believed to be long gone, it snags on something and half of my belongings come crashing to the ground.

I jump backward to save myself from it and back right into Hannah, who yelps.

I turn around just in time to save her from falling to the

floor. And there she is in my arms, damn near parallel with the floor, her doe eyes wide open, hands clutching my shirt.

She's the first to break into a sheepish grin. "Thanks."

I prop her back on her feet, fingers lingering at her sides until I know she's back in her equilibrium.

"Don't thank me. That was all my fault. Sorry about that."

"No big deal," she says, eyes on the floor. "And it looks like it was all worth it." She bends down, retrieving the tripod from where it had fallen.

"Oh, perfect," I say, bummed we don't have more time.

"Guess I'd better get going. Thanks again for letting me borrow this."

"No problem, at this rate, you should probably keep it. I'm clearly not going to use it any time soon."

She lets it dangle from one finger. "You sure?"

"Absolutely. You said your other one is broken. Consider this your replacement."

Her signature wide smile stretches to full capacity as she clutches the tripod to her chest like it's something truly priceless. "I guess I would hate to see it get lost in Narnia," she says, gaze gliding to my mess of a closet.

Note to self: clean and organize the damn closet.

"Yeah," I say, kicking a stray boot back toward it. "We wouldn't want that."

Chapter Five

Hannah

It's an odd sensation, being abundantly happy for your sibling while also being abundantly miserable in your own life. Add in the fact that I showed up at Miles' apartment this morning thinking he wasn't home, only to be greeted by him in nothing but his boxers. He was so adorable, all sleepy-eyed, with his overgrown hair sticking out in every direction. I'm also not proud of the way I ogled his muscular chest and shoulders—or the way my gaze followed the trail of hair leading from his navel and under the waistband of his black boxers. And I'm pretty sure he noticed. I can always count on myself for new footage to cringe over at three in the morning when I can't sleep.

When I brought it up to Holt, all he said was, "Hmm, I must have had my weekends mixed up," then immediately changed the subject.

Suspicious.

I still can't believe today is the day my brother is asking his soulmate to marry him. I didn't know how romantic Holt could be. When he told me his idea, I was pleasantly surprised —and even more excited to photograph it. Serena's been through so much in her life, she deserves someone who worships every step she takes, and I believe she truly found that with Holt.

HOLT

Leaving the car now

The plan is, they're going to take a quick stroll through the park, something they enjoy doing together. I'm hiding in a wooded area near the picnic space he styled with my help. Underneath a tall oak tree with plenty of character and spindling branches, there's a sea of battery powered votive candles lighting up the scenery. In about twenty minutes, the lighting will be perfect, giving them just enough time to get here. I have a perfect vantage point, and we made sure it was somewhere I wouldn't be visible. I even bought a camouflage sweatshirt to blend in.

HANNAH

I'm ready. Good luck!

Something I hadn't been expecting was tears. Before they even arrive, I'm wiping at my eyes. This isn't even my first proposal. I guess they've all had me in my feelings in their own way. But I have heightened feelings, knowing it's my brother who's about to get engaged.

I take photos as soon as they appear in the spot we practiced. They look too adorable hand-in-hand as Serena looks up at Holt with so much love in her eyes. Then she turns and sees the little area we set up before Holt went to pick her up. She stops to look at him in surprise. *Snap.*

What is this? I read from her lips as she looks between it and Holt.

They talk back and forth, but I'm too far away to hear. But it's clear where the conversation goes when Holt drops to one knee, and Serena's hand claps over her mouth in surprise. My shutter goes off non-stop, the entire moment feeling like an out-of-body experience.

It's obvious Serena says yes as she covers her mouth, then drops to her own knees to throw her arms around Holt's shoulders.

They pause for a moment as Holt slips the ring on her finger. Then they're embracing once more. By the time Serena tackles Holt flat to the ground, I know I've gotten plenty of great photos. I continue snapping until I notice Holt pointing into the trees, and I know that's my cue. I pop up out of my hiding spot with all my gear in hand and wave as Serena's tears fall to her cheeks. Even Holt's eyes are wet, and of course, so are mine.

"Congratulations, future sister-in-law," I say, running to wrap them in a hug. "I'll give you guys a minute to bask in the moment, then we'll take some photos to remember the day, okay?"

"Okay," Serena says, blubbering.

"Oh," I say, rubbing her back. "Holt, come here and console your girl."

Then I back away, feigning messing with my camera settings, when I'm really taking photos of their cute moment together as Holt whispers sweet nothings as he wipes under Serena's eyes.

"Good job, brother bear. You did great. Both in picking out a wife, and asking her to marry you. Love you, Holt."

Holt hugs me back. "Thanks, sis. I'm glad you said that." There's a pregnant pause as they glance at one another. "I have just the person."

"That's unnecessary, Holt. You know I'm not dating right now."

Chapter Six

Miles

It's Friday night, and Holt and Serena threw together an impromptu engagement party. I've spent the whole day (and past week) anticipating seeing Hannah again. I haven't been able to get her out of my head. Which is why I spot her the moment she walks into my bar.

Her deep blue maxi dress swishes at her feet, her auburn hair in soft curls. She looks beautiful and nearly takes my breath away when she and her moss green eyes rimmed in jet black turn on mine. She smirks, but the eye contact doesn't last long, her attention stolen away by one of her dad's friends sitting at a table near the door. She's flanked by her best friend, Val, and Val's boyfriend, Brody, who I've come to be friends with over the past several months.

I run a hand down my dress shirt, straightening it unnecessarily as I attempt to look anywhere else in the room. I traded out my usual attire of a t-shirt or henley paired with my favorite black jeans for tonight's occasion, which only adds to my discomfort.

I help Edith behind the bar as an onslaught of newcomers shows up all at once. Soon enough, I've got Brody standing in front of me, an odd look on his face. After a moment's stand-off, his mouth cracks into that smile he always seems to wear.

"Miles, the pub looks great."

"Thanks for coming in. What can I get you?"

"I'll have a Corona with lime and two of those fruity, pink drinks everyone's walking around with." He says, twiddling his fingers in an all-encompassing circle.

"Tab or close it out?"

"Tab please," he says, holding out his card to me.

I hand over his beer and set two glasses on the bar and whip up the two fruity drinks, using extra care to make them well, knowing one will be Hannah's.

As I'm adding the garnishes, I look up. The space is really filling in quickly as guests arrive for Holt and Serena's celebration. They still haven't arrived yet.

I set the two drinks in front of Brody and my eyes flick in Hannah's direction of their own volition, meeting her gaze that bounces away almost immediately. I turn back to find him giving me a knowing smile. "Enjoy," I say, then turn away toward the next customer. It feels like he knows something he shouldn't.

A cheer rings out amongst the patrons who are strewn about, and I turn to the door as I pull the tap handle on one of the most popular seasonal beers we stock. I find the reason for the commotion at the door. Holt and Serena just walked in hand-in-hand. They look every bit the happy couple I know them to be, but with an all-new engagement glow about them.

Great. As if I didn't already feel single as fuck. But I am happy for them. Besides, I knew this day would come sooner than later.

Even the people who didn't show up at the pub specifically for them cheer and clap. That's the type of person Holt is in our community. He's the guy with a smile always at the ready. The one who has not only built wealth in the short time since he graduated college but also uses it to help those in need. I'm aware I couldn't have done better at picking out a best friend.

He turns to smile and wave at me. After a few hugs and hellos, they're both heading in my direction.

"Congrats again," I say as I smack Holt's back, then turn to Serena. "Now let's see this ring."

She flashes me a megawatt smile before thrusting her hand in front of my face and wiggling her fingers. The move makes the rock on her hand sparkle. "It's as beautiful as the person wearing it. Congratulations, Serena, and welcome to the family." I throw an arm around Holt's shoulders as I say, "I promise to help keep this guy in line, and to make sure he's bringing his best back home to you, as I always have."

"Aw, thanks Miles," she says, throwing her arms around me in a hug. "You really are sweet when the words finally come out. I bet if you tried that with more girls, you'd be next in line behind us to get married."

"Alright, that's enough, you two," Holt says, pulling his girl out of my arms and into the barricade of his own.

I have to laugh, because for some ridiculous reason, Holt believes he needs to guard his girl from me. My smile falters when I turn to find who just walked up beside us. So much for keeping my cool.

"Hey," Hannah says. Her eyes are on me when she says the greeting, but they quickly shift to Holt and Serena standing beside me. "Sorry to break up your little powwow. Mom and Dad are trying to get everyone to go to the back room. I figured if you two walk that way, everyone would follow."

"Makes sense," Holt says, smacking me on the arm. "You'll meet up with us when you can?"

I nod, watching him lead his fiance away.

I turn to Hannah, who's already looking at me. "Thanks for letting them take over your pub tonight. Don't work too hard. And come see us, okay?"

"Will do," I say, catching her smile before she turns away, my whole body itching to follow, but I've got a job to do.

"You're staring," Edith whispers from the side of her mouth.

My gaze snaps to hers. "Excuse me?"

"It's a bartender's job to be observant. And I can't help but notice your eyes have been tracking the same person all night long." She nods her head in the direction Hannah just walked. "That girl in the pretty blue dress who just came out of the bathroom. It's her, isn't it? Your best friend's little sister?"

I knew as soon as I looked at tonight's schedule that Edith would make it a priority to give me endless shit about Hannah after what she said the other night in Hodges. "She's his *younger* sister, yes," I correct, hating the descriptor *little* anything when it's pertaining to Hannah. She's a grown-ass woman. "What about her?"

"You've been making eyes at her, Miles." I turn my don't-fuck-with-me gaze in her direction, but she doesn't bristle the way most people do. Instead, she laughs. "Don't look at me like that, and don't you dare try to deny it. I'm great at noticing these things."

"Are you, now? And what's next? You going to psychoanalyze me?"

She shakes her head, smiling up at me. "No, I was going to say go for it. You two have known each other for a long time, yes?"

I roll my eyes, finally giving in to her need for control in this conversation. "Yeah, her brother's been my best friend since I was eight."

"Then let me let you in on a secret," she says, leaning in. "The people we know the longest make great lovers."

I brush a hand down my face, "Edie," I warn, feeling this

turning into an HR nightmare as we speak. "I know I'm pretty lax, as far as bosses go, but you can't go around saying shit like that."

She laughs again. "You should see your face right now, kiddo. You're all sorts of red, but what I'm trying to say is, my Archie was *my* brother's best friend. And after my brother got his head out of his ass and accepted our feelings for each other, it turned out to be the best relationship I could have asked for. You know why?"

"Because you already knew each other?" I ask, taking an educated guess.

"Yes!" she says, pointing her finger at me. "And relearning the things we thought we knew about each other was half the fun."

I scratch the back of my neck, wiping up a small spill on the bar in front of me. "Yeah?"

"It was," she says, setting a hand on my shoulder and leaning in close. "Now give me this," she says, ripping the rag from my grasp, "and get your ass in that room and celebrate that engagement and stop avoiding the poor girl."

"I'm the owner, Edie. You can't exactly tell me what to do."

Her smile turns sympathetic. "Whether you make a move on the girl tonight, Holt strikes me as the kind of guy who only gets married once. Do you really want to miss out on his only engagement party?"

Our gazes tangle in a stand-off that I know I won't win, but dammit. I'm making headway with my employees. I can't let this conversation make me look like some little high school boy with raging hormones that takes nothing seriously.

"Fine," I say, taking one last look around the room. "I'll go, but come get me if there's another rush. I'll only be a few steps away."

"Wait, one last thing," she says as I move.

I turn to find her holding out an uncapped Blue Moon. I

smile and shake my head as her smile lines all become more pronounced on her face. "Thanks, Edie," I say, grabbing a frosted mug and orange slice to top it all off.

When I cross the threshold of the back room, Holt is the first one to spot me. "Hey! There's my guy," he says, and the rest of the room joins him, erupting in cheers and clapping, and I absolutely hate the attention.

"Miles, come sit with us," Bobby says, slapping the table next to him, where there's an open spot between him and Hannah. "You've worked enough. Now it's time for some play."

Bobby's personal motto.

I smile kindly, already feeling my skin prickle with the gazes of far too many people at the table as I round it and do as the man I've always considered my second father asks.

When I pull out the chair, he stands to hug me. He's barrel chested, and his arms are huge. He now sports a bald head where there used to be thick brown hair like Holt's. "I know I say it every time I come in lately," he says, finally sitting down as I follow his lead, "but you've sure done some great things with the place, Miles. Jenny and I sure are proud of you."

"Thank you, Bobby. Means a lot."

I settle into my chair, accidentally bumping into Hannah.

"Sorry," I whisper, but she's too focused on whatever Val's saying on the other side of her to turn. Instead, she taps my arm a couple times without even looking as if to say no problem. I don't know why, but the gesture feels more intimate.

"Hey, you two," Serena says, weaseling between both our chairs a minute later. "Do you have a minute for Holt and I?"

"For sure," I say, as Hannah says, "Yeah, of course," at the same time.

I let Hannah stand first, then follow behind her to a quiet corner of the room where Serena and Holt stop, smiling back at us.

"So what's up?" Hannah asks, voicing my thoughts.

The two lovebirds look at each other with excitement all over their faces. "Well, for starters," Serena says, "We got to talking last night, and we decided we'd rather have a quick engagement than a long one, so we're hoping to get married soon, but we'll see."

Holt takes her hand and adds, "Of course, Hannah, we'd love to have you as our photographer if you'd be willing," then he looks at Serena with so much love in his eyes. "Since we've got you both here right now, we have something to ask you both. With how small of a wedding we're thinking about having, we're each going to have one person standing up with us on our wedding day." Holt wipes at his eyes with his free hand. "So, Miles, will you be my best man?"

And even though he already pretty much told me this was happening, I'm feeling emotional too as I say, "Yes, of course I will, Holt," bringing him in for a hug.

Then before I pull away, Serena says, "And Hannah," we break apart and I watch as Serena takes her hand, "you've made me feel like your sister since the day you met me. And there's no one else I'd want standing next to me when I marry your brother. Will you be my maid of honor?"

Hannah covers her mouth and nods vehemently as her tears fall. "Oh my gosh, yes! Of course I will. Thank you, Serena," then they're hugging as Holt and I watch on, smiling.

When they pull apart, Serena says, "I know it won't be very traditional, since my maid of honor and the photographer will be the same person, so we'll need to brainstorm how it's all going to work, but we're pretty laid back, so it shouldn't be a huge deal."

"Where are you thinking of getting married?" I ask.

They share another look before Holt says, "We haven't made any concrete decisions, but we're throwing around the idea of an intimate ceremony at the cabin by the lake."

Cabin is a modest name for the six-thousand square foot monstrosity nestled in the wilderness outside of Durango,

Colorado. Bobby Hawkins' father was the owner of the place, but passed it on to all of his children when he passed away. The five brothers and sisters all spend their fair share of time there. Bobby and Jenn have brought me on plenty of family trips to the cabin over the years.

"That would be perfect!" Hannah says, truly crying now. Before I can talk myself out of it, I put my arm around her, rubbing my hand up and down her bare arm until she finally wraps her arm around my waist, leaning right into me.

"And if it isn't too much, we'd love any help we can get with the wedding planning. But only if you're free," Serena adds.

"You know I'm in!" Hannah says, doing a little happy dance and making my arm bounce on her shoulders.

"Miles?" Holt asks. "What do you say?"

Planning a wedding is about the last thing I'd like to do, but I know Holt would jump at the opportunity to help if roles were reversed.

"Yeah, what about you, Miles? You game to help plan a wedding with me?" Hannah says, her pink-painted lips spreading into a smile.

And that right there is the reason I never knew I needed to help my best friend plan his wedding despite how busy things have been at the bar.

The prospect of extra time spent with his sister.

"Yeah, of course," I say, a smile spreading on my own lips. "I'm happy to help."

Chapter Seven

HANNAH

It's my first wedding-free weekend since spring began. I was looking forward to sleeping in this morning, but Serena has other plans.

Instead, I wake up to a quick succession of dings from my nightstand. I open my phone to find Serena's started a group text.

SERENA

Hey, friends. Thanks again for agreeing to be a part of our day! Love you guys!

MILES

Y'all are up and at 'em early.

HOLT

You know how I feel about early rising, Miles.

MILES

Let me guess, you've already gotten your run and green smoothie in for the day. More power to you. But some of us had a bar to close last night and have another two hours of sleep before we're ready for the day.

40

SERENA

Crap. Sorry, Miles!

HOLT

Don't apologize, babe. He'll be fine. I'm sure he's just glad it wasn't a wake up call in the form of Hannah breaking down his door again this time. Speaking of…Hannah, where you at?

HANNAH

Was trying to catch my own beauty sleep. It's my first Saturday with no weddings in a month. But hello, everyone!

SERENA

I always forget you work primarily on weekends. Sorry!

MILES

Yes, some of us have non-traditional jobs and don't get to leave the office on a Friday night at 5. Solidarity, Hannah. Glad you have the weekend off, though.

HANNAH

9 to 5, ick! One more session this evening stands between me and a stiff drink.

MILES

Hey, my pub is full of those. Come in and see me later. Sounds like I'll be working at the pub all night. I could use the company.

HOLT

Wasn't the whole point of owning the bar so you don't have to work nights and weekends anymore, Miles? What's going on over there?

MILES

There's this thing called ownership. If no one else can cover it, that job falls on me if I want to keep the doors open.

HANNAH

You know, I might have to come visit. But I will be a PAYING customer. Friends don't let friends lose their bar by giving away free booze.

HOLT

Gee, thanks for the invite.

MILES

It's an open invitation to anyone in this chat. Come see me anytime!

SERENA

We'd love to, but it's date night and we're going to figure out some potential dates for the wedding. Does next Wednesday work for everyone to get together and talk timeline?

HANNAH

My night is free!

MILES

I'll make it work!

SERENA

Yay! See you then!

My shoot tonight took place just before sunset, so it's dark before I get back on the road that leads to home. I've been thinking about Miles' invitation all day today. Did he really mean it, or was he just being nice? If I show up, will he be annoyed?

Gah, I've been out of the dating scene for long enough that I don't even know the signs of whether a guy is interested. Or maybe it's just Miles. I've known him since we were kids. He and Holt have been inseparable for as long as I can remember. But when the two of them got on each other's nerves—which was always, since they're nothing alike—Miles would sometimes hang out with me instead. Especially if we were somewhere that he couldn't ride his bike home when he got bored. Like the time my parents took the three of us to the beach.

I was playing on my own in the water, and could hear Miles and Holt bickering like an old married couple back on the beach. Miles used to be a hothead, and Holt has always been sensitive, which caused many spats and disagreements.

In the end, I decide to go. Because even if Miles didn't think I'd show, he's still the type of guy who will make me feel welcome. And whether there's a deeper meaning behind the invitation, we're going to be busy planning a wedding together for the next several weeks, and it's about time we reconcile our friendship that has been on the back burner for far too long— and if there's a chance to turn it into more? I just might take it.

When I walk through the door, I get a perfect view of Miles throwing his head back in laughter as he stands across the bar from two of the regulars I remember from back when Miles was only a bartender. They're upward of seventy and I can tell they really adore him. Even better, they love giving him shit.

In fact, when I come into view, the one in a trucker hat says, "Oh, Miles, maybe this beauty would date you."

Oh, if you only knew.

His head whips in the direction of their gaze, and his smile is a sight that hits me so hard, my breath catches in my throat.

"Gentlemen, this is Hannah. You remember Holt right?"

"Of course we remember Holt!" One of them says.

"Hannah is his sister, and a good friend of mine, so be nice." He turns to me, his stern look turning into something much softer. "Glad you could make it."

The one sitting closest to me swivels on his chair to give me a smile. "Nice to meet ya darlin'."

"Likewise. You two already have my respect, keeping this guy on his toes. Mind if I sit here?" I ask, pointing to the stool right next to the one with the smart mouth.

"Oh, honey. I'd be honored," he says with a hand to his chest.

"Don't let him give you shit, Han," Miles says. "What can I get ya?"

I look behind him at all my choices and give him an over-exaggerated smile. "How about you surprise me?"

The corner of his mouth tips up and he gets to work. I watch him as he works meticulously with each bottle, cup, and even ice cube until he sets it in front of me.

I pick it up and inspect it. "What's this?"

He smirks. "Something I've been thinking about putting on the menu."

I raise my brows. "And what, you want me to be your guinea pig?"

The way he smiles at me, I forget about everyone else in the room for a moment. "Maybe. Drink up and tell me what you think."

I eye him as I sniff the drink. It's that perfect mix of fruit and alcohol that singes all my nose hairs. "What's your plan, making me drink this?"

He shrugs. "I trust your judgment." he breaks eye contact, staring down at the bar. "I know you'd be honest if it was a bad idea, so I wanted you to be the one to try."

That reply was too nice, so now I *have* to drink it. I swirl the tiny straw, then take a sip. It tastes like juice. No alcohol detected by my taste buds. I set the drink back on the bar and catch Miles still staring at my mouth, but look away before he realizes me noticing. "Whoa," I finally say.

"Too much alcohol?" He grimaces. "I've been working on the ratio. I'll keep trying." He reaches for my glass, but I pull it closer to my chest.

"No, Miles. I meant *whoa*, as in, that's freaking delicious. It doesn't even taste like alcohol. I could drink these all night and get so hammered. They're dangerous."

"That could be their name," the guy sitting next to me says. When Miles and I both swivel to look at him, he says, "Dangerous. You could name 'em that on the menu."

"I like the way you think, Chuck," Miles says, reaching for the drink in my hand again. "Can I try?"

I smile as I hand it over, and it's my turn to watch his mouth and try not to think too hard about the fact that his lips are where my lips just were.

"Whoa is right," he says, looking between me and the glass. "Dangerous, indeed." He says it in such a way, I'm unsure whether he's talking about me or the drink.

He hands it back because there's a customer waiting for a drink at the other end of the bar. I have no shame watching his backside as he crosses the floor.

"He likes you, honey," the guy Miles called Chuck says from beside me, clearly catching me watch him like a hawk.

I smile, "We get along pretty well," I say, playing dumb.

He shakes his head. "Oh no, that's not what I meant. He has feelings for you. Trust me, I can see it in his eyes when he looks at ya."

"He's right. It's very clear. We noticed the last time you were in here." He holds his hand out to me, "Oh, I'm Freddie, by the way. And this goon is Chuck. We were both friends of Miles' grandpa, Lyle."

I shake hands with both of them. "Nice to meet you two. Lyle was a great man," I say. "Now, do you have any dirt on Miles here?"

Chuck throws his head back and laughs, "Oh boy, do we! Known that kid since he was in diapers. He'd been through hell and back before he even reached the age of ten, and he turned out to be one of the good ones, Hannah."

Everyone's been pretty quiet about Miles' past around me my whole life, and I've been too scared to ask questions. All I know is that he lost his little brother at a young age, but none of the details.

"I agree with you there. He's one of the good ones." Miles walks up in time to catch the tail end of that sentence.

"Talking about me, huh?" Miles asks, smiling as my cheeks flush.

"In fact, we were," Freddie says, "They were saying how good of a kid you turned out to be."

"I'm damn near thirty, Freddie. I'm hardly a kid anymore."

Freddie makes a sound with his mouth that sounds a lot like a fart. "Nonsense. That's still a kid to me."

"Agreed," Chuck says, patting the hand Miles has sitting on top of the bar. "Speaking of which, it's always a pleasure, Miles, but I think it's time for this old man to head home for the night."

"I second that," Freddie says as they both stand from their stools. "Good to meet you, Miss Hannah."

"It was good meeting you as well," I say, waving to them both as they scoot out the door.

"Good night, boys," Miles says.

Once the door slams behind them, I turn to Miles. "They're really cute."

He leans over the bar and quietly says, "Yeah, if you find nosy shit-talkers cute, I guess."

Chapter Eight

"So, how was your photoshoot?" I ask as Hannah settles deeper into her bar stool as we slowly become the last two people in here.

"It actually went pretty well. I think the couple will be fun to work with at their wedding."

"That's good."

"Yeah," she says, then glances around the room. "Sorry if you didn't expect me to accept your invitation tonight. I just felt like I could use a drink. And I feel like we barely see each other anymore, and since we'll be spending some time—"

"Yeah, why is that, Hannah?" I ask, cutting her off, and looking far too interested in her answer.

The deer in the headlights look I get has me realizing that asking may have been a mistake. But I can't deny the fact that I want to hear the answer.

"I don't get out much. Turns out running a business takes up a lot of your time."

I look around the bar. "Yeah, that sounds about right. But you're sure that's it?" She looks at me like there's something she wants to say. When she doesn't speak, I continue digging myself a hole that'll be hard to climb out of. "Because I used to see you multiple times a week. Then it was like you disappeared."

"I moved in with Val. Of course, you didn't see me as much."

"Huh, must have been a coincidence then. But promise me something?"

It takes a moment for her eyes to find mine. "Yeah?"

"You're done being a stranger."

A smile breaks on her face as she nods. "I'm done being a stranger."

"Good. Now that we've got that out of the way, will you help me with something?"

She eyes me skeptically, "Yes?" Her answer comes out in a question, like she's not sure she should agree to anything when it comes to me.

Fair assessment, honestly.

I waste no time grabbing the supplies I'll need before she can change her mind. A glass, a shaker, ice. When I come back to my workspace with a bottle of my best bourbon, what I can only describe as a squeak falls out of Hannah's mouth.

"Wait, what are you doing?" I meet her gaze as I shake up the contents of my signature concoction—the one I've spent years perfecting since the last time she drank it. She doesn't look at me, instead stares at the glass I'm filling. "Is that what I think it is?"

"Miles—"

"High Club Soda," We both finish the name in unison as she recognizes the ingredients.

"I thought I told you I'd never drink that again after that one night."

That one night she's speaking of is when Holt and I threw a small party at his parents' house while they were out of town. He was in charge of Hannah, who made us let her join in on the fun, unless we wanted her to call and tattle on us. We'd been seniors in high school, and she was merely a freshman, so neither of us liked the idea of her attending a party, but let her after making a pact to keep her safe from the idiots we knew would be in attendance. Long story short, we turned our backs for one second and she had a beer in her hand.

I was the one who caught her with it. And since I've always had a soft spot for her, all it took was a quick bat of her eyelashes to get me to let her keep it. But I got the last laugh when she took a chug before I could change my mind and ended up coughing.

"It's an acquired taste," I'd said, smacking her back until she was breathing easy again. "You okay?"

"Uh, yeah. But you can have it," she said, handing it over.

By the end of the night, and when I'd been a few drinks in myself, she brought me something from her dad's secret stash in the basement—bourbon whiskey. And after scrounging the fridge for something to mix it with—since I knew there was no way she was going to drink it straight—the Miles High Club Soda was born. We'd come up with the ridiculous name together that night.

"Well, I think you've got more of a tolerance than you used to, and I became a bartender, so I've perfected the drink since then."

She's still grimacing at her glass. I inch it toward her.

Her gaze flicks to mine and we're so close, I can see the tiny flecks of gold in her otherwise green eyes.

"Fine," she grumbles under her breath before snatching the glass and downing a sip. A rather large sip, if you ask me—something she comes to realize quickly. But after the initial reaction wears off, I watch as it changes into surprise. "Oh wow, that's good, Miles. What's in it?"

"The same ingredients as before, just got them in the right proportions this time."

Her teeth rake across her bottom lip, catching a rogue

drop of liquid, and I have to force myself to look away. "Do you think it's good enough to add to the menu?"

"I can see myself asking for it again, and I think other people would like it too." I smile down at the stack of glasses drying in the under bar. "So you're really doing it, aren't you?"

"Doing what?"

She lifts her hands and swivels from her torso, encompassing the entire space. "This. The bar. You've talked about it for ages, and here we are. You're all in, aren't you?"

I can't help but laugh at the innocence of her question. "What, the spending of my life's savings didn't clue you in enough?"

"Miles," she chastises. "You didn't really spend all your money on this, did you?" She looks around, admiring all the details. "I mean, it looks great, but are you sure that was smart?"

I look around at all my favorite updates, telling myself it was worth it, even when my conscience is screaming otherwise. "A guy can hope, can't he?"

"Updated drink specials seems like a good place to start. And while I'm here, maybe we can come up with a few other ideas?"

I wipe down the bar again, and I think it's the cleanest it's ever been at this point. "I'll take any ideas you have," I say, walking away to help close out the pub's last customers for the night. When I return, I ask, "So, whatcha got for me?"

"A few months ago, I did a shoot with a local business. Rise Bakery, have you heard of them?"

"Oh, that's the bakery in Freeport, right? I actually went there a couple of weeks ago because I've been seeing their advertisements everywhere. Their croissants were delicious."

"Exactly!" she says, throwing her hands up. That, mixed with the excitement on her face, tells me she'll be jumping into one of her spiels about things she feels passionate about. One of my favorite things about her.

"That's exactly what I mean! They did a rebranding shoot with me to get tons of new photos to use in their advertising efforts to get more people through the door of their struggling business. And look—it worked! It got you in theirs. And I think we could do the same for this bar."

"Re-what?"

"Rebrand."

"What the hell does that mean?"

She bites her lip, most likely thinking of the best way to dumb it down for me. "Say you're a person who hasn't been to this pub in a few years. What are a few things that you'd use to describe the place you remember it to be?"

"Dingy walls, my favorite liquor out of stock at all times, and the same five regulars belly up to the bar?" That answer came to me far too fast, the main reason I made so many changes to the place.

"And is that what you'd like people to see it as today?"

"Hell no."

"Enter rebranding," she says, waving her hand in front of her. She takes a hefty sip of her drink, causing the telltale gurgle of an empty glass as her straw sucks up the last of the liquid between the ice cubes in her cup. As she explains, I busy myself with making her another. "Rebranding is a great way to take away the assumptions that people may have about your business, especially with all the effort you've put into making changes. It can start by changing a logo or business name. Or the drinks you're wanting to introduce to the general population. That's also a form of rebranding. And I think you could profit from not only making those changes, but advertising the fact that they've been made."

When I set her fresh drink in front of her, she holds her hands up. "I'm not sure if I should. I still have to drive home."

"Come on, no one else is here." At that, she looks around

like she's only now realizing we're the only two people in the place. "I'll lock up and you can come sit in my office and tell me more about demanding—"

"Rebranding," she corrects.

"Right. Then I'll give you a ride home."

"You don't have to do that."

I lean against the bar. "I'm not getting you tipsy, then letting you drive yourself home, Hannah."

I slide her drink further in front of her as she slides a twenty-dollar bill in my direction. I slide it back. She pushes it back in front of me.

"I'm not letting you get me tipsy, then not take payment, Miles. Especially after you just told me you spent all your money remodeling the place. How will you make any money if you keep giving out freebies?"

I laugh at the way she made that parallel, then reluctantly make change. "Point taken. I could use someone like you as a business coach to tell me everything I'm doing wrong."

"Ahh, you couldn't afford me."

That I know is true. I hand back her money and pretend not to notice the way she stuffed it into the tip jar when she thought I wasn't looking on my way to flip the locks on the front door.

On my way back, I turn off one light at a time until it's only us and the dim security lights and lead Hannah to my office, where I set my cash register drawer on my desk for counting. I push my comfortable computer chair in her direction and pull up a folding chair for myself and drop into it. Hannah doesn't sit right away, instead taking it upon herself to look around the space I've tried to turn into my own in the past several months.

My gaze follows her around the room until I realize what I'm doing, and I busy myself with counting the drawer for the night.

"What's this?" She asks, pointing to a large print I have

framed on my shelf of a landscape that holds many memories for me.

"That's one of my favorite places in Colorado. I used to go every summer with my Grandpa Lyle."

"Aw, have you been back since he passed?"

"Not yet. I always tell myself I will, then don't."

"Hmm," she says, going back to looking around. It makes me antsy, watching her look around at my things. "You should."

"I can't, now that I've shackled myself to this place."

She sighs and turns to me. "From one business owner to another, take breaks. It's easy to get caught up in the numbers and work yourself into exhaustion to make sure you're turning a profit, but you have to give yourself some time away too. Especially for you, since you live upstairs."

"Okay, I'll think about it," I say, knowing damn well I won't. But with all these people hounding me about it, I just might have to. "Now come over here and tell me more about reprimanding."

"Rebranding."

"Yeah, that."

Over the next several minutes, I listen to her tell me what I need to do with the place, ideas buzzing through my head the whole time as I jot them down on a scrap piece of paper.

Then, when the gurgle noise returns from Hannah's glass, I take it as my cue.

"Alright, let's get you home."

There's a sparkle in her eye when she smiles at me. "Okay, chauffeur."

I walk Hannah to the passenger seat of her RAV4, her hand in the crook of my elbow.

"Thanks, Miles," she says, her smile wide as she drops into her seat, crumpling in that way she does when she's a little tipsy.

I catch myself smirking on my way to the driver's side and shake my head at my ridiculousness.

"God, who drove this last, a toddler?" I ask, falling into the driver's seat, my back and knees smacking into the back of the seat and the steering wheel all at once. I feel around for the lever on the side of the chair and slide it back until I can swing my legs in.

"It's not my fault you're ginormous."

It's true, I may be six foot four, but she's no shorty either, with the top of her head coming up to my nose. Something I've found convenient for covertly smelling her hair when she's near. Is that creepy?

"Those drinks really got me. I didn't realize I was buzzing until I stood up and walked out here."

"Yeah, that bourbon sure sneaks up on you. Aren't you glad your bartender is giving you a ride?"

She giggles. "You gonna carry me in the house, too?"

"Absolutely," I say as I navigate the few streets between the place she lives with her best friend, Val, and my bar. Another reason I've been so annoyed that she hasn't come around recently. It's so close she could walk to my pub. And that's exactly why I assume I'm the issue.

"Wait, that was a joke."

"Too bad," I say, pulling into her driveway in the spot I know she always parks. I turn to her with a smile. Before she can see it, I round the vehicle to open her door.

"You coming?"

A laugh bubbles out of her. "You're not carrying me, Miles."

"Okay, fine," I say, stepping away from the vehicle. She finally gets out and stumbles, so I catch her around the waist and hoist her over my shoulder.

"Miles!" she yelps, but she's laughing, so I start toward the house. "Wait, Miles! My camera bag. It's still in the car."

I turn in the direction she's pointing, her arm sticking out at an odd angle, and find the bag in question sitting in the back seat. I bend to grab it, throwing it over my other shoulder and heading up the sidewalk to the house.

I knock since my hands are full. Val answers a moment later in a messy bun and sweats, a bewildered look on her face.

"Miles? Hey," she says, her head turning sideways, taking in the pair of legs that are dangling from my shoulders. "Wait, Hannah? What is going on here?"

"Can we come in?" I ask as Hannah yells unintelligible things from behind me.

"Oh, duh. Yes, just dump her onto the couch," she says, backpedaling out of the way.

When we're in front of the couch, I let Hannah's limp body slide down my own until her feet touch the ground. Then her forehead lands on my chest and at first I think she might be crying, but when I pull her back to look at her, she's laughing hysterically.

"Okay," I say, unable to hide my smile. Something that happens often when she's around. "Let's get you sitting down, Hannah."

She does a trust fall with the couch, laughing when she bounces once before settling into their overstuffed cushions.

"As glad as I am that you enjoyed yourself tonight. We might have to skip the bourbon next time."

Chapter Nine

Hannah

"What was that?" Val asks, sitting on the couch after Miles walks out the door.

She's got one of her favorite binge TV shows paused on the screen, and I laugh at the freeze frame that has one of the main characters resembling those photos you see of Olympic divers in midair.

"What do you mean?" I ask, playing coy. If anyone in my life knows about my *Miles feelings*, it's Val. But I'm just tipsy enough to make this into a game.

"Hannah. Miles, the guy you've crushed on for ages just brought you home from his bar and you're drunk."

"I'm not drunk, I'm—" hiccup, "tipsy. There's a difference."

"Yeah, but with you, it's not much."

She's right. I'm a certified lightweight, and I knew I was in trouble as soon as Miles slid that darn drink in my direction, taunting me with memories and that sparkle in his eye. The one that always gleams just before a smile appears, because with him, they're not so easily earned.

"Okay, I know. And that's the only reason I let Miles drive me home."

Val gives me a knowing look. "The only reason?"

"Shut up," I say, rolling my eyes. "Do you remember that drink he made me back in high school? That party they threw while my parents were out of town?"

"The one I didn't get to go to because my grandparents were visiting?"

"The very one. He made me that drink tonight, except this time it was delicious."

"That only explains how you got drunk, not how you ended up with Miles."

"Oh, right, I forgot," I say, holding my head in my hands for a moment to regroup. "This morning, he told me I should come visit him for a drink after my session since he'd be bartending tonight. I didn't actually plan on taking him up on that offer, but I was driving past on my way home and decided *what could it hurt?*"

"And how did it go?"

I smile, thinking back on our easy conversation. "It was really nice to just be around him, you know?"

Val doesn't answer, but smiles in that knowing way she has whenever we're discussing Miles.

"Don't do that."

"What am I doing?"

"Making this into more than it is."

"Okay. I distinctly remember you doing the same when I told you that Brody and I were just friends."

I pull the blanket from the back of the couch and wrap myself up in it, sinking back onto the armrest. "Yeah, but that's different."

"How? I ended up with the guy I crushed on years ago. Is it so odd to think the same might happen to you?"

"Yes."

"Why?"

This is the question I always avoid answering. It's the douse of cold water on my burning heart. The reason that even if my feelings were reciprocated, Miles and I would never work out. "Because Holt would never approve of it, and I care too much about him to make that mistake. Nothing would be worse than ruining their friendship and my relationship with my brother in one fell swoop."

"Are you sure that's how he feels, though? He seems just sentimental enough to approve of you two falling in love."

I toss my arm over my eyes as if that could really close me off from this conversation. But I get lucky, and Val just pats my knee and says, "I'm not trying to force you into anything, Han. Just playing devil's advocate here."

Wednesday night, I get to my brother's place a few minutes before seven and knock twice, then let myself in since I usually get yelled at for knocking *because you're family*.

When I walk through the door, Holt and Serena turn their attention from the binder lying on the counter in front of them and smile when they see it's me.

"Knock, knock," I say.

"Psh, you know you don't have to knock here, especially when we told you to come over," Serena says. I laugh, not only because I called it, but because it's not technically her house, although she's here all the time. She's held onto her apartment in the city, blocks from where she and Holt work for their entire relationship. But now that they're engaged, she's letting her rental agreement come to a close, and in a few weeks, they'll finally be living together. The timing's so perfect, I have a feeling they planned it this way. Knowing them, they probably did.

"I know, but it still feels weird," I say, opening my arms to her as she reaches me. I wrap her in a hug, and she squeezes me even tighter. Not only did my brother find the jackpot in a future wife, but he's given me more than I could ask for in a future sister-in-law.

It's not long before Holt comes up behind her and wraps his arms around both of us. The Hawkins family has never shied away from showing each other affection, something I never saw as a blessing until I was older and met people who weren't fortunate enough to have the same upbringing.

The door opens behind us and we all break apart to turn and find Miles taking us in from the doorway with a look that says, *not this again*. One we've seen from him many times. If the affectionate Hawkins family was category A, Miles' family was firmly in category B. But that's not his fault, and he's warmed up to the Hawkins way plenty throughout the years.

"Bring it in, brother," Holt says, opening his arms.

"I'm good."

"Miles," Serena says, because she too had a category B upbringing.

"Let's hear these wedding plans," he says, attempting to change the subject.

He makes a beeline for the fridge, where I know he plans to grab a beer, but I hook an arm through his and pull him toward our little group smiling to myself at the look of shock on his face before we bring him in for a hug.

He grunts and we all laugh, but just before we let him go, he sinks into the gesture like he may have needed it more than he realized.

"See, that wasn't so bad, was it?" Serena asks, patting his back. She opens the fridge, pulling out a beer to hand to him.

"I suppose not," he says, taking a turn looking at all of us. He looks at me last with a lift to the corner of his mouth like we're in on the same joke.

Or maybe he's thinking about how ridiculous I was the other night when he took me home.

My cheeks flush and I look away. When I do, my gaze

snags on the binder Holt and Serena are leaning over once again.

"What the hell is that thing?" I ask, looking at a thick binder stuffed with papers of every color. The open pages read, *THE I DO TO-DO LIST*.

"I second what Hannah said—what the hell is that?" Miles asks.

Serena slaps a hand over the list and giggles like she's actually embarrassed by her over-the-top planning skills. "Ah, yes. This ol' thing. It's everything we've come up with so far."

"Wow, you two work quick. When are you getting married…tomorrow?" Miles jokes.

Holt laughs, "Well, we're actually hoping to be married by the middle of July."

"What?!" I ask, sharing an incredulous look with Miles. "You two realize that's less than two months to pull this off, right?"

Holt puts both hands up like he's warding off an angry bear. "I know, and that's why we wanted to talk to you both before we make any concrete decisions."

"Holt, it's wedding season for me. My life is about to get insane as it is. And you want to throw another wedding into the mix?"

"I know, it's crazy. But it's going to be quick and painless for everyone." He shares a look with Serena. "As long as everyone can pitch in a little beforehand to help us plan it."

"So what you're saying is," Miles says, looking at me, then back to the couple. "It won't be quick and painless whatsoever."

Serena drops her face into her hands, then looks at Holt. "You know what? They're right. This is crazy. Let's just go with Plan B."

"But babe, you wanted—"

She covers his mouth before we find out what Serena wanted, but it's enough to make me feel terrible. If anyone deserves a wedding day that's exactly what they pictured, it's Serena. She's been through so much in her twenty-eight years, and her life turned around the moment she and Holt found each other.

"No, no. I'm sorry guys. Of course, we can make it work. Tell us what you need, and we'll help, right Miles?"

I turn to him, pleading for him to read my mind and agree.

He swallows hard, then nods. "Yes, of course. Let's do this."

Serena wipes a tear, lifting her head from Holt's chest to look at each of us in turn. "Are you sure? I know it's fast."

Miles surprises me by crossing the kitchen to hug her. "Yes, now let's get you two married."

Serena's smile turns bright, and she reaches for the thick binder that sits ominously between us. By the end of the night, we've divvied up all the tasks that will need to be finished in less than eight weeks.

Chapter Ten

Hannah

The following week, Miles picks me up for our first adventure in wedding planning.

"Not sure what type of person lets someone else choose what's on their registry," he says as soon as I'm buckled into the passenger's seat of his truck.

"I know, but in true Serena fashion, there are specific instructions on what they're looking for."

"How's your week been?" Miles asks once he's on the road.

"Good," I say.

"You ready to scan some shit?"

"Oh, born ready. How about you?"

"I can't wait. What do you say we put at least one stupid thing on their registry at each store since they're making us do this."

I bark out a laugh. "That's a great idea. I'm in."

I turn in time to see his lips curve up in a smile.

"I love when you do that," I say without thinking.

His brow furrows, staring at the road ahead. "Do what?"

"Smile."

His smile grows bigger. "Stop."

"No, Miles. I'm serious. I don't know why you rarely smile, but it makes me sad."

"Don't be sad for me, Hannah," he says, gripping the wheel tighter. "I rarely have anything to smile about, so I don't. End of story."

"Sure you do." I say, turning the volume dial down a few notches so we're no longer talking over it. "You've got a bar all to yourself, good friends, and a beautiful face somewhere under all that beard."

He laughs, running a hand through the unruly scruff on his face. "A bar, a best friend, and a beautiful face. That's all a man ever needs, isn't it?"

I chuckle, reaching into the backseat for our copy of the infamous wedding binder I brought with me—yes, Serena made two. "So I was looking through this bad boy the other night," I say smacking the cover. "There's a master list of the things they're looking for, down to the color."

"Should be easy enough, then," Miles says, pulling into the parking lot.

It turns out that making a wedding registry is more fun than I expected. I went into the experience thinking it would be like one of those montages I've seen in the movies where the guy and girl are both carrying around a handheld price gun, laughing, pointing, and shooting at everything in the aisle. Behind the back, point, shoot. Through the legs, point, shoot. Close your eyes, spin, point, shoot. And laughing, lots of laughing.

Instead, everything is basically mobile now. Technically, if they'd been thinking about it, Holt and Serena could have done all of this online, but we're using our phones to scan barcodes as we walk the aisles and adding things that way. We try to keep to the list as much as possible, but Miles and I stick to the rule we made in the car, adding anything we find completely ridiculous to their registry.

We're now at the third, and thankfully, last place, and Miles just rang up a ceramic, metallic gold giraffe that would serve literally no purpose in Holt and Serena's house besides making both of us laugh every time we visit.

"I really hope someone buys that for them," I say, giggling as we walk away.

"You've said that after every random item we registered," Miles says, matching my stride.

"I know. I just want to see Holt's face when they open every single one of them."

He laughs, "Yeah, you're right. That would be worth it."

"Miles, is that you?" a female voice asks from the end of the aisle. Miles straightens, turning comically slow in the direction of the voice he clearly recognizes. That makes two of us.

The blonde bombshell he dated during his senior year of high school stands stock still, with one hand on her hip and the other on the handle of her cart filled with overpriced home decor.

"Eliza, it's been a long time."

As soon as she knows it's him, she runs straight into his arms like the aisle just transformed into a beach and they're long lost lovers in a rom-com.

Only Miles doesn't get the memo. The entire exchange is awkward and stilted. His hands dangle at his sides as her arms wrap tightly around him. I nearly laugh, watching him awkwardly pat her back right as she backs away.

"How have you been?" She asks, injecting fake enthusiasm into the words.

"Great," comes Miles' one-word response. I always forget how quiet he is around other people because he's so himself around me and my family.

Eliza looks around, finally noticing my presence over Miles' shoulder.

"Oh wow, Hannah, right?" She looks between us. "Wait, are you two together now?" A laugh bubbles out of her throat. "Oh, you used to have it *bad* for Miles when we were together. I always felt for you, the best friend's little sister with hearts in her eyes. I'm glad to see things finally worked out for you, though."

I'm stunned speechless, my jaw falling open and slamming shut several times before Miles cuts in.

"If you mean together as in, in each other's company, yes. We're helping plan Holt's wedding. So if you'll excuse us," without another glance in her direction, Miles lugs me to the end of the aisle and out of her sight.

I'm leaning against some throw pillows on an end cap when I realize Miles is hovering over me.

"I'm sorry about what she said," he says, one hand still lingering on my hip and driving me crazy. "She's always known how to make her words cut the deepest."

"So you knew?"

A muscle in his jaw ticks, a quick ripple of his beard. "Knew what?"

"About my silly little crush all those years ago?" The words come out almost breathlessly, my staccato heartbeat drumming in my ears, anticipating the answer that just might be the death of me.

"Hannah, just because I'm a quiet man doesn't mean I don't have eyes." He leans closer. "You still look at me the same way you always have, and if your eyes were open, you'd see me looking at you the same way, too."

My body has sunk into the pillows behind me, something I don't realize until he's already walking away and I have to right myself.

I follow Miles' retreating form out into the golden sunlight of the spring evening. The sun is warm on my skin; the birds are chirping, and Miles may as well be fuming, his entire body vibrating with tension where he leans against the door of his truck.

"What are you doing? We aren't finished." I don't know whether I'm talking about the registry or our conversation at this point.

"Doesn't matter, we're leaving," he says, rounding the vehicle and opening the passenger door, looking anywhere but at me while he waits for me to obey his unvoiced demands. *Get in the car*, his body language says.

Instead, I lean against the bed of his truck with my arms crossed. Two can play this game.

"Hannah, I swear I will toss you in here myself if you—"

"I dare you."

His eyes flash to mine, surprised by my choice to challenge him. Then, in two large steps and a quick maneuver, he's got me over his shoulder. This entire scene is reminiscent of that night in my driveway. Except I'm sober, and every hard plane of his body feels like heaven against mine. He uses careful consideration, lowering me into the truck, his hand on the crown of my head so I don't smack it on anything.

He rights me, savoring every moment of our bodies sliding against each other until I'm in my seat. Even then, his touch lingers. He spreads one large palm across my thigh, the other on my opposite biceps.

I look up, and that's when I finally see it, his eyes deep earthy brown, pupils blown wide. He's finally letting me in on the secret. He wants me too.

But before I can beg my muscles to move, his touch is gone, the door slams shut, and I inflate my lungs, desperate to catch my breath before he rounds the vehicle.

We're both completely silent as he turns the key and backs out of the spot.

I stare at the big white letters on the storefront. I think we got eight items on their registry before all hell broke loose.

Sorry, Holt and Serena, you won't be seeing any gifts from the fancy-schmancy home decor store. Oh, and I broke your best man's brain. My bad!

Miles has been brooding from the driver's seat, sighing with each red light we hit. We're about halfway home when I finally gather the courage to speak.

"So, are we going to talk about what happened back there?"

"No. We're going to do what we do best."

"And what is that?"

"Ignore it until it goes away."

Chapter Eleven

Miles

"Miles, how have you been? Is there anything new you'd like to share?" Dr. Rosenburg asks with her usual upbeat tone.

I've been warring with myself about whether I'll bring up Hannah today. I know our complicated relationship is something I could use some clarity on, but voicing it out loud makes me nervous.

I chew on my lip, scratching at a loose thread on my favorite pair of worn-in black jeans. "Uh, there's definitely some news to share. But if I tell you, there's no returning to the before, if you get what I mean."

"I think I understand where you're trying to go with that thought. I would need more clarity to know for sure. It's, of course, up to you how much you tell me. Let me ask this," she says, readjusting her glasses on her nose. "Is it something to do with the pub?"

I can see why she'd ask that. I've been bitching about the place to her for weeks. "No, surprisingly enough, it has to do with something else entirely." I avoid her gaze while she does that thing where she pauses to let me decide what I'd like to share. I stare at my bouncing knee until I realize I'm doing it, and place my foot flat on the ground and finally look up. "I've got a guilty conscience."

"Okay, and are you finding this guilt to be debilitating?"

I chuckle. "Yes, very. As you know from my last session, my best friend is engaged and they're throwing together a wedding pretty quickly. Because of that, it's an all-hands-on-deck situation. I've been put in charge of a laundry list of things to do, but I'm not doing them alone."

"Okay, and who are you working with? Your best friend?"

"No, his younger sister. And she's—" I shake my head, trying to find the right words to say. "She's fucking amazing. I've thought so for as long as I can remember. She was someone I considered a friend back when we were kids, but those platonic feelings have gone out the window as of late."

"Is this what's making you have feelings of guilt?"

"Yes," I say with more conviction than necessary.

"Why?"

With that question, I meet Dr. Rosenburg's gaze. "Holt is my best friend, and I've never told him about my complicated feelings for his sister. I've been feeling this way for a long time, but I'd let myself believe the feelings were gone because it had been a while since we've interacted. But with the sudden change, we've seen each other a lot lately. And it feels like her feelings might match mine."

"Do you consider her to be a friend as well?"

"Yes, of course. I was never as close to her as I was to her brother, but she's right there in so many of my memories from childhood to recent years. For no reason that I'm aware of, it felt like she avoided me for months until we were paired together to plan this wedding."

"Can you think of anything that may have happened to make her retreat from your friendship?"

I bite my bottom lip, thinking back on exactly when it was that she started pulling back. Due to my own estranged family dynamic, I spent both Thanksgiving and Christmas with the

Hawkins family, as they never let me spend a holiday alone. Hannah was her usual self during Thanksgiving, chatting my ear off and laughing with abandon. Then at Christmas, about a week and a half after she'd gone into the ditch, she barely acknowledged my existence.

That night she went in the ditch, her parents were on a trip for their anniversary, and Holt was away on a business trip. It was snowing like crazy, so naturally, the pub was hopping with rowdy patrons who were praying for a snow day the next morning. It was a miracle I'd noticed my phone ringing through all that noise. When I heard the fear in Hannah's voice, I told the other bartender I'd been working with that I needed to leave, hopped in my truck, and drove like a bat out of hell to a notoriously shitty road outside of town where Hannah had taken snow photos for one of her couples.

They'd been having a good time, so the shoot went late, and by the time she left their property, the last burst of daylight had already disappeared beyond the horizon. There was a curve in the road, but with the snow coating everything in white, Hannah had lost track of where she was, and ended up in the ditch. She called me in hysterics, so I knew something was wrong the moment I answered.

I'll never forget the pure terror of seeing her RAV4 sitting at an angle in that steep ditch. It was like an electric strike ran through my body, and I ran down that hill on pure adrenaline without a care that there was snow soaking through my favorite pair of boots.

Her mascara was running down her cheeks, and she had her camera bag clutched in her hands when I finally got to her. I had to dig through inches of snow with my bare hands to even wrench her door open.

"Miles," she said, relief clear in her tone. Looking back, that was the moment I knew my feelings were one hundred percent real. The moment I knew I'd do anything for this girl without her even having to ask. And that there'd be no one on this earth I'd rather protect with all I have. It's the closest thing to love I've felt in my life. Well, besides Grandpa and Holt, but that type of love feels different.

And I've been holding it in ever since, afraid I'll lose Holt and Hannah, and my second parents that feel more like family to me than my own do.

At the time, I'd been shaking so damn bad after my thoughts ran wild on my way out to her. We sat in my truck outside her house after we got back to town, and I hugged her like I'd never let her go. Hell, I didn't *want* to. But I eventually walked her to her door. I pressed my forehead to hers, my entire body buzzing with the need to show her how I felt, although my mind was telling me it wasn't the right time. I'd almost said to hell with it in that moment. I can still feel the puff of breath against my lips when she exhaled just before pulling away. I can still see the way she looked at me, faces merely inches apart before she walked inside.

The next morning, I arranged the tow truck and had her RAV4 sitting in her driveway by the afternoon. Then, after thanking me profusely for everything, it was like she suddenly fell off the face of the earth.

I'd been too busy with the pub after that to put two and two together.

"Yeah, I suppose there was," I say, with more questions now than I had when I sat down.

Chapter Twelve

I've had a handful of photography sessions in the week since the night Miles and I did the gift registry, but it's another weekend with no wedding. So Serena, my mom, and I are making the most of it by going dress shopping. Secretly, I'd been wishing today would have involved something to do with Miles, since I've heard nothing but silence from him since he dropped me off at home the other night.

I returned to the home decor shop yesterday to complete the registry since I felt bad leaving it unfinished.

"Hannah, did you hear me?" Mom asks, breaking me from my reverie.

"Sorry, what?"

"I asked how things are going with Miles?"

I can feel my face drain of blood at the unexpected question. "What?"

"Haven't you two been working together a lot lately?"

"Oh," I say, taking a deep breath to get my breathing back under control. "Yeah, we have. I feel sorry for him, since he's already so busy with the bar, but it's been fun having him around. It had been a while."

"He's one of the good ones. Do you know—is he single?" One blink. Two. I stare at my mom so long that she adds, "I'm only asking because—have you seen the way he looks at you?" Her eyes light up the way they always do when she's up to something. "I've always thought you two would make a cute couple. Don't tell your brother."

I see the moment sitting right in front of me and take it. "Why? Do you think he'd be mad?"

She furrows her brows, thinking long and hard about her answer, which I appreciate. "If it were any of Holt's other friends, I'd say yes. He'd be pissed, but with Miles, I'm not so sure. He's a great guy with a good head on his shoulders. He's nothing like Holt's immature friends. They're more like the boys you used to date, which I think is why they were so protective of you. If you recall, Miles was right there alongside your brother, intimidating the boys who tried to date you. He really cares about you, sis," Mom says, calling me the nickname she's used for me ever since the day Holt started calling me by it. "Why? Are you interested?"

I'm contemplating confiding in her when Serena comes walking out of the changing room in a gorgeous, intricately beaded bridal gown over my mom's shoulder.

"Wow, Rena. You look amazing!"

Mom turns at the sound of the dress swishing as she walks toward the three-way mirrors we're seated in front of. She gasps when her gaze finds Serena.

And even though I'm glad the fire is off me for the moment, I find I wouldn't mind confiding in her. To ask her for some advice. But instead of dwelling on a conversation I probably shouldn't be having, I give myself over to the moment as we find the perfect dress for Serena to marry my brother in.

And we do. I'd be lying if I said I didn't love every single dress Serena tried on. She's thin, tall, busty, and blonde, so everything works on her effortlessly.

But I think we all know the moment she walks out in an ivory, floral lace number, she's found the one. Her entire demeanor changes and the three of us all have tears in our eyes. The moment ends with hugs, smiles, and laughter in the mirror. I'm so glad Mom and I can be here for someone so deserving of all the love we have to give. Serena has always felt like a part of the family, especially since the diamond winking from her finger landed there. The first twenty years of her life were so hard. I hope Holt gives her the beautiful future she deserves. I know planning this wedding must be as hard for Serena as it is happy. Weddings tend to be a family affair, and she made the hard decision to cut ties with hers years ago. I'm so glad to see her smiling.

After she takes a photo with their *"I Found my Dress!"* sign with Mom and I, we head over to the bridesmaid area and Serena shows me the shade of blue she likes so I can start looking for a long dress to wear for their ceremony.

On the following Thursday evening, I pick Miles up behind the bar. I had to fight him on it for over an hour, but he finally agreed to let me drive us to our cake tasting appointment.

"Hey," he says, folding into the passenger's seat, and like every other time I have him this close, those stupid little butterflies in my belly are full of hope, fluttering like crazy at the sight of him.

"Hey, how have you been?" I ask, unsure whether I should avoid mentioning the crater the meteor of our feelings left when it crash landed between us.

He nods, "Good."

I give him a weird look, but he doesn't meet my gaze. "What a shining review of your life, Miles," I joke, only to receive a half-assed smile. "Okay, what's wrong?" I ask.

He combs his fingers through his hair. "Nothing."

I turn back to the windshield and drive us back to the road. "I know you're a private guy, but on the off chance you think you don't have anyone to confide in, you've got me."

I turn my gaze on him at a stop sign, only to find an intensity I hadn't been expecting to see. "Good to know," he finally says. "I just deal with things on my own, so other people don't have to deal with my bullshit."

"Well, from now on, your bullshit is my bullshit. We are basically family."

He squeezes my hand. "Don't do that."

"Do what?" I ask, playing dumb.

"Minimize our relationship by pretending I'm just like a brother to you. We both know I'm protective of you, but brotherly is the last word I'd use to describe our relationship."

My breath catches in my throat. I can hardly handle the way he's spoken to me lately, or that we each have unspoken feelings we refuse to acknowledge head-on.

"So, back to my question…" I trail off, and when I glance over quickly, frustration is clear in his expression.

"It was a rough day," he says, swiping a hand along his beard. "Buying the bar was a good thing, and I know that. It's already been a blessing for me, and I'm happy I did it." I wait as he stares out the passenger window. "But there are days I'm less grateful for it than others. Like today, for instance, I did the financials for the month and we're not where I was hoping to be by now. I had to close for a while to get everything done. That, plus the money we spent on the actual updates, has got us in the red pretty badly right now."

"What are you thinking could help you with that?"

"That's the thing. I want to update the drink menus, and maybe add daily specials to pull people in. I know you said I should utilize social media, but if I'm honest, I don't know how social media could help a small town bar gain some traction. Isn't that stuff only reserved for people in big cities?"

"No," I say, feeling the same excitement I always do when

I get to talk to a fellow business owner about what helped me get mine off the ground. "It's definitely for everyone. You just have to be strategic about it. Like," I stop to think about it, "Do you have any daily specials? A lot of restaurants use social media to remind their followers and customers of things like that to try to get them in the door. Or a special limited-time menu item? Like seasonal drinks?"

He nods slowly, looking out the windshield. "Okay. That makes sense," he says, lifting off his seat to pull something from his back pocket. He flips open a small black notebook and a small pen. I'm not sure why I find that so endearing. "God, I have so much shit to learn."

I've got plenty on my own plate, but I don't even think twice before saying, "I'll help you."

He waits until I meet his gaze before he asks, "You'd do that?"

"Of course," I smile. And although the one he returns isn't at full wattage, he still smiles back.

We're only a few minutes from our destination when I yawn so wide, I swear I could break my jaw. We're near a coffee shop, so I maneuver into the turning lane, rather than the one we'd been in, waiting for the light to turn green.

"Where are you going?"

"Coffeeeee," I say, letting the last syllable linger a moment as I turn into the parking lot. When I pull up to the speaker, I turn to Miles. "Do you want anything? It'll be my treat."

"I have a hard and fast rule against drinking coffee after four p.m."

"Okay, suit yourself," I say before turning and ordering an iced white chocolate mocha. It's a flavor Val got me hooked on, but where she's a hot coffee girl, I prefer it cold. I started adding cold foam and a caramel drizzle, and now I can't get enough.

"I've never understood the point of cold coffee. That

sounds disgusting," Miles says after I pull up to wait in line for the window.

"You are such an old man sometimes."

He scratches at his beard. "I'm only three and three-fourths years older than you."

"That is oddly specific. And that's not what I meant. Old men are grumpy about things like ice cubes in coffee." I pull up to the window and pay. When the barista hands over my coffee, I shake it up real good, stick the straw in and hold it out to Miles.

"I don't want any."

The person behind me in line honks, and I watch Miles' brow furrow as he turns in his seat to give them a glare.

"Guess you better take a sip, because I'm not leaving until you do."

He grumbles, taking the cup.

I shift into drive even though he's staring at it like I've asked him to take a potion that will make him love me forever.

I stop at the exit. "Alright, time for a sip."

"Did I mention that coffee is for mornings? I never drink it this late."

"Okay, old man. Me too, most days, but after this appointment, I'll be up all night editing." And by editing, I mean moving the sliders back and forth in my photo-editing software and finding that I'm still not happy with any of it. "Besides, I thought you said you've been putting in the same hours at the bar lately?"

He sighs. "Yeah, I suppose you're right."

He takes a careful sip, like he's afraid of the contents. But I see it on his face as soon as my drink hits his taste buds. His eyebrows jump on his forehead and his quick sip turns into a slow chug.

I smack his arm before he can gulp too much of it down. "Okay, okay," I say. "Give it back."

He lets me have it, but I forget all about the drink,

watching him lick the leftover drips from his lips. "Alright, I guess it wasn't terrible."

"Wasn't terrible? That's not what the look on your face said, but I'll let you pretend you hated it. I know the truth."

I take a sip, unable to stop thinking about how Miles' lips were just where mine are.

"I'll admit, I didn't hate that caramel drizzle on top," he says.

I smile, feeling pretty smug about my current victory, but it drops off my face when Miles' phone goes off a second later. He checks the screen and clearly doesn't like what he sees, because he silences the ring and tosses it in the back seat without a care of where it lands.

"Whoa, who was that, an ex-girlfriend or something?"

"No," he bites out. And just like that, his good mood has vanished.

"Do you want to talk about it?" I ask, aware I'm poking the bear. Miles *never* wants to talk about it.

"Not really, Han," the words come out so soft, I can't detect his earlier frustration, like he's controlling himself so he doesn't take it out on me.

I'm impressed.

"Do I need to remind you that your bullshit is mine, too?" I stare at him while stopped at a red light, hoping he'll look my way.

He finally does, a muscle ticking in his jaw before he sighs. "That was my mom. Want to take a guess when the last time we talked was?"

"Hmm, a month ago?"

He laughs, leaning his head back against the headrest. "Try six."

"Six months? But Christmas was only five months ago, Miles. She didn't wish you a Happy New Year? Nothing?" He shakes his head. "Well, do you want to call her back?"

"It's not that easy."

"Why?"

He laughs. "What's with all the questions? You're not my therapist."

"Well, it's not like you have one, so maybe you need to get these things out." There's a pause, and I glance away from the road to see Miles' furrowed brow. "Do you...have a therapist?"

He taps his fingers against his knee. "I do, actually."

"Wow," I say before I realize how that reaction could be misconstrued, and quickly add, "I'm proud of you, Miles. Have you found therapy helpful?"

"Yes, surprisingly enough, I have," he says, picking up my coffee from the cup holder and taking another swig when he thinks I'm not looking. I knew he liked it.

When I'm parked outside the bakery, I smile at him. "Good, I'm glad."

"Thanks. This doesn't make things weird between us, does it?"

I turn further toward him. "No, why would it?"

He shrugs. "I just don't want you to think differently of me because I asked for help."

I tap his hand that's resting on the center console between us. "I think highly of you, Miles, and I don't think much could change that."

"Good," he says, his dimple popping with his smirk. "Now let's eat cake, shall we?"

"We shall," I say, getting out of the car and grabbing the wedding binder. I find Miles' phone sitting right next to it, and decide to grab that, too. I catch up to him, where he's holding the door open for me and place it in his hand.

"Thanks," he says, and we share a prolonged look until another patron nears the door and I'm forced to move.

"Don't you find it odd that Holt and Serena wouldn't want to do the cake tasting on their own?" Miles asks as we wait at the front desk. "This is the best item on the to-do list. Why would they give something like this to us?"

I quirk a brow. I hadn't thought about that. "You're right, it is kinda weird. But they're also that couple who wake up before the sunrise and train together and rarely eat sweets. Their one contribution was requesting the original wedding cake. They had no flavor combinations requested and gave us free rein to pick."

"Welcome to Frost. How can I help you?" The attendant asks when it's finally our turn.

I take the lead, knowing Miles isn't much of a conversationalist. "Hi, we're actually here for a cake tasting."

"Oh!" She jumps, excitement painting her expression as she looks down at something on the counter. "You two must be the future Mr. and Mrs. Hawkins, for 7pm?"

I'm about to correct her when Miles cuts me off. "Yep, that's us."

The store attendant smiles as Miles' arm wraps around my shoulder, setting all my nerve endings into freak out mode. "Perfect. Take a seat at any table you'd like and I'll be with you in a moment."

He smiles at her, "Thank you." Then, in a surprising move, he pulls on my hand, leading me toward a table near the window.

"What the hell are you doing?" I whisper-yell.

"Just go with it," he says, smirking as he pulls out my chair. I go against my instinct to continue asking questions and do as he asked—just go with it, watching him take the seat across from me.

"Sorry about that wait, you two," the attendant comes to our table a few short minutes later with a tray of a few different flavors of cake. "Before we get started, let me make sure I've got everything right here in my notes. You are Holt and Serena. Last name will be Hawkins. Wedding reception is happening in Wellford, and will be delivered to the address below," she says, setting her clipboard down on the table next to me.

I find my parents' address printed on the sheet and nod. "Yes, the address is correct."

"Alright," she grabs the clipboard, before adding, "Date is August 5th. Your preferred flavors are in the chocolate and vanilla families. Does this all sound correct?"

She's looking right at me, so I force myself to smile and say, "Yes, sounds great!" With a little more enthusiasm than necessary.

"Perfect," she says, "I'm going to start you off with our most popular from the categories you put in your top three. The ones I have in this batch are the wedding, which is a vanilla with buttercream, the double chocolate, frosted with chocolate mousse, and last, the chocolate with a salted caramel frosting."

"Yum," I say out loud at the sound of the last one, making both Miles and our attendant laugh.

"Well, I'll leave you two to it," she says, smiling as she backs away from our table. "Let me know if I can get anything. My name is Kat, if you need me."

Miles hands me one of the tiny forks Kat provided us, and when she's out of earshot he says, "With the way you're eyeing that piece of cake, I'm assuming you're no longer feeling any remorse about pretending to be who we're not."

I tear my eyes away from the cake and smile at him. "One thing you need to know about me is I'm slutty for anything salted caramel flavored."

He tries to hide his smile by looking down at his lap, but I catch it. "Glad to know that about you, *Serena*." He says the name that's not mine pointedly, and I'm not gonna lie. I hate it.

"Call me Serena all you want, but you won't catch me calling you by my brother's name." I cut into the cake I've been salivating over.

I'm bringing it to my mouth when Miles asks, "Is that because it disgusts you to find yourself attracted to your brother?"

My fork pauses halfway to my mouth as it contorts in disgust. "Uh, yeah, that disgusts me. And who says I'm attracted to you?" I make a show of rolling my eyes. "Now stop trying to taint the experience of trying this cake, because I won't let anything ruin it."

He cough-laughs into his hand.

"What?"

"You said taint."

I drop my face into my hands. "Oh my gosh."

He plays with his fork, twirling it from hand to hand as he smirks at me. Finally, I bring the piece to my mouth, closing my eyes when the salty goodness hits my tongue and mixes with the chocolate cake they've paired it with. A moan escapes me before I remember where I am and snap my eyes open.

Miles' eyes have darkened since the last time our gazes met, and he's fidgeting in his chair. No way did my enjoyment of this delicious morsel of cake spark such a reaction in him. I'm ready to do it all over again.

"Yes?" I ask when his gaze wavers.

"If you keep making noises like that, I don't mind making us look like the insatiable newlyweds in the corner."

I instantly feel my cheeks heat. "Miles," I scold.

He stabs the wedding cake, taking his sweet time to bring it to his mouth and licking the fork clean. Damn.

"Yes?" He asks, firing it back with the same amount of attitude I used a moment ago.

"You can't just talk to me like that." I look around the room, finding no one paying attention to us. "And especially not in public!"

"Then why do you like it so much?"

That, dear reader, is a fantastic question.

Chapter Thirteen

I was excited about the cake-tasting appointment. As excited as I can be about this wedding bullshit, anyway. What I hadn't realized was how enjoyable it would be to have Hannah sitting across the table from me, sampling like each morsel is her own personal heaven.

Kat brings us yet another tray. This time they're plain. Some with berries on top, others with berry filling or frosting.

"How's everything tasting?" Kat asks.

"Oh," Hannah says, patting her belly like eight half slivers of cake could really cause her to bloat. "Everything's delicious, Kat. I don't know how on earth my fiance and I will pick."

Hannah and Kat are so busy talking, neither of them notices me staring at Hannah. She called me her fiance, and I know she was kidding, playing the part. But damn, does hearing her call me that—even if it's pretend—do something to me. I've never bothered to look into the future to see myself as a husband or a dad, but something has come over me lately, because I can suddenly see it. And I have an odd suspicion that change is because of the girl sitting across the table from me.

The past several weeks have been stressful as hell, but somehow, Hannah has always been right there to make it better. I take a deep breath and let it out slowly, trying to find a way I can salvage what's left of the electricity between us.

Kat smiles, like it's exactly what she wanted to hear. "Well, lucky for you, I'll let you go home and think things over tonight before making you jump on a decision."

Hannah holds a hand over her heart. "Oh, perfect. I think we'll definitely need it."

"Most people do," she smiles, then leaves us to our own devices.

"Which one do you want?" I ask, plotting something in my head that I know might get me smacked, but I don't care.

"That one," she says, pointing at the one with the line of berry filling between the two layers of cake. If I'm honest, it's the one I would have gone for too, and even though we've been sharing this far, I'm about to try something a little different.

I give her a shit-eating grin and grab it with two fingers.

"Hey, what are you doing? I said I wanted to try that one!"

"And I want to try that one." I point to the one with berries mixed into the frosting. "Now grab it and follow my lead, honey bear. It's time to practice feeding each other like we will after we cut the cake on our big day."

She's a deer in the headlights. It's well past our platonic, friends with feelings line we've tried like hell not to cross, and we both know it.

Suddenly a smirk forms on her delectable lips and she's grabbing for the sliver of cake with hell burning in her eyes, like it tends to do when she looks in my direction.

"Ready?" I ask.

She nods, her grin widening as she leans across the table.

Each of our hands crosses into the other's space, mine

moving nice and slow. Then, out of nowhere, Hannah launches at me, the piece of cake landing hard against my half-open mouth. As revenge, I catch her finger between my lips, licking it with a swirl of my tongue before she can pull away.

I don't miss the intake of breath she takes at the feel of it. I really can't blame her. It causes a similar reaction in me below the belt. Despite that fact, I'm the one who's grinning when she pulls away, back to her own side of the table. Miles, one; Hannah zero.

"My turn," I tease.

"Don't you dare!" She wags a finger in my face.

"Whatever do you mean, snookums?" I ask, feigning innocence. I lean back across the table and stuff the piece of cake into her mouth—just enough to the left to leave some frosting behind. Before she can lick it away, like I did with the damage she left moments before, I lean even further until our faces are millimeters apart. "You missed some," I say, dipping to plant an open-mouthed kiss just past the corner of her mouth, lapping up as much frosting as I can.

I pull back slowly, watching her the entire time. She's rigid in her chair and refuses to meet my eye.

Miles, two; Hannah, zero.

"Oh my goodness, you two are the cutest." Kat returns with some papers in her hand and a huge smile on her face as Hannah wipes her mouth with a napkin. "You know, I see a lot of couples in here, so I feel like I have a sixth sense at this point of who will and won't last. You two are definitely in the former. The playfulness between you is something special. Never forget what it feels like right now. Keep that in your relationship, and you'll be golden."

Her assessment of us immediately brings a smile to my face and I lean across for Hannah's hand, splayed out on the table in front of her. She fires a look at me that certainly doesn't scream doting fiancé.

"Yeah, babe," I say, "Keep being playful." Then I lift my eyebrows, tilting my head toward Kat to remind her we're supposed to be in love.

She shakes her head, snapping out of her drug-like trance. "Yeah," she says, turning toward Kat as she squeezes my hand like it's a neck she's trying to choke—envisioning mine, I'm sure. "We love messing with each other. But we'd probably better head out before this guy has any bowel problems. He's lactose intolerant, but refuses to stop eating things that contain it."

Kat's eyes go wide, but before I can explain that Hannah's a dirty rotten liar, she's ripping my arm out of its socket to pull me out the door.

Alright, there you have it. Current score: Miles, two; Hannah, one—or was that low blow worth two?

Chapter Fourteen

Hannah

"Oh, it's beautiful!" Serena says the following Wednesday afternoon as I try on my dress for her. "It's exactly the color I imagined, great pick," she says, picking up the jersey material and running it between two fingers. "And it'll be so comfortable. That's something I love about my dress, too."

I run my hands down my hips, looking in the mirror. "I know. It's so comfortable. I can't believe it's a bridesmaid's dress."

"Yay, one more thing to check off the list. And Holt should get back any minute from shopping for wedding clothes with Miles."

My ears perk at the mention of Miles. It's been several days since the cake testing where lines were crossed a few times by both of us. "I'm surprised you didn't join them."

She waves off my worry. "Nah, your brother wears enough suits for work. I trusted him to find something that looks good. Besides, I showed him what I'd been envisioning over the weekend, so he won't veer too far from the original plan. At least I hope not. I don't think I can handle having to redo much else."

"Uh oh, what happened?"

She shakes her head, looking past me. "It's nothing."

I set my hand on her shoulder. "Rena, what happened?"

She takes a deep breath and laughs. "Well, all of our signage showed up this morning. I paid extra for immediate shipping and it showed up in the wrong color with a different couple's name on it."

My jaw drops. "You're kidding."

She shakes her head. "I wish I was. I had a good long cry, so I feel a little better now. Plus, the girl who made them apologized profusely and promised to have them finished and shipped by tomorrow morning, so we'll see what happens."

I examine her bloodshot eyes, coming up with a great idea. I fire off a text to the girls. Val and I are hosting wine night, something we've been doing with our friends Lainey and Ella, who we met through Val's boyfriend. I receive an influx of affirmative answers from our group text, a plan forming in my mind.

"Anyway, Holt and I are so grateful for you and Miles. You two have been so helpful. We wouldn't have been able to plan this wedding so quickly without your help."

Without another word, I pull my future sister-in-law in for a hug. "Of course, Serena. If you need more help, ask."

When she pulls away, there are tears in her eyes. "I refuse to put anymore on yours and Miles' plate. I know you're both busy enough as it is. How's that going, by the way?"

"Oh, it's been fine." I say, downplaying it majorly as I feel my cheeks heat, thinking back on the happenings at the cake tasting.

She furrows her brow, smiling at my non-answer. "Are you two getting along? I know he can be a grump, but you seem to vibe well with each other most of the time."

"Yes, well," I squint, trying to find the right words that won't get me in trouble when she reports back to Holt later. "We were both a little hesitant about the pairing at first, but it's been going a lot better these past couple of weeks. Dare I say I've actually had some fun at times?"

She smiles, like I've given her the right answer. "I know this will sound like I'm trying to put ideas in your head, but I've always thought you and Miles would make a great couple."

I look up at her and she's giving me a Cheshire smile, and I wonder if she knows something she shouldn't. "Oh, really?"

"Yes," she smacks my arm playfully. "You know he's freaking cute, obviously. In my time with your brother, I've always felt that—of the two of them—Miles is actually more defensive of you. Don't you agree?"

I look back, a very specific moment in his bar not so long ago coming to mind. "Yeah, I guess you could say that, but it's just brotherly stuff." The lie tastes bitter on my tongue.

She lifts her brows and gives me a look. "Whatever you say, Hannah."

I crack a guilty smile. "What?"

She puts two hands up in the air, palms out. "All I'll say is the way he looks at you when you can't see doesn't say *brotherly* to me."

I can't hide my smile. Her smug look says she got exactly the reaction she was looking for. But all I can think is, if she sees it, does Holt see it too? And if he does, what must he think?

Thankfully, before I build the courage to ask her, she makes for the door. "I'll let you change. I'll be down in the kitchen."

"Wait, Serena," I say before she can escape. She turns back to me and I add, "Val and I are hosting a wine night tonight with a couple girls at our house. You should come."

She screws up her face. "Ah, I don't know. I've got a lot of wedding stuff left to finish. I should probably stay home and get that done."

I give her the same look she threw at me a few minutes ago. "At least think about it."

"I will," she says, giving me a polite smile that tells me she doesn't plan on doing that at all.

I change quickly and walk down the steps with my bridesmaid dress in-hand. Right when I reach the landing, the front door opens and I make it to the kitchen just in time to see Holt and Miles walk through it.

"Oh, hey, Han," Holt says.

Miles walked in with his head down, but it pops up when he hears my name. My belly flutters. Hell, maybe Serena's onto something, and we should actually see whether these feelings could lead to more.

"Hey, guys. How was wedding shopping? Find yourselves some pretty dresses?"

Miles looks extra grumpy at the mention of their shopping trip. Makes sense, since you rarely find him dressed in anything other than his usual grayscale, while the wedding colors contain shades of blue. "Let me just say I much prefer to shop with you than with your brother. He's a dick about my style choices."

I eye his ensemble today—a signature black t-shirt and dark jeans. Then there's my brother's grey dress slacks and light blue button-down shirt, unbuttoned at the neck with the sleeves rolled. "Well, I think we can all agree, your styles aren't exactly complimentary of each other. So I guess that doesn't surprise me."

"Let's see what you guys got," Serena jumps in suddenly, and I know it took everything in her to wait this long to do so, which makes me laugh as Holt takes the bags from Miles and dumps them on the oversized, white marble island. We all watch on bated breath as Serena looks over their selections.

I sneak a peek at both boys as she unravels a pair of navy pants. Holt's too busy waiting for his fiancé's approval to notice, but Miles turns to me and smiles like we've got a secret. I guess we do.

"These are good." Serena says, stealing our attention. "Did you get any pictures of you two in them?"

I laugh because that's preposterous, but laugh harder when Holt digs his phone out of his pocket, surprising the hell out of me. Christ, Serena has whipped this boy into shape, and I couldn't be more proud.

"Oh god, I've gotta see this," I say, peeking over Serena's shoulder as she looks through the photos.

The first is of Holt, and I have to admit, he looks great. In fact, I can't wait to photograph the details of their wedding now that I know what each of them will be wearing. Then Serena swipes to the next photo of Miles. I damn near salivate at the sight of him in formal clothes, both because it's something I don't see him in often, and because he looks absolutely delectable—until my gaze reaches his face.

I bark out a laugh. "Miles, you look constipated."

Serena had swiped past the photo in question, but I reach over her and swipe it back. She laughs along with me, covering her mouth as if that will save Miles from the humiliation he's trying his best to hide underneath the grumpy look he's aiming at me.

"Let me see," Holt says, taking his phone from our hands and zooming in. He laughs too, "Oh, I have to heart that one."

"For the last time, Holt, it's called *favoriting* it when it's in your camera roll," Serena says. He rolls his eyes.

"Anyway. Did you two want to go for a drink at Miles' bar? We were going to celebrate getting another thing checked off the list today."

"Make that two things," I say, dangling my dress hanger from a finger. I check the time, realizing it's past the time I'd meant to get home. "And I'd love to, but it's wine night and

I'm late." I look up at Holt, hoping our sibling telepathy works like I know it can in my next words. "I invited Serena, but she says she has too much wedding stuff to do."

Holt turns to Serena. "Babe, you should go." He says, playing right into my hand.

"See?" I say, tossing an arm over Serena's shoulder. "You should come."

"I don't want to intrude, besides," she says, turning around to pick up her wedding binder, and she smacks the cover. "I've got plenty to do here."

Holt takes the binder in two hands and pulls, but it doesn't leave her clutches. "Babe, let go. You deserve a night off. Doesn't she deserve a night off?" He asks.

"Absolutely, after the day you had," I say, then look toward the door where Miles is still standing, giving him a look until he bounces to attention.

"Yeah, Rena. You deserve a break. Let Hannah get you good and tipsy tonight and you can worry about wedding stuff in the morning."

I smile at Miles as Holt whispers something I'm glad I can't hear in Serena's ear. Whatever it was, it must have worked.

"Hannah," Holt says, pulling my attention from his best friend.

"Yes?" I ask, nervous he's catching on to what's happening with those looks.

"Do you promise to get my future wife, your future sister-in-law, drunk tonight?"

I cross my arms, tilt my head and take a much-needed deep breath. "You know it."

An hour later, the five of us sit in Val's and my living room with our wine in-hand like an extension of our bodies when

Serena says, "Alright, ladies. I'm going to need y'all to vote here. All in favor of Hannah boning Miles, please raise your hand."

She raises her hand high in the air like an overeager student. Meanwhile, everyone else in the room looks between us with wide eyes, wondering what they should do.

Serena looks incredulous when no one joins her. "Are you guys serious? No one here is Team Miles?"

And just like that, the girls I once considered my best mates all turn on me at once.

"Oh, I'm Team Miles. Always have been, always will be," my oldest friend in the world, Val says, finally raising her hand as she looks pointedly at me.

"I've actually never met him, but I've seen pictures," Lainey flashes a seductive smile around the group. "That's enough for me to know that I'm Team Miles, all the way. That and the stories I've heard. He sounds dreamy."

"If I wasn't one-hundred percent in love with Holt," Serena starts, her eyebrows threatening her hairline, "I'd go after him myself. That, and I'm smart enough to realize the poor man only has eyes for our Hannah." She smiles at me then, leaning over on the couch to pat my knee.

I roll my eyes, but I'm secretly loving all the support in favor of my feelings for someone I've always believed I'm not supposed to want.

"Technically, I'm Team Hannah," Ella says all matter-of-fact, "So I'll go along with whatever she wants. But damn, girl. You know he's got the hots for you. I say go for it. Collect a few orgasms along the way, if nothing else. To hell with what your brother thinks," then as an afterthought, she adds, "no offense," in Serena's direction.

Serena throws up her hands. "Trust me, none taken. I love the man, but wow, is he dramatic sometimes." We all laugh. "But I'm serious, Han. Why haven't you kissed the man already?"

"We've never kissed, per se," I say, swirling the wine in my glass. When I look up, Serena's hanging on my every word. "But we have had some close encounters. I think we both know we shouldn't, so we haven't."

"But you should!!" Lainey yells from across the room, making everyone laugh.

"Trust me, it's getting harder not to. He's been very obvious about how he feels as of late."

"Do tell," Serena says, inching closer.

"At the cake tasting appointment, he licked frosting off my finger."

The entire room gasps except Val, who already knows all the details.

"That's hot," Ella says, lifting her head from where it was buried in her phone.

"You have no idea. Then there are the two kisses that I think were supposed to be on my cheek, but landed suspiciously close to my mouth. Actually, one was more of a frosting incident than a kiss."

"Okay, so what did you do about it?"

I laugh, "Nothing. He does these things to make me feel like he's interested, then acts like it didn't happen the next. I don't understand."

"He's probably warring with himself on his feelings because he knows he'll have to tell Holt eventually," Val says.

I toss that thought around in my head, because she's probably onto something there.

"If you two don't date so I can live vicariously through you, I'll be pissed," Lainey says when I'm done, causing the room to erupt in laughter.

"Or you could finally give Mal a chance," Ella says, challenging her younger sister with a raised brow.

"He's dating someone," she says, rolling her eyes. "Which is better off, honestly. It would never work with us living so far apart."

"Who's Mal?" Serena asks, not realizing she's opening Pandora's box with that one question.

Ella wastes no time fielding the answer. "Her lifelong best friend and soulmate. Also, a hottie minor league baseball player."

"Ooh," Serena says, bouncing her eyebrows, which makes us all giggle.

I listen intently as everyone fills Serena in on the weird dynamic I've barely begun to understand between Mal and Lainey.

"I know Val's happily attached. How about you, Ella? Give me all the gossip."

"I'm single, nothing to tell," Ella says, staring down at her phone again.

"Bullshit," Lainey says. "I bet if I looked at your phone right now, I'd see Andrew's name on the screen. Wouldn't I?"

Ella glares at her sister, setting her phone facedown on her lap. "No."

"Sounds like everyone's either in a good relationship, or straight up lying to themselves," Serena laughs, but no one denounces her theory.

"That might be true," Lainey says. "But I think Hannah's the only one in the position to change that right now."

"Yeah, but he's at the bar—with my brother."

"Alright, ladies! Drink up," Ella calls. "This DD is driving us to the bar."

"What?" Lainey whines, "I'm practically in pajamas," she says, motioning to her comfy sweats with her high school's mascot on the thigh. "How am I supposed to pick up a man looking like this?"

Ella shrugs. "Guess you should've thought about that before you went out in public dressed like that. Besides, it's not you I'm worried about." She looks over at me. "Hannah here needs to go get her man. And we're going to help."

Everyone whoops and hollers, making it clear I won't be

getting out of this. So instead of fighting it, I jump to my feet, a pang of nerves spiking through my chest at the prospect of what I'm about to do.

Chapter Fifteen

Holt is in the middle of a story from work when the bar door opens with a bang loud enough for me to think I may have to replace it, stealing both Holt's and my attention as a rowdy bunch comes through it. "Holy shit," he says, just before I recognize who's in the doorway.

"Rena, baby. What are you doing here?" He asks as she slips into the booth next to him.

Serena's telling him something that doesn't compute because she isn't the one who snags my attention. No, mine is on the red bombshell who comes up to the table next. The one wearing a knowing look.

"Well, this is a surprise," I say. That's when I notice two brunettes bringing up the rear. I know without having to ask that they must be the two sisters they met through Brody.

They greet me with various *heys*.

The shorter brunette smacks Hannah's arm, whispering in her ear without taking her eyes off me. Hannah's cheeks tinge pink as she comes up beside our booth, scooting in beside me with the secretive brunette, as the other goes to squeeze in with Holt and Serena.

"Where's Val?" I ask.

Hannah points to the bar. "She lost the game of *Rock, Paper, Scissors* and had to buy the first round."

Across the way, an uncharacteristically tipsy Serena is currently lavishing her fiancé with a very x-rated kiss, right here in front of us all. A heavy-lidded Holt pulls back, seeming to suddenly remember he's in his own sister's company.

"Wasn't sure you two were ever gonna come up for air," the girl sitting on Serena's other side says, making the rest of us laugh. Hannah takes the liberty of introducing us all to each other and I learn that the girl next to her is the eldest sister, Ella, and the one across the table is Lainey.

"Nice to meet you. I've heard a lot about you both. It's good to put a face with the names finally," Holt says.

"Yeah, what he said," I say with a nod as everyone turns to me.

"I hear you've been spending a lot of time with Hannah lately," Ella says, leaning around the girl in question with a knowing smirk.

My gaze flicks to Holt out of habit. He's too busy listening to Serena whisper in his ear. Just to cover my bases, I add, "Yes, we've been doing a lot of wedding planning for these two," I say, pointing my thumb in the insatiable couple's direction.

Hannah's hand pats my thigh, just above my knee, and suddenly all my nerve endings are on high alert. I brave a glance her way, only to find she's already smirking like she knows exactly what she's doing to me.

"Who needs a drink?" Val asks, coming up to the table with both hands full.

The table erupts in whoops, but I don't join in. Mostly because Edie's standing behind Val helping her deliver several beers. Her gaze flicks between Hannah and me with a conspiratorial smirk as her drawn-on brows bounce on her forehead.

I shake my head and look at Holt to make sure he's not catching any of this. He's still too fixated on his soon-to-be wife to notice anything but her. Thank goodness.

The boundaries between us have been tested lately, but Hannah hasn't pushed them further, so I've tried to keep it to small lingering touches and suggestive language to test them. I broke my own rules last week thanks to a bit of sugary frosting and her creamy white skin that was even sweeter. Out of fear that I took it too far and blew things between us, I've avoided contacting her since. But I knew that wasn't the case as soon as she walked into the room at Holt's earlier. The way she looked at me, I'd been wishing for a moment alone with her. Now that she's here, maybe that option is still on the table.

"Hey, man. Sorry to cut the night short, but I think I'm gonna get this girl home," he says, pushing an errant hair behind Serena's ear, looking at her like she hung the moon.

"Yeah, that much was clear the moment she walked in. You two have a good night."

"You sure you'll be okay? You'll be the only guy left."

Serena laughs, "Oh, look at him," she's looking at me, but talking to Holt. "He's shaking in his boots, thinking about being the only guy in the company of four gorgeous girls. Poor Miles."

"At least you'll have Hannah and Val, though, right? You get along with those two just fine."

"Yeah, at least I'll have them," I say as everyone shuffles around to let them out of the booth. They practically run toward the door. It's weird though, because in all the years I've known Serena, she's never been the type for public displays of affection, yet she's been all over Holt since she sat down. I'd say it's because she got drunk with the girls tonight, but that isn't it either. She seemed like she'd been feeling tipsy enough to have rosy cheeks, but I've seen her good and drunk. Tonight, she wasn't.

"Oh good, our plan worked," Lainey says, looking at the door as she settles back in.

Val sends a warning glare at her friend, who suddenly becomes very interested in the drink she's holding.

"What plan?" I whisper in Hannah's ear.

She screws up her face and shrugs, but her pink cheeks are a telltale sign that I'm not getting the truth.

"I know there's something you're not telling me, but it's okay because I'm glad I got to see you again."

She turns, her gaze piercing me like she can see into my soul. Then she smirks, "Me too."

"Do you think we could go talk somewhere?" I ask before I can think better of it.

"It's almost like you have a place right above this bar."

"I didn't want to be too forward."

Hannah takes a nice big chug of her drink. "One could say, Miles, that you aren't being forward enough."

That statement is a slug to my chest. One that seems to answer a lot of the questions I still have about us, and I can no longer wait to find out. "Alright, let's go then."

Hannah turns to Ella, who smirks as she lets us out of the booth. "Don't do anything I wouldn't do, you two," she whispers as the rest of the girls whistle and cat call on our way to the door. As I turn, my gaze snags on Edie behind the bar wearing that damn teasing smile. I'll be hearing about this later, that's for sure.

But that's all forgotten when Hannah smiles up at me as she leads us out the back door. By the time I'm past the threshold, my blood feels too heavy for my body, the weight of what's to come—the choices I have yet to make, causing every step up to my apartment to land like concrete blocks.

She moves to the side when we reach my door. I smile and open it for us, propping it open for her to walk through.

The last time she was here feels like forever ago. Back before I dared let her have a glimpse at my feelings that seem to be growing out of control. I just hope whatever she's about to say doesn't have me regretting the whole damn thing.

Hannah's standing in the middle of my kitchen, her arms wrapped around her middle and her top teeth sunk into her lip.

I feel like I need something to do with my hands, so I walk to the fridge. "Beer?"

"Actually, do you have any bourbon?"

I close the door and turn to look at Hannah. Her smile takes up her whole face, and the sparkle in her eyes tells me she's up to no good.

I find the dusty bottle of Hillrock bourbon I have high up in my cupboards.

"How do you want it?" The words feel like an innuendo.

"Surprise me."

I plop two large ice cubes in the only two fancy tumblers I got from Jenn and Bobby one Christmas, then pour us each a glass.

I turn around and hand one to Hannah. At some point, while I had my back turned, she hopped up on the island counter. With her shoes kicked off, a pair of tiny cutoff jean shorts, and a tank top so thin, I can see the color of her bra through it, I realize I could get used to seeing Hannah so comfortable inside my space.

"To…" Hannah starts, holding her drink out to me.

"Us," I finish for her.

"To us," she says, her cheeks tinged pink.

I clink my glass with hers and she smiles, leaning imperceptibly closer. "To us," I say, leaning against the counter right next to her thigh.

We both assess the other over the rim of our glasses as we take a sip. Hannah's cool facade fades as she coughs at the first taste, making me think back on that night many moons ago when I caught her with her dad's bottle of bourbon.

"You good?"

She chuckles. "Yeah," she says, taking another gulp as if to prove her point.

I had strictly platonic feelings for Hannah back in high school, but I considered her a good friend back then, as well as every year before it.

I could tell all she wanted that night was to fit in with a bunch of kids who were used to drinking on the weekends. I've always recognized that in her, that need to feel like she belongs somewhere with people who see her heart. It took me a long time to realize that all the conversations we'd had over the years were us finding that person in each other. I wonder if she sees it that way. If she ever could.

"So you gonna tell me what you lured me up here for?" I ask, even though I fear the answer.

She leans back on one hand; the position bringing her closer to me. Close enough, I can smell the coconut scent on her skin. "It's your apartment. If anyone's doing the luring, it's you."

I smile into my glass. "Left the door unlocked. You're free to leave at any time, Hannah."

"And what if I don't want to?"

"Then tell me why you're here."

She takes a deep breath, resting her glass on her thigh. "Do you feel it?"

"Be more specific."

She lifts her hand to talk with it, something that happens when you really get her going. "I don't know. I've felt a shift between us these past several weeks."

All the air in my lungs whooshes out between us. "Yeah, I've felt it too." Admitting that feels like an out-of-body experience after all this time. I've thought about this moment a million times, and it's finally out in the open.

She looks up at me through her lashes. "So your flirtatious ways recently haven't been just you trying to mess with me?"

There's a stray hair in her face and I finally let my inner thoughts win and push it back behind her ear. "Hannah, my flirtatious ways recently have been the product of my inability to control myself around you any longer."

"So, are you officially done controlling yourself around me?"

I chew on my lip, trying like hell to hold myself back until she gives me the go ahead. "Do you want me to be?"

She smiles, never taking her eyes off of me. Her fingertips find my beard before her palm settles on my cheek. "Yes. Lose control with me."

Her gaze drops to my mouth as she leans. I set my glass on the counter and step between her spread thighs. Her fingers grip the front of my shirt, pulling me in.

"Are you sure?" I ask, leaning my forehead against hers, silently begging her not to change her mind.

Instead of answering, she pulls me in the rest of the way, our lips finally colliding. It's unlike anything my imagination could have conjured. Finally having her this close. This indescribable throbbing, burning sensation in my chest spreading as our lips learn each other's for the first time.

Her hands grip the material of my shirt at my shoulders as mine find her lower back and slide her body closer to mine and she wraps her legs around my hips. Before I can deepen the kiss, Hannah's hands push me back just enough to look at me, but those long legs stay in place.

I search her gaze, looking for any indication she doesn't want this like I do. Then Hannah's mouth breaks into the biggest smile I've seen in a while. A smile I can still feel when her mouth lands back on mine.

When her hands snake themselves around my neck, I lift her from the counter, causing her to squeal into my shoulder on our way to the couch.

I sit with her straddling me and it suddenly feels like everything just got a lot more serious. I set my hands on her thighs and wait for her to meet my gaze.

She does, and the flush of her skin offsets the freckles peppered across her cheeks. "This is crazy, isn't it?"

I rub circles on her inner thigh with my thumb as I contemplate the best way to move forward without scaring her off. "Maybe, but I'm not ready to ruin whatever's happening right now by overthinking it."

She runs a finger down my chest. "I like the way you think, Miles."

I'm completely content watching her explore with her hands—my chest, my forearms, my hands. "I can't believe this is happening right now," she says so quietly, it's like she's in a trance.

"Me neither, if I'm honest."

Her nose crinkles, "Really?"

I pull at a strand of her hair, wrapping it around my finger nice and slow. "You're so far out of my league, Hannah."

She laughs, but when I don't join, she asks, "Wait, you're actually serious?"

"Of course I am. When was the last time you saw me date anyone? There's a reason for that." I don't dare tell her it's because I've spent the past few years holding out for exactly this.

"So? I haven't dated anyone in a year because of my track record. We're both a mess. In fact, you should probably just kick me out of your apartment and save us both the trouble."

I hate that the joke actually has me thinking about everything that could go wrong after what we just started. What's our next step? Telling Holt? Running around behind his back? Deciding it's not worth it and ruining the friendship we were finally rekindling?

"Miles," Hannah says with a palm against my beard like she'd been trying to get my attention for a while.

"Yeah?"

"We don't have to have this all figured out right now. All I know is that I really like you, and if recent events are any indication, you like me, too. I want to see where this could go. Do you want that too?"

"Yes."

She smiles. "Good." Her fingers weave through the short hairs at the back of my head as she pulls me in. The feel of her lips turns off the background noise inside my head momentarily, and I'm grateful for the reprieve. But she breaks away quickly when there's a buzzing sensation coming from the back pocket of her shorts.

"Shit, it's Val," she says, pulling out her phone, unknowingly shoving her chest closer to my face. "I should take this."

She drops a chaste kiss to my lips before hopping up from my lap and answering on the last ring. I try not to eavesdrop as I walk her to the door, but Val's talking so loud, I can hear every excited word she's saying—many of them about me.

"I think I'll stay a little longer. Miles will make sure I get home okay," she says, turning to smile at me.

I'd fully expected her to leave with her friends, so the fact that she wants to stay is definitely a good sign.

Chapter Sixteen

Miles

"Are you hungry?" I ask after Hannah pockets her phone.

She follows me back out to the island to grab her glass, taking a small sip before answering. "I could eat."

I pull the ingredients for my famous grilled cheese out of my fridge. As I toss them in a pile on the counter, I hear Hannah's gasp from behind me.

"Please tell me you're making what I think you're making."

I look at her over my shoulder and say, "They don't call me the grilled cheese king for nothing."

She laughs at me then, throwing her head back. "Nobody calls you that, Miles."

She's right, but anyone who knows me knows the name fits. I've never had a grilled cheese better than the ones I make at home.

I guess I'd blame it on the amount of times my parents left me to my own devices growing up. When it came to food, I fended for myself, and there were times that nothing was in the house. One day, we had little else besides cheese and bread, so I cut slices of a few different cheeses left over from when my parents had guests over and it was the first of many I've made since.

Of course, that first recipe wasn't perfect, but with time, I was making money and able to buy the ingredients myself. And much like the Miles High Club Soda, I've perfected it with time.

"Can I watch?" Hannah asks, appearing at my side.

"Of course," I say, setting my skillet on top of the burner. "But no sharing my secrets with anyone else, got it?"

She glances up at me, hearts in her eyes. "I wouldn't dream of it."

"So first things first, you need a good skillet," I say.

"Guess I have to come to you for a grilled cheese, then. Because Val and I don't have one."

"I'll make you a grilled cheese anytime, day or night."

She smiles, but tries to hide it behind her glass. "Noted."

"Once your pan's hot, then comes the fresh parmesan," I say, sprinkling the cheese in two bread-sized piles on the skillet.

"Yum."

"French bread," I say, picking up my partial loaf from beside Hannah and cutting off several pieces.

"Let me guess, butter next?"

I chuckle. "You're such a good student."

"I'm a good listener," she says, and my mind goes off on a tangent, imagining her taking orders.

Hannah listens intently through the last several steps of my process. And while they sizzle on the skillet, I can think of exactly one way I'd like to spend my time.

"And while they do their thing," I say, my hands finding her hips. I prop her up on the island counter as her legs instinctively wrap around my waist. "You let your girl keep you occupied.

And when I lean in, ready to continue what we started earlier, she welcomes me with open arms.

I'm walking Hannah home after we finished eating our grilled cheeses, which were delicious, by the way. We decided to take the long route, which means we're just walking around, and not really in the direction of her house.

"Thanks for letting me talk to you tonight. I know we kind of ambushed you. I'm sorry about that."

"Hannah," I say, bumping my shoulder with hers, "it's an honor to have my plans interrupted by you. As long as it's you, you'll never hear me complain."

"Careful, Miles. You might get me thinking that I'm your favorite Hawkins."

"You always have been, don't tell Holt."

She giggles, leaning against my shoulder as we navigate a narrow sidewalk. This night has been full of surprises, and I'm not sure where we'll go from here. All I know is I plan to savor her attention while she's willing to give it.

"So, this is all pretty new. Can I ask where your head's at?" I ask, surprised by my straightforwardness.

"I'm glad you asked," Hannah says, looking up at me. "I've been a little nervous about how this could all pan out. You're obviously best friends with my brother, and I don't want to ruin anything going on between you two. I do know I want this to happen again."

We made it to the park that's a few blocks in the opposite direction of Hannah's place, so instead of continuing on in the wrong direction, I pull her over to a bench to sit for a minute.

There's not much light around, but we're just close enough to a streetlight that I can make out the features of her face.

"I want that too," I admit. "I want that very badly."

She chuckles, picking at her fingernails. "It's so weird to hear you say that."

"It's so weird hearing myself finally admit it out loud."

"This is crazy," she says, echoing her thoughts from earlier.

"But in a good way, right?" I ask, suddenly self-conscious and worried she's second-guessing everything.

She leans across the space between us, kissing me quick on the mouth before she says, "In the best way." She takes my hand, looking down at it as she continues. "If you hadn't already guessed, the girls devised a plan for me to get to spend time with you tonight. Ella was the mastermind of it all. Serena was supposed to seduce my brother to get him to want to leave."

"I knew she was up to something. She never acts like she did tonight, even when she's drunk."

"Yeah, the girls wouldn't listen to me, otherwise things would have happened a lot differently."

"Well, considering everything that transpired, I'm glad it happened."

"Me too. Actually, Serena is kinda the reason we got on the subject of you tonight at all, so I guess it's a good thing I talked her into coming. She promised not to bring it up to Holt, but I know they tell each other everything."

"That's what I'm afraid of. What do you mean by her being the reason?"

"I guess she notices the way we look at each other. She was onto us and asked everyone else if they were Team Miles."

I smile at that. "Team Miles, huh? What was the consensus?"

"Let's just say you have fans," she says, and it makes us both laugh. It feels good, laughing with her. It's been so long since we've been ourselves around each other. Something in my chest locks into place at the thought.

"Do you think he'll freak out when he finds out?" she asks. The question is a total mood killer.

I appreciate the way she says when rather than if, like him finding out is an eventuality, rather than a possibility. "It's hard to say. He knows we've always been close, so it can't be that surprising, right?" I ask, trying to manifest the best-case scenario.

"The wedding's only three weeks away. Maybe we should lie low until afterward. It gives us time to figure things out for ourselves before involving anyone."

"That might not be a bad idea," I say, not a huge fan of having to keep secrets from my best friend, but I've been doing so this long. What's another few weeks?

"So we're doing this," I say.

"We're doing this." Hannah says, her palm landing on my thigh. "On a—trial basis."

"I don't like the sound of that," I admit

She sings the lyrics to "Dirty Little Secret" by The All-American Rejects, making me laugh. "Stop it right now."

"That song was a banger," she says.

"I was partial to "Gives You Hell," actually."

She laughs, and I laugh right along with her. "Damn, Miles. Who broke your heart?"

I laugh, and Hannah pokes my cheek and exclaims, "Dimple sighting!"

"What on earth does that mean?" I ask, grabbing her hand and holding it between us. I can't get over how easy this feels. The touching, the banter, all of it. I enjoy it when it's happening, then crave it when she's gone.

"You don't smile enough, and I get excited every time I get to see your dimples, even if they try to hide under your beard."

I'm still grinning when I shake my head at the ridiculous notion. "You continue to surprise me, Hannah."

"There will be plenty more where that came from, but for now, I should probably get home. Walk me?"

I'm on my feet in an instant, lifting her to standing as she leans in for a kiss. I get lost in the moment, just the two of us there in the middle of the park, hidden from the rest of the world.

Christ, I'm already gone for this girl and she doesn't even know it.

Chapter Seventeen

Hannah

This night still feels surreal. Especially as I walk up to my front door with Miles' hand in mine.

"Thanks for walking me home." I say, swinging our hands between us. "You're such a gentleman."

"I can be sometimes," he says, his eyes dark and promising.

He leans me back against the side of the porch, closing me in with the bracket of his arms. I'm surrounded by his cedarwood scent, which I've always found intoxicating. But I never imagined I'd get to experience it in this way.

"I don't know how I'll ever get enough of this," he murmurs against my mouth, going back in for more.

He lifts my leg high on his hip, leaning his pelvis against me until I can feel the hardness in his jeans. His hands only add to the sensory overload. He's gripping my thigh with one hand, my waist with the other. I can't get enough of his glorious mane.

I've spent years wanting to touch this man's hair, and now I have free rein to do so. What is my life? Holy shit. I'm in way over my head with this man.

We're just finding a rhythm with our mouths, his tongue tasting mine when I hear footsteps approaching.

"No fucking way," a voice that's far too close says and we shoot apart.

I turn to find Brody standing in the middle of the sidewalk, his hands up in front of him like he's trying to prove he means no harm. "Shit, I'm sorry. Let me just—" He walks on his tiptoes, as quiet as can be, but the harm has already been done.

"Brody," I say, it comes out as more of a warning than a greeting.

Miles steps in front of me, even though we both know I don't need protecting from the bespectacled man my best friend is in love with whom just interrupted us mid-make-out.

"Great timing you've got there, Brody," Miles says.

Brody grimaces, trying to sidestep us, even though we're right in front of the door. "I know, and I'm so sorry. For what it's worth, I like what's going on here."

The door behind us opens. "Brody? Oh, hey you two," Val says when she sees all three of us standing there. I can only imagine what's going through her head.

"Miles just walked me home, and Brody just got here."

"They were kissing, and I accidentally interrupted," Brody blurts.

"Brody!" All three of us yell for our own reasons, and I'd find it comical if I wasn't so uncomfortable.

"You didn't need to tell her that," I say.

Val turns to me, mouthing, *I'm sorry.*

"I mean, even if I hadn't walked up on you two," Brody adds, digging himself an even deeper hole. "It's pretty clear what you've been up to. You have beard burn, Hannah," Brody says, making everyone laugh.

We stand around on the porch, none of us looking one another in the eye. Miles is the first to make a move. "Alright. Hannah, I'll call you tomorrow. Have a good night," and despite the awkwardness of the moment, he kisses me on the forehead. "Thanks for…everything."

"No problem," I squeak. He gives me one last parting smirk before turning back down the sidewalk.

Val, Brody, and I stand and watch him until he disappears into the night.

"That was so hot," Brody says.

I'm still so dumbfounded by the night's happenings, I don't have a more exciting reply than, "I know."

"I'm so mad I missed it," Val says.

Chapter Eighteen

Miles

"Hey, boss. I just opened the last box of Absolut and thought I'd better tell ya," my hardest-working bartender, Carolina, says from my office doorway Friday morning. She's also the most infuriating behind Edie. They both enjoy giving me shit.

"Thanks, I appreciate you letting me know."

She smiles and nods, then disappears.

I had to call a meeting with all my employees a few weeks after I took over as owner after my uncle, Stu. He hadn't run a tight ship while here, which could have had something to do with the turnaround in employees we experienced during that time.

When we ran out of something, customers were forced to go without until the next shipment came in. At the time, I was a bartender, and always got an earful when we were out of something.

It wasn't until I took over that I realized what had been going on. Back then, I thought he'd been lazy about orders, getting the amount of inventory wrong every time we turned around. But it wasn't that he was forgetful or not paying attention. There was just no money.

And from that moment of realization on, what I thought would be an easy transition turned out to be a huge fucking mess.

Employees were used to his lax management style. They were used to getting away with things like not notifying management of low inventory, freebie drinks for their friends while bartending, and on occasion, even getting drunk on the job.

A few people were let go after that first meeting because they refused to change their ways. Instances like those are the worst part of my job, since I hate confrontation—or any kind of attention on me, for that matter. But those who stuck it out spoke up after they were out the door, and it sounds like they'd been needing let go for longer than I'd realized.

After a few new hires, things are going well with our small team. I'd hoped a spruced up storefront and some simple word-of-mouth would help us drum up more business from our little town, but it hasn't been the case. At least most of our regulars have stayed with us, except for the few I've watched take a look at the new interior and grumble something under their breath about "youths," like an elderly version of Schmidt from the sitcom, New Girl, and walk right back out the door.

It's fine though. It's just growing pains (I hope) and not everyone wants to be a part of that.

As I'm preparing an order to send off to my supplier, I yawn. I woke up pretty early this morning, considering how late I sat here in this chair last night. When I went to my coffee maker, I cursed myself for my decision to put in another long night, rather than getting groceries like I should have. My bag of coffee grounds had run out the morning before, so it's been a no coffee morning for me.

I send the email I'd been working on and get up out of my

chair, my back screaming at me for the way I've been hunched over in it all morning.

After making sure I have my wallet and phone, I make my way through the bar toward the front door. "Heading out for some coffee. Do you need anything?" I say to Carolina, who has her back turned. She volunteered to come in early to help deep clean the bar this morning. I was grateful for the help.

She points across the bar to where an extra large to-go coffee cup sits. "Already stocked for the day, but thank you."

I nod and push out into the sunny spring morning. One of the best parts of Wellford is its Main Street. O'Harrow's Pub, along with many other small businesses, line it. There are black lampposts erected from the sidewalks, which hold hanging baskets of various bright colors, and they're bursting from their pots now that it's mid-summer.

It's the third of July, so there's a group of people in town who spend an entire day just before Independence Day, putting up American flags that line the entire street. They're all blowing in the wind above my head as I walk, and I'll never stop thinking the view is incredible.

Tonight is the town's Fourth of July festivities, only happening on the third because we're a small town they want to give the surrounding cities a chance to outdo us on the actual holiday. But everyone knows, Wellford is the place to be if you want a light show on the third.

I let my mind wander as I walk, and no matter what corners my train of thought turns down, it always pulls up to Station Hannah Hawkins.

I'm still dumbfounded by the fact that she searched me out the other night and initiated our first kiss. It was a fantastic kiss, and a fantastic night. One I wouldn't mind repeating as soon as possible.

When I finally get to Brew & Bean, the local coffee shop, I pull open the door as several people walk out. I'd be annoyed, but every single person says thank you with a smile on their face. Iowa nice is a stereotype that was coined for the way people around here will treat you upon meeting, and it's especially true here in Wellford.

If you're some stranger passing through town, after everyone has whispered about you, trying to figure out your story to no avail, they'll welcome you with open arms.

When I get inside, the cash register is open, so I walk right up to it, where Belinda—Bindy for short—is standing there, smiling as usual. She's in her early fifties and if you walk through the door of her establishment, she will immediately consider you a friend. See? Iowa nice.

"Miles! It's been a while. But I still know your usual," she taps her forehead and says, "Black coffee, your darkest roast, none of the frills. Right?" She relayed my usual order in a growly voice that I assume was meant to sound just like me.

I chew on my lip, almost embarrassed by what I'm about to do. "Actually, do you make white chocolate iced mochas here?" I ask, hoping I didn't just annihilate the name Hannah rattled off to her barista that day in the car.

"Do you mean an iced white chocolate mocha?"

"Yes, that. And there's this stuff on top—"

"Whipped cream?" I shake my head. "Cold foam?"

"That sounds right, yes."

"Could I interest you in a caramel drizzle as well?"

"The drizzle is a must," I say, then immediately wish I could take it back.

"Alright, this is new. But I'll have it ready in a moment."

I sit at a table off to the side of the pick up counter, scrolling through my phone to pass the time. My emails are all promotional bullshit, so I close the app. Instead, I click on the app I rarely open. I have a generic username, and I'm pretty sure my name isn't even attached to it, but it's where Hannah shares her photos. Both her professional ones, and her self-portraits. I follow celebrities, and some friends on the app too, but it's Hannah's latest self portrait that pops up first on my homepage.

The sight of it knocks my breath straight from my lungs. Her creamy white skin is glowing in golden light, her hair taking on that coppery appearance it tends to in the evening light. She's surrounded on all sides by a tree with white blooms.

"Miles, your order is ready," Bindy calls, making me jump and look around to make sure no one saw me ogling Hannah's picture on my phone. I pocket it and walk up to the counter just as Bindy sets down a drink that looks identical to the one Hannah made me try a couple of weeks ago.

"Thank you," I say, sliding it closer to myself and slamming the end of my straw onto the counter two times to open the wrapper and stick it into the drink, my mouth already watering for a taste.

The door behind me opens, momentarily letting noises from outside traffic into the building. I'm just turning toward it, straw poised in front of my mouth, when I run into Hannah.

She's free of makeup, which makes her freckles pop, and her auburn hair is in a knot on the top of her head. I can't think of anything else besides how badly I want to kiss her. I'm so stunned by the sight of her, it takes me a moment to register why her eyes are as wide as sand dollars, and her mouth is dropped open as she points at my hand.

"See? I knew you liked my coffee!" she says in an accusatory tone.

I pull my cup away and look at it like it's done something to offend me. And as I wrack my brain for something to say that will save my dignity, I realize I've got nothing. She caught me red-handed.

I shrug. "Just trying it again to determine whether it's actually good or not."

She nods slowly, her expression the description of doubtful. "Right," she turns toward the counter, "Hey, Bindy. I'll have what he's got, please."

She nods. "See, I thought that was your order, but I didn't want to say anything."

I sip on my drink before I pull my credit card from my wallet and give it to Bindy.

"You don't have to do that, Miles," Hannah says, looking around the space, because god forbid anyone see us conversing in public. She must have forgotten the woman standing behind the counter is currently enemy number one.

"A small price to pay to keep you quiet about my drink of choice. What are you doing here?" I take in her appearance as I walk back into the dining area, where Hannah leads us to one of the booths. She's got her camera bag slung over her right shoulder, and is wearing bright purple leggings and a white tank top that leaves nothing to the imagination. I force my gaze away from it.

"I'm actually meeting another photographer here in a few minutes, then probably going to camp out here and try to get some work done. My home office feels kinda stuffy these days."

I almost tell her to come to the bar for a change of scenery, or even my apartment, but imagine Holt walking in on that with a million questions and think better of it.

"Oh yeah? Do I know her?"

She grimaces. "No, you don't know *him*," she says, annunciating the last word. "His name is Cameron, and we have a wedding coming up where he'll be my second shooter, so we're just trying to get on the same page about things."

"Oh," I say, trying to tamper down my sudden jealousy at the thought of her having a coffee date with some guy I don't know.

"Miles," she says, tilting her head down and looking at me through her lashes. "You know I meant everything I said the other night, and having to meet a guy—another photographer —for coffee is just a part of my job, right?"

"Yeah, of course," I say, mentally shaking myself out of it. "Sorry, I don't do this often."

"What, have feelings for your best friend's sister? Good, I was hoping I'd be the only one."

That makes me smile. "You are."

"And so are you. I've held out hope for this chance for years. You won't find me doing anything to jeopardize that."

"Good to know," I say, taking a sip of my iced coffee, a burst of delicious flavor hitting my tongue. Hannah watches my mouth the whole time. I lick my lip, and she bites hers. I'm about to throw caution to the wind when Bindy calls her name from the counter.

Hannah jumps up, and instead of going to the counter like I expected, she jumps into my side of the booth and pulls me in for a kiss.

It's hurried and cautious, but it's enough to settle the storm brewing in my mind. She smiles as she pulls away, and I haul her back for one more kiss, this one deeper. We both exhale into it and I swipe my tongue across her lip as she opens up for me. I'm just starting to lose myself in her when she pulls away. Looking at me with her bright green eyes wide open. And not just in the literal sense, but I feel like I could see all her thoughts churning inside her mind if I tried just a little harder.

She sets her hand on my chest. "Pick me up on your way to my parents tonight?"

I nod before I can even register what she's asked me. "I'll pick you up at 5:45."

"Okay. I'll see you then," she says, standing up out of the booth and backing toward the counter. "See you then."

There's a guy approaching the front door as I walk through, so I hold it for him. He's what most would call attractive, by Western standards. He nods in thanks, then makes a beeline straight for my girl. But I don't sweat it, because she's across the way, smiling back at me.

Chapter Nineteen

Miles

Despite my feeling there's plenty left to do at the pub, I leave myself plenty of time to get to Hannah's several minutes early.

I'm three steps toward the house when she bursts from the door looking much different than she had at the coffee shop this morning. Her auburn hair is slightly wavy, and although she's wearing minimal makeup, whatever she did to her eyes makes them stand out against the rest of her face. She's wearing a flowy white t-shirt and those damn shorts that I can't get enough of.

Her sandals smack against her feet as we both take large steps to close the space between us. I don't know what I was expecting when we finally meet in the middle of her sidewalk, but her jumping into my arms wasn't on the list. But I'm not complaining when her legs wrap around my waist, her arms around my shoulders. I widen my stance as I wind one arm around her back and pull her mouth closer with a hand in her hair.

"You look beautiful," I say against her lips. Then our mouths meet in a slow, sensual kiss. We take our time, right there in the middle of the sidewalk, for the whole neighborhood to see and I can't find it in me to care.

"We should probably go," Hannah says, breathless, with her forehead resting against mine.

"We should. Good thing I accounted for just enough time to kiss you.

She laughs, her whole body shaking in my arms. "Yeah, I was happy when I realized you were early. You know how Holt gets when we aren't punctual, especially if he sees us show up together."

I pat her ass with the hand that found its way there naturally during our kiss. "Alright, let's go then. Wouldn't want to make a lady late."

I turn toward my truck, but Hannah's hand stops me mid-turn. She reaches up to pull me down to her for one last quick kiss, which I savor. But it's the look in her eyes that really gets me.

That sparkle I'd been missing for months is back to its full luminosity. I hadn't realized how much I'd craved that look until it's right here in front of me. I lace my hand with hers and pull her toward the truck before I make us late.

On the short drive to the Hawkins house, we have the windows rolled down. The breeze blows Hannah's tropical scent all throughout the cab, and I'm a lucky asshole lying on the beach sipping Piña Coladas.

The juxtaposition of our trip to the truck and our trip from the truck is comical. Where we looked like a couple leaving Hannah's, we look like two strangers who carpooled for the good of the environment when we arrive at the Hawkins residence. Hannah runs ahead, pushing open the front door while I take my time.

Nobody even notices Hannah and I show up together, thanks to the fact that the house is buzzing with guests. Neighbors, friends, and family members all flit about the place, but the true party is in the backyard.

Bobby Hawkins is a grill master. When he got his first meat smoker, his game stepped up even more. As soon as I step into the backyard, I'm hit in the face with the smell of barbecue and the sound of laughter and happy chatter everywhere.

I look around for Hannah, but already seem to have lost her. Instead, I make my way to Holt, who is talking animatedly with one of his dad's friends on the patio.

He doesn't miss a beat, smacking me on the back mid-conversation and grabbing me a beer from a nearby cooler. "How you been?" Holt asks when his dad's friend walks away to mingle with other guests.

"Good, you?"

"Great."

Holt laughs. "Look at you all chipper," he says, and I don't realize until then that I have a permanent smile on my face.

I shrug and wipe a hand across my mouth to get control of myself.

"Things going well at the pub, I take it?"

I should be offended that's the first thing he thinks of that could be going right for me. But I'm like a dog with a bone and run with it, burying the truth in the backyard with the rest of my secrets. "Yeah, things are looking up. Still a little nervous to leave them to their own devices here in a little over a week, but I just keep telling myself it'll be fine. How are you feeling about the wedding?" I ask, trying to shift the focus off myself.

I listen intently as Holt talks about everything we've accomplished for his wedding in the short time since they got engaged. I feel a little swell of pride I hadn't expected when I think of Hannah and our part we played in it all. If it weren't for this wedding, I have to wonder where we'd be right now.

Would we still be avoiding each other? I unfortunately feel as if that might be the case. I wasn't sure how this would all pan out, but Hannah and I kiss to greet each other now. I'd say that's worth the insane to-do list we were given.

"Thanks for letting us help with things," I say honestly.

Holt looks at me, surprise apparent on his face. "I thought you hated it."

I shrug, hiding so many feelings within that one gesture. "Yeah, but it wasn't all bad." Over Holt's shoulder, I meet Hannah's gaze across the party. She's giving me a secret smile as she talks to Val and a few of their friends from high school.

"I knew you'd be here," I say when I find Hannah sitting alone in front of the evergreens at the edge of the yard, hidden from the rest of the party.

"I was hoping you would," she says, her smile lighting up the night as I sit down on the blanket she's got sprawled on the grass.

"Sorry it took me a while. I had to ditch your brother with Serena so I could come find you."

It's no secret that this was our favorite spot to watch the fireworks growing up. Not all of us, just Hannah and I. We've managed to watch many firework shows from this very spot throughout the years. The Hawkins' backyard has a fantastic vantage point of the light show, located only about a block away from the site where they shoot them off. But this spot right here is top tier, with nothing blocking the view, and no one else knows about it.

"I think you made it just in time," she says, pulling me in for a kiss just as the first firework trails up into the dark sky.

The popping noises and flashing colors feel a lot like the feelings inside my chest begging to make themselves known.

"Tell me, have you ever been kissed under the fireworks?" I ask.

She pulls only far enough away for me to see her smile

grow wide. "Never. You?"

"My first time, it's kind of romantic, isn't it?"

She chuckles. "Yes. And you're going to make fun of me for this, but—" she stops, suddenly bashful.

"What, honey?" I ask, brushing her hair behind her ear so I can see her face more clearly.

"I imagined this exact scenario every year you sat here next to me."

I shake my head. "There's no way you mean that."

"I do. I've thought about it every July third leading up to this one, where it's finally happening."

"Even that year you were dating that weasel named Rowan?"

She throws her head back, laughing. "Yes, even then. Especially then. He was a terrible kisser. I would have spontaneously combusted from the comparison alone."

"Did you just call me a good kisser?"

She lands a light smack on my chest. "You already know you're a great kisser."

"I don't know that at all, actually. I know you're a fantastic kisser, though."

"Shut up," she says with a laugh.

"I mean it, Hannah. Best game of tonsil hockey I've ever played."

"Oh, gross!" she shoves at my shoulder with that one, exactly the reaction I'd been hoping for. We're both laughing until on my back, with her straddling me with her hands on either side of my head. This position sobers us real quick.

"Now get down here and show me what I was missing all those years."

There are explosions of color lighting up the sky above Hannah's head just before she leans in, taking up my whole view.

And with her beautiful mouth to distract me, I miss every single one.

Chapter Twenty

Hannah

Serena was very much against having a bachelorette party in the traditional, girls-gone-wild, drinking-all-night-long sense. So instead of completely skipping a party, I planned a night of friends and relaxation for her and a handful of girls. I get her to the spa on Friday afternoon with Holt's help. I've heard her say she's been wanting to try this place out for months.

They walk in the door hand-in-hand right when I told Holt to show up. She thinks she's here on her own, but Val, Lainey, Ella, and three friends of Serena's from work and college all stand up with squeals of excitement when she reaches up on her toes to kiss Holt goodbye. She turns at the noise, smiling when she recognizes us.

I meet them at the door. "Hope you don't mind us joining you. I had to figure out a way to surprise you, and Holt agreed to help get you here," I say as I wrap my arm around my brother, leaning my head on his chest as he returns the side hug.

"Of course I don't mind," she's covering her face, wiping

a tear from the corner of her eye as Holt kisses her forehead. "Thank you for this, Hannah."

I smile, pulling her in for a hug. "I know you don't want a wild and crazy night. So we're going to get pampered, then go out for some good grub afterward. Now get over there. Everyone's excited to see you and celebrate you."

She smiles at me, gives Holt another kiss, then she's walking across the room to greet everyone.

"Thanks, Han. You and Miles have been working your asses off these past several weeks, so for you to do this on top of everything else means a lot." The sincerity in my brother's voice eats away at my soul a little, knowing what I've been keeping from him. "I know tonight's going to mean a lot to her. Last night she opened up about her family—something she's only done a handful of times since I've known her. She's really glad to have you in her corner. I hope you know that."

"I know, and I'm glad to have you both too," I say, pulling him in for a hug. "What are you going to do without your girl tonight?"

"Miles and I are gonna eat something, then probably turn in early in preparation for the bachelor party tomorrow."

"Ah, what's the plan for that? Gonna hit up the strip club?"

"Absolutely not. Hey, you've been with Miles a lot lately. Has he mentioned anything about a girlfriend?"

I can suddenly hear my heartbeat in my ears. "No, why do you ask?"

His brows furrow. "I don't know. I have a hunch that he's keeping something from me, and he's on his phone a lot when we're together. Maybe it's nothing."

"Yeah, I'm sure it's nothing."

Holt's face breaks into a smile and he pats my shoulder. "You're probably right. You better get going, though. Looks like they're all waiting for you."

I turn back to the group as Holt waves to his bride. "Yeah, okay. Have a good night, Holt. Tell Miles hi."

He nods, then turns and walks out the door.

"That was friggin' amazing," Serena says, walking out to where the rest of us are getting mani-pedis. She walks like she's floating on a cloud and I mentally pat myself on the back for the full body massage and body treatment package all of us girls chipped in on. I know she's stressed from the last-minute details that haven't gone as planned. On top of that, we'll be traveling for the wedding. I wouldn't blame her if she's second-guessing the decision to do this all in our family's cabin on the lake in Colorado. Then my parents talked them into a party in their backyard a few weeks later so more people could help celebrate, even though that went against Holt and Serena's entire plan.

"You look relaxed," I say, standing up from my massage chair. "Here, sit. I was keeping it warm for you."

She smiles, doing a little shoulder shimmy as we switch spots and I stand next to her chair. "Was that your first massage ever?"

"Yes," she says with a groan as she goes boneless in her chair, "But it's not gonna be my last. This is perfect, Hannah. I can't thank you enough. With us leaving soon, I've been nothing but anxious. This is exactly what I needed."

"I hoped you'd like it. And talk to Val. She'll be the first one to tell you that there comes a certain moment in event planning where you just have to decide to let things be as they are. As much as we want to, we can't control everything, you know?"

"Damn straight," Val pipes in from a few seats away. When I look up, I realize everyone's been listening in on our conversation.

"Yeah?" Serena asks with her never-ending smile, even though I can tell she's unsure of the validity of that advice.

Serena's nail technician gets started as Val gives her some event-planning advice and I'm hoping by the end, she's willing to implement at least a few of her ideas because I think it would save us all some headaches.

Later, when everyone is about finished paying, save for a few stragglers who are still under the lamps, I pay for my nails and the spa treatments Serena received. My phone vibrates from my purse as I'm putting away my card. When I see the unknown number flashing across my screen, I know exactly who it is, and confirm it when I look out the large glass windows in the front of the spa to find our transportation waiting there for us.

"Our ride is here, ladies! If you're all set, let's get out there!"

My instructions are met with excited whoops all over the place.

"So there were too many people around to ask at your parents' barbecue, but how are things between you and Miles?" Serena asks when we're seated next to each other in the back seat.

A flash of nerves flutters through my belly, remembering what Miles said on the phone that night. But I trust Serena's word enough to know she won't go behind my back with the information I'm willing to give her.

"We haven't put any labels on it, but he's a fucking amazing kisser, Serena."

She laughs. "Is it bad if I say I'm not surprised? I always imagined he would be."

"So, do you think it was just a onetime thing? Or will you explore things further?"

"It definitely wasn't a onetime thing, but I think we'll wait until the wedding festivities are over to complicate things too much. All I know is I'm having a lot of fun."

She grips my knee, shaking it back and forth. "I'm so excited for you, Han. You deserve happiness, and so much more."

I lean over until my head brushes the side of hers. She tosses an arm over my shoulders as I say, "So do you." I lean up again to look at her. "So tell me about you. Less than two weeks. How are you feeling?"

"Is it rude to say I'm ready for the day to get here and be over with already? I'm not usually one for large crowds, so I'm excited to get hitched, take a bit of a break, then get the big reception back home out of the way."

I don't think either Holt or Serena was exactly happy when my parents came to them with the idea of a reception, and I completely understand why. But they obliged. I know Holt was fully prepared to stand up for his future wife and tell my parents no, but she's too nice and agreed to the plan, anyway. Because nothing screams wedding like feeling like you have to please everyone and their brother with an invitation to consume food and drink, free of cost.

"If it makes you feel any better, my parents are used to hosting events, so they'll take care of everything, and you'll only have to be there."

"In front of a huge group of people, as one of the two people at the center of attention. Yes, I know, and that's what I'm afraid of." Serena has social anxiety, which I don't really notice much anymore since she's been around our family for so long that the symptoms rarely show when we're all together. It only seems to rear its ugly head when we're meeting people she doesn't know, or large groups.

I think that was why she initially declined my offer to join us for wine night, but I was glad to see her warming up to my friends. I only invited my friends tonight when Holt assured me she came home and was raving about everyone afterward.

"You'll have Holt by your side all night. And me. And so

many others who are in your corner. Always. You know that, right? I'll always be here for you."

She squeezes my hand. "You're right, I know that. It's that my head tells me differently sometimes. Thanks for reminding me of that. I'm so excited to be your sister, Hannah."

"I'm so excited to be yours. Although, I guess it already feels like you are. It has for a long time."

She smiles, "I know. We're just making it official."

I look around the limo and thank my lucky stars I get to call these girls my people.

Chapter Twenty-One

Miles

"She came home last night so relaxed. Hannah did a great job."

Something jolts in my chest at the mention of Hannah. We're currently on hole number six of our second round of golf for Holt's bachelor party, which means everyone's either tipsy or trashed by now. Holt is the latter, and I'm the former. But apparently I'm teetering on the line between the two, because I say, "Yeah, Hannah's the best."

It really shouldn't be a weird thing for me to say. Holt knows she's been a part of my life for as long as I can remember. He's even been a witness to many of the things she's done for me that made me care for her the way I do. And I guess that's why it feels like a confession this time—we've had moments together that Holt knows nothing about.

It's such a mind-fuck, sitting here next to my best friend, knowing I'm falling for a girl I can't tell him about. Ever since I can remember, he's been the first one I turned to when I had news.

"Yeah, I know she is," Holt says, pulling me from my thoughts. "And you know what?"

We're waiting in a long line of carts for our turn to go, so listening to drunk Holt's chatter is inevitable. "What?"

"Maybe I shouldn't say this, but I think you'd be good for her."

Suddenly my ears are burning, and it's not because of the eighty-degree and sunny, humid Iowa weather. This can go one of two ways: deny, deny, deny, or I can go out on a limb and hope it doesn't break, bringing everything I hold so dear crashing to the ground. I choose option number two.

"You think so?"

He scrubs a hand down his face. "I wasn't supposed to tell you that. That thought is supposed to be locked up here in the vault."

"Oh, okay. So you don't really believe that, then?"

"Miles, any woman would be blessed to have you in her life, my sister included. I see both sides—you both needing someone, and can't stop thinking that you'd actually be great together."

"I don't *need* someone, Holt." That statement feels like a lie.

"Oh, but you do. You just don't see it yet."

If we'd been drunk at the golf course what seems like ages ago, then we're hammered as we pile off the party bus who's dropping us off at our third destination. The sun went down long ago, and I've been drinking water between each beer for the past hour, trying to be the one and only responsible one in the group of idiots I call friends.

Our friend Jeremy bellies up to the bar first thing, buying the group a round. I keep hearing whispers about the strip club down the road from here, even though Holt was adamant that it wasn't on tonight's agenda.

I lean against the bar when I hear a greeting from my left side.

I turn to find a blue-eyed, blonde-haired woman smiling back at me. "Hey," I say, instantly wishing I was at my bar with two and a half feet between me and anyone else. Especially when she swivels her barstool to run her foot up and down my pant leg.

I back away quickly, which only makes her laugh. Luckily, one of the smarmy guys Holt works with swoops in and I'm able to walk away, although I do feel bad for leaving her with him.

"Has Miles lost his game?" Holt says, holding a beer out to me when I reach his side.

"What?"

"I saw that," he points to the girl. "You practically ran away from her. What's up with that?" I shrug, knowing I'm being evasive as hell, and that he's bound to put two and two together at some point. Luckily for me, he's too drunk to see things clearly tonight.

"Miles, Holt!" I hear our names being called from the corner of the bar and turn, thankful for the reprieve.

"Oh my god," Holt says, making a beeline for the voices I still haven't put a face to yet. I follow him anyway, only to find Val's boyfriend Brody at the table with another guy that looks oddly familiar, and that's when I remember the bar we're in is in Brody's hometown.

Brody waves as we walk up, throwing his arm around each of us as we stand at the end of their table. "Tonight's your bachelor party, right?"

Holt's smile widens as he closes his eyes and nods. "Is my inebriation that obvious?"

"Yes," he says, and we all laugh. "Guys, this is my best friend, Malakai Moore. He's the one I was telling you about that plays for the Nashville Salamanders in the minor leagues, although there's been talk of him moving on up sooner than later."

"No shit?" Holt says, turning toward Malakai in awe. "How does it feel to be living my dream there, Malakai?"

He flashes a bright white smile. "It feels pretty damn good, actually. But please, call me Mal. And you are?"

"I'm Holt Harris. Maybe you've met Val's best friend, Hannah? She's my sister."

"Oh, right! Yes, I actually have met her a few times now. She's great."

And I don't know why, but hearing this tan, tall, and muscly guy with perfect teeth compliment Hannah in any way makes me want to fist my t-shirt with both hands and rip it in half in a show of pure male dominance. Which is the moment and turns to me and smiles. "I didn't catch your name."

He's holding out his hand and I take it, squeezing with more force than necessary. "I'm Miles O'Harrow, Holt's best friend. Also close to Hannah."

Brody's resulting smile is proof enough that I'm being territorial as fuck. He definitely knows about Hannah and me.

"Oh, nice to meet you."

"Likewise."

"This guy doesn't talk much," Brody says, smacking me on the shoulder. "But get to know him, and he's a big ol' teddy bear."

"Yeah, I think not." I say, unintentionally making the whole table laugh.

"Oh my gosh, hey!" a feminine voice says from behind us. I turn to find Val, followed by Lainey, as they appear to be returning from the bathroom.

Val hugs both Holt and I, and I hear Brody whisper, "See? Total teddy bear."

"What are you guys doing here?"

"Oh, just making the rounds for my bachelor party."

"Oh, duh," Val says, smacking her forehead. "I remember Hannah and Serena mentioning that now."

"Speaking of Hannah," Lainey says from her place at the table next to Mal, who's currently got an arm slung around her shoulders in an equally territorial move as my outburst a moment ago. *Interesting.* "I wish she had a job where she doesn't work practically every weekend. Otherwise, she'd probably be here with us right now."

"Yeah," Holt says. "But she's great at what she does. I couldn't see her doing anything else with her life."

"True that," Val says. "She certainly found her calling." She elbows me in the arm lightly. "All thanks to this guy."

Holt gives her a confused look, no doubt thinking about the financial contribution he gave to get her business off the ground almost two years ago. Even I am not sure what Val is talking about.

"What do you mean, all thanks to Miles?" He asks.

Val smiles at me, then looks around the table before she says, "Because Hannah got her first camera from Miles, and she hasn't stopped taking pictures since."

My stomach turns inside out at her words. It's not like I don't remember giving her a camera when she was young, it's just that I never really bothered to put it together that I had a hand in Hannah finding her calling.

When we were young, Grandpa found one of his old cameras from the seventies and didn't have a use for it, so he gave it to me. I brought it along when I stayed at the Hawkins house for the weekend.

I let Hannah borrow it, and it became an extension of her arm by the end of the weekend. Since I always had a soft spot in my chest for her, I gifted it to her when she tried to hand it back to me at the end of the weekend.

She carried it everywhere with her that summer, snapping photos, changing out the film, and learning all the tricks of photography. And for many summers after, she carried that old camera around, learning and growing as a creative, and I still remember the way my chest would swell with pride each time she'd run into the living room to squeeze between Holt and I while we played video games with a stack of developed photos, making us promise not to get our grimy fingerprints all over her favorite shots as we fought over who got to look at them first. She has a natural eye for beauty, which can't be hard when she sees it each time she looks in the mirror.

I wonder if she still has that old thing somewhere. It seems it's been long forgotten ever since her parents started seeing serious potential in her work and splurged on a high-quality camera she'd begged for continually for years until they finally bought it for her fifteenth birthday. Ever since, she's been upgrading to the next best thing when she hits new milestones in her business. It's now been almost two years since she finally quit her shitty retail job and took her passion full time.

"Holy shit, I forgot all about that!" Holt laughs, smacking me on the arm on the opposite side of Val. "Good job, man."

I'm an introvert hiding in my shell after that, observing and listening to the conversation taking place between this oddball group of people where half of us could have gone our whole lives without meeting, but when we all get together, we somehow fit perfectly.

I'm not even sure how long we're there before Val declares it's time to go because she has to get up early for some event she has in the morning. She works as an event planner in the next town over.

"It was good to see you guys," Holt says, and I nod in agreement as we all share hugs and claps on the back as we say our goodbyes.

Holt and I take a seat at the now vacant table, looking around for the friends we came with. But the bar is much less crowded than it was when we walked in. "Wait, where is everyone?" I ask, looking around, but not finding a single one of the guys who was on the bus. What are the chances they're all in the bathroom at once?

"Uh," Holt says, squinting as he tries to place our friends with his beer goggles on.

"I think they left us," I say.

"What?" Holt asks incredulously, a step behind my thought process.

"You sit tight, I'm gonna go check the bathroom," I walk toward the back of the bar and there's no line, so I walk right in. There's a guy I don't know at the urinal, and an unfamiliar pair of shoes peeking out from underneath one of the stalls.

I walk out, doing a hot lap around the bar and only stopping when I reach a droopy-headed Holt. "Our friends left us, man. Let's go outside and see if the bus is still here."

He laughs. "Twenty bucks says it isn't."

Betting against that guess is pointless.

When we reach the parking lot, our suspicions are proven correct.

"Well damn, it's too bad we didn't realize this before Val and Brody left. They could've given us a ride. Do you have either of their numbers?"

"No," I say, refusing to tell him I have had Val's number for years because I know without a doubt that she's going to be staying in town with her boyfriend and as nice as she is, I'm not making her give us a ride to the town she wasn't even planning on staying in tonight. I look at the time on my phone. "But I bet Hannah's done with her wedding by now."

I barely get the words out before Holt's phone is at his ear.

"Hannahhhh," he says, a few seconds later. His ear piece is just loud enough that I can hear both sides of the conversation.

"Holt, is there a reason you're calling me during your own bachelor party?"

"Our friends left us, and we need a ride home. I was

gonna call Serena, but I didn't want to get in trouble, so Miles had the bright idea to call you."

"Wait, your group left you? Why would they leave the bachelor behind?"

Holt huffs out a laugh. "They wanted to go to the strip club, and we didn't. I think they left us while we had our backs turned. Oh! We saw Val, Brody, Lonnie and Melrose."

"You mean Lainey and Mal?"

"Yes, them."

She laughs. "Why didn't you ask them for a ride?"

"Because we didn't know our friends left us until they were gone."

"Wow. Well, what nice friends you have."

"Yeah, but I've still got Miles here. He's a keeper."

"That he is," she says, and I wonder if she knows I can hear her. "Can you send me your location? I'm almost back to town, so I'll come find you."

"Han, I'm far too drunk to try to figure out how to do that right now."

"I've got it," I say, loud enough she should be able to hear me. "Hannah, I'm sending over my location right now." I fish my phone out of my pocket, which flashes a low battery warning as soon as I open it up. "If you need anything, call me. Your brother is too intoxicated to be his usual helpful self right now. See you soon. And thank you!"

"Bye, Han. I love you!" Holt says as the line disconnects. Suddenly, he disappears. No, scratch that, he lies down in the middle of the sidewalk at the side of the building that everyone uses to get into the bar.

I roll my eyes, giving in to the ridiculousness of the moment. "What are we doing down here?" I ask once I'm on my back, the concrete biting into my shoulder blades.

"Lookin' at the stars."

"Of course we are," I say, fully aware that we've done this

about a million times since we were kids. I can't say it's something we've done in the past ten years, though.

"You know I've always been obsessed with the stars, man. To the naked eye, they're beautiful, right? But there's so much more to them than what we can see from here." Holt goes off in his drunken psychobabble ways. "It's like the difference between my earlier friendship with Serena, and when I finally let her in for real. She helped me see how beautiful life can really be. She's like my first telescope, man. Life just looks so much clearer with her in it. I hope you find your telescope someday, Miles. You deserve someone to share life with, too."

I wonder if he'd still feel that way if he knew the one person his monologue brings to mind.

I thought hiding this for a few weeks was going to be easy, because Holt is preoccupied with his wedding. What I hadn't thought about was all the little moments between the start and end point that we'd have just the two of us, and how it would feel like one huge lie until I tell him the truth.

But before I can act on the thought of telling him, the sound of a car pulling up to the curb has me attempting to sit up before someone finds us this way. But I sit up too fast and get a head rush, all the alcohol I had today dancing around in my vision.

When I've finally got my head in control, a car door slams and my favorite voice in the entire world asks, "What on earth are you two doing?"

Chapter Twenty-Two

HANNAH

I'm already confused about having to pick my brother up at his own damn bachelor party. But when I arrive at the location they've sent me to, only to find them lying in the middle of the sidewalk, I look around for Ashton Kutcher, because I'm clearly being Punk'd.

"What on earth are you two doing?" I ask, rounding the car.

Holt is still on his back, but Miles looks like he's trying to sweet talk his head into stopping its spinning, and failing. It's delayed, but I see the moment he registers the sound of my voice, because he removes his hands from his face and looks up at me like I'm his North Star, the one thing his eyes can find and know he's on his way home.

And maybe it's post-wedding day emotions still pumping through my veins, but my eyes water at the sight of him.

"Hannah," my name comes out breathless, making so many questions pop up in my mind.

But the sound of my name suddenly rouses Holt, who pops up to a sitting position next to Miles. "Hey, Han!" He yells, transferring his weight to his hands and knees more quickly than someone at his level of intoxication should be able to.

"Hey, Holt."

Before I can blink, he's on his feet and tackling me in a hug. I can smell the liquor wafting from his pores, and can't help but laugh because this is so unlike the Holt I know and love. Sure, I've seen him drunk, and sure, he hugs me all the time, but my brother isn't a lush who begs for a ride home often. He's so *on* all the time, it's kind of nice to see him seem so…*human*, for once.

After one last squeeze, he suddenly extricates himself from the hug and throws open the back door to my car and dives in face-first.

I turn to Miles, shaking my head as I round the vehicle. "You really did a number on him tonight."

"That wasn't me, it was everyone else. Besides, he's been drinking since seven a.m. It was bound to catch up with him at some point," he says, getting in the passenger's seat.

"So they really left you?" I put the car in reverse, focusing on backing out of my spot. "Should I drive by the strip club to see if the bus is there?"

Miles looks down at his phone. "Nah, I already got confirmation that it was."

"What assholes."

"Yeah, well, don't tell anyone I said so, but I'm kinda glad it ended up being only Holt and me. We ran into your friends, which is most likely when they hightailed it out of there. I feel bad you had to pick us up, but I'm not exactly sad I got to see you." He says that last part in a whisper.

"Yeah, me neither," I say, patting his thigh.

"Augh," Holt moans in the backseat, which is my reminder not to be too explicit while he's in the vehicle.

"Don't you dare get sick back there. You'll be cleaning it up," I yell.

Miles laughs. I turn toward the sound as I slow at an intersection because there's something so open and happy about the sound. He's always had a sober personality, even when we were children, so every time I hear his laugh, I want to capture it in a jar to set free on a rainy day.

The light turns green in my peripheral, so I turn back to the road, but I can feel Miles studying my profile until he reaches over to intertwine our fingers. I let him, surprised by how natural it feels.

I look over quickly to find so much admiration in his eyes in the low green light from the accessories on my dashboard. It catches me off-guard, that look. Because until this point, I'd half-believed there was no way his feelings matched mine. But he must be just tipsy enough that his mask has fallen out of place, because I see it.

"You two are really cute together," Holt says from the back seat. We disconnect our hands as Miles turns around to look. "What you talking about, Holt?"

"I don't know." The intoxication is clear in the syllables that twist and curl in all the wrong places. "It's just that when I see you two together, I can't get over how well you two would fit, you know?"

Miles turns to me with a *what the hell is happening* look. "Holt, your head is facing the back of the car. How could you possibly see us right now?"

"I've seen you two together enough to know what I'm talking about. I wouldn't even have to see your faces to be able to tell. I just know."

We're quiet the rest of the short drive home.

I pull up as close as I can to the bottom of Miles' stairs in the back alley of the bar.

I look back at Holt, who is not moving a muscle in the back seat.

"You think you'll be able to get him up there on your own?" I ask Miles, but get my answer when he yawns so big, I have a perfect view of the back of his throat.

I sigh, and get out of the car, and when I open the back door to see a passed out Holt slumped over in the back seat, I know this won't be easy.

"Holt," Miles yells a few inches from his face, smacking him on the cheek. "Wake up, man."

"Huh?" he asks, cracking an eye open and leaning up long enough to get him on his feet.

He sways, but we somehow get him to the stairs. Miles goes first, and if he were sober, I know he'd be the one at the bottom. At this point, I know it'll be a miracle if we all make it out of this alive.

"Oh my god, Holt. If you don't get this ass up the steps right now, I'm just gonna let you tumble down and sleep at the bottom for the night." I've got both hands on my brother's ass, trying to shove him up a flight of stairs. It's what I get for trying to be a good person.

"I'm trying, Han. Damn!" He says as he trips over yet another step.

We finally make it through the door, and Miles heaves Holt over his shoulder, much like he did with me, but he's less careful.

I laugh from the doorway, watching Miles try to wrestle off Holt's shoes. Holt, who's trying to cover himself with the blanket draped over the back of the couch, isn't helping.

When Miles makes it back to the doorway, he's breathing heavily, with a nice sheen of sweat on his forehead. "Sorry you had to witness that."

I toss my hands in the air. "Don't worry about me. I'm highly entertained. I just wanted to make sure you were good before I head home."

"You sure you don't want to hang around for a minute?" he asks, leaning in closer. I'm not sure if it's intentional, or if he's swaying on his feet from drinking all day. The latter, if I had to guess.

"Oh my god, I'm gonna puuuuke," Holt calls from the couch, making us both jump.

"Nah, I think that's my cue to leave. You have fun with him, though."

"Gee thanks," he jokes as I turn toward the door.

"What, no kiss goodnight?" He whispers, catching my hand before I get very far.

"Holt is right there."

He pulls open his door, stepping out onto the landing, and I follow. When the door is closed behind me, Miles pushes me up against it. "There, problem solved."

I laugh, but he leans in, kissing the smile right off my face with his hungry mouth.

He tastes like bourbon and mint, and my heart thumps against my chest wildly at the way his hands squeeze my waist with urgency.

"I'll never tire of kissing you, Hannah."

His drunk words knock the wind right out of me.

"I hope that's a promise."

His eyes are half-lidded when his gaze meets mine. "It is. I'll prove it."

Please do. I pull him in for one more quick kiss, and leave before he can change my mind.

"Good night, Miles."

Chapter Twenty-Three

Hannah

The morning we're set to leave for Colorado, I'm running around the house before dawn breaks, making sure all the little piles of things I need are ready to go. I didn't realize how much shit I'd have to take with me when not only am I *in* the wedding but also photographing it.

When my family goes to the cabin, we usually drive and take the long way. It's roughly a seventeen-hour trip, about seven of those hours spent cutting across the most barren land known to man—AKA Nebraska. I'm glad we're flying this time, even if I fear for the weight of the bags I'm bringing along.

"You about ready to go?" Val asks, appearing in the doorway of my office.

"Yep, just making sure all my batteries are charged, then we should be ready," I tell her, shoving another battery, along with its charger, into my bag, which will also serve as my carry on. No way in hell am I allowing any of my beloved gear out of my sight during the flight. "My parents should be here anytime," I say, looking at my watch. A bunch of us are carpooling together to the airport.

After I finish saying so, there's a knock at our front door, then footsteps make their way inside. "Good morning, ladies," a voice I hadn't expected to hear bellows from the front of the house.

Val and I stare at each other in surprise.

"Your pack mule is here. Load me up!" Miles says, humor dripping from his tone.

Val leans into the hallway. "Hey, come on in. Hannah's finishing up, then we're on our way."

When he appears in the doorway, he's dressed in black jeans that fit him so perfectly. I'd think they were tailored if I didn't know Miles was one of the most laid-back men on earth. He's wearing a charcoal gray henley, one of his thinner one, being that it's mid-July. If it weren't summer, he'd be wearing his leather jacket on top. I meet his gaze, his teasing smile proof my perusing didn't go unnoticed.

"Did you come here with my parents?"

He nods. "Yeah, a last-minute addition. That okay with you?"

"I'll let you two talk. I'm gonna grab my bags," Val says, heading for the door.

Miles stops her with a hand on her shoulder. "No, let me get them. That's what I'm here for."

Val raises her eyebrows, "You two catch up," she looks pointedly between us, "and I'll be upstairs retrieving my bags," she pats Miles' chest. "Don't be dense."

He smirks, watching her leave, then turns to me. I take a deep breath, finishing the task I'd been working on and avoiding his gaze. "Hannah."

I put my last battery and charger in its rightful place inside my bag, finally meeting his gaze. "Miles?"

"Hi," he says, extending a hand. I zip my bag and drop the strap into his grasp with a sly smile. He rolls his eyes, swinging the bag over his shoulder, holding his hand out to me again. I finally drop mine into it and he helps me off the floor, pulling me closer until we're touching from knee to chest.

"Hi," I say, breathless from our proximity, as I wrap my arm around the small of his back. He does the same, one finger pushing a piece of stubborn hair behind my ear. His gaze doesn't leave my own the whole time.

"This just feels right," he whispers against my skin as the tip of his nose trails a line down the bridge of my own. "Doesn't it?" He asks, his lips only a hair's breadth away from mine.

"Yes," I whisper breathlessly, a zap of electricity coursing through my whole body as my mouth barely brushes his, setting an inferno of lust alight between us. I pull at the back of his head, lifting to my toes to kiss him.

He's strung so tight, he's practically shaking, but as his lips move with mine, his whole body relaxes. I forget where we are, what we should be doing as he deepens the kiss and our limbs tangle. A moan escapes the back of my throat when his tongue brushes my own, sending a spike of warmth low in my belly.

The sound of the front door crashing open is a glass of ice cold water poured over my head. "Let's go!" my mom's voice yells as I touch my fingertips to my lips, staring up at Miles, who looks as dumbfounded as I feel.

"Hello?" she yells, her voice closer this time, setting us into motion.

"Mom, I'm in here. Almost done," I say, turning back to the desk to pull my laptop from its charger and pack both into a carrying case.

"Oh, there you are," she says as she rounds the corner. "Are you about ready to go? I told you no later than 2:45," she checks her watch. "It's 2:47. Get your shit and let's go. We've still got a two-hour drive to get there."

Have I ever mentioned how well my mother works under pressure? I love her dearly, but we are so different.

"I know. I'm double-checking all my camera stuff is here. You know, to photograph my brother's *only* wedding?"

"Quickly," she says, flinging one finger in a circle. Then she turns to Miles, grabbing his forearm and dragging him into the hallway. "Miles, I saw Val heaving her bags down the stairs. Can you help her?"

He smiles back at me, then disappears out the door.

Despite my mother's insistence that I'd make us late, we catch our flight on time and make it to Durango by 1 p.m., Mountain Time. Holt, who arrived on Monday with his bride-to-be, is waiting for us with the rental Suburban he got for the week. My mom is the first to run up to him, peppering kisses on his cheek and squeezing him hard enough it's a miracle his eyes don't pop out of their sockets.

"Can you believe it's your wedding week?" She asks.

He scratches the hair at the back of his head. "It's surreal, but I'm more than ready. How was the trip?" He looks around the group as he asks and his eyes land on the luggage he bought me for my high school graduation—which is currently in Miles' arms. He insisted on carrying everything but my camera bag, so I took Val's carry-on, which I realize now wasn't much of a coverup.

I swear, by the end of this trip, Holt's going to catch on because of Miles' chivalry alone.

"It was great," I say, pushing both Miles and Val from behind. "So, should we get going?"

"Yes, we should," my mom says, finally on my side for once today, but only because she doesn't realize it.

I shove into the SUV after Dad takes Val's bag from my hands. I jump into the back seat with my camera bag on my lap. Val packs in next to me, as Mom and Dad take over, Tetrising the hell out of our luggage.

I turn and find Holt and Miles with their heads bent together. Holt glances my way. They continue talking, but where they'd usually be laughing, or at least smiling, they're both far too serious. It all makes me nervous.

"What do you think they're talking about?" I ask, still staring in their direction.

Val looks, "It's hard to say, but you seriously need to chill, Hannah. Even if your brother finds out about you two, don't forget that it would be a good thing. You don't want to be running around behind his back anymore. Just try to keep that at the forefront of your mind right now, okay?"

As soon as the words are out of her mouth, Miles glances our way.

"Ugh, I hate this." That terrible feeling in my gut only worsens when everyone's packed in the SUV and Holt pulls out onto the road. His eyes find mine in the rearview mirror as Mom rambles about something from her seat between Holt and I.

We're sitting at a red light that I wish would change.

"Okay, maybe you should be a little worried," Val whispers.

"Not helping," I mutter, looking out the window.

Holt drops us off at the hotel located only an eight-minute drive from the cabin to unpack and get settled before he grabs Serena, who stayed behind to get some decorating done.

Mom and Dad are the first to get checked in, and when they have their keys in-hand, they head up to their room, which is a godsend because I really need to talk to Miles without my mom lingering around a corner. As soon as the elevator doors hide them from sight, I hand Val my credit card. "Here, put this on file. I'm going to go talk to Miles."

He's sitting in a chair in the lobby on his phone. I hear the words *order* and *kegs,* and it isn't hard to deduce that he's talking to one of his employees back at the bar. He looks up at the sound of my footsteps and smirks before saying, "Keep me updated, but I've got to go. Bye."

"You can take the bar owner out of the bar," I start as soon as he pockets his phone, lifting to his feet.

He huffs out a laugh. "Yeah, something like that," he looks toward the front desk, then asks, "you okay?"

I look down at the strap of my backpack and graze my nail over the stitching, suddenly nervous. "Yeah, I'm good. I just wanted to check the same is true for you," I toy with my messy bun. "It seemed like you and Holt were having a pretty serious conversation outside the airport. Made me kinda nervous."

"Oh, no. It was nothing. Everything's all good."

His nervous babbling doesn't soothe my worry, but I smile anyway. "Okay, well. Guess I'll see you at dinner then."

He smiles, "I guess you will."

This is going to be one interesting trip.

Chapter Twenty-Four

Miles

I'm quickly realizing how hard it is to hide my growing feelings for this girl—especially while surrounded by her family. We've barely glanced at each other, let alone interacted, and I feel like that is going to be our downfall. We're always chatting with each other at family dinner.

"Did you hear me?" Holt's voice pulls me from my reverie as I finish buttering my complimentary bread. I've already eaten three from the basket in the middle of the table.

"Sorry, what?"

Holt smiles, "I said you seem distracted, and you just proved my point. Everything going okay at the bar without you?"

"Oh," I try to laugh it off, because if he's noticing how weird I'm acting now, that's not a good sign. "No, everything's good. They are calling me every five seconds, though, it seems. I never realized how many questions I get asked until I leave the building."

He picks small pieces off his bun and tosses them in his mouth one by one. "Hey, man. I know it's a few weeks away, but would you mind keeping Hannah company at the reception? Like, dance with her and stuff?"

I look up to find him giving me a pleading look. "What makes you think she needs company? She's a grown-ass woman who can take care of herself." I say, coming to her defense too quickly for a man trying to keep a secret.

"I know, I know that. But the thing is, there will be a few guys I'd rather keep away from her. Unless you were actually planning to cash in on that plus one I gave you."

Actually, I'm hoping to, but not in the way he thinks.

I scan the table, finding Hannah deep in conversation with Val and Serena a few feet away. Good thing she can't hear this conversation. I know it would piss her off to know Holt's trying to control her. But since I know standing up for her right now might do more harm than good, I go against my usual instinct. "I would have done it without you asking, man. And not in a possessive way, but because I care about her, too."

"Good deal, thanks, Miles."

And with that conversation, my appetite goes right out the window.

Later, when we're back at the hotel, I'm tucking my towel into itself at my hip post shower when there's a knock at my door. I use the peephole and find Hannah's auburn curls on the other side as she looks up and down the hallway like she's about to commit a crime.

I swing open the door.

Hannah's gaze finds the white towel draped around my hips first, then finally meets my eye.

"Uh, I'll just come back."

I grab her hand as she walks away. "No, stay. I was getting

out of the shower. Let me change quickly and we can talk. Just —" I gesture to the room, "make yourself comfortable."

Every muscle in my body is flexed—about ninety percent showing off, ten percent nerves—as I retrieve my boxers, sweatpants, and an old comfy t-shirt I've had as long as I can remember from my duffel.

"I'll be right back."

Hannah's cheeks are painted red with embarrassment when she nods with a soft smile.

I toss my towel over the hook on the wall and make quick work of my clothes. Unzipping my toiletry bag, I swipe on some deodorant, then stare at the tiny bottle of cologne I've had for more years than I care to admit. After much deliberation, I spray one pump in the air in front of me and walk through it, hoping it won't be totally obvious I used cologne at 9 p.m. after a shower.

When I come out of the bathroom, Hannah's sitting gingerly on the edge of my bed like she feels completely out of place.

"Hey, so what's up?" I ask sitting down about a foot away from her to give her some space because I can tell she's about to run.

She shakes her head. "Nothing, really. Val was on the phone with Brody and I left the room to give her a little privacy, and I ended up at your door. But now I see this was a mistake. I'll go."

She lifts to her feet, but I catch her hand before she can walk away. "Wait. Why was it a mistake?"

She turns back to me and I realize I don't know this version of her at all—the one who shrinks into herself.

"Because this is so new, and we're here for my brother's wedding. This hotel is crawling with my family members. I don't need my mom and dad catching me leaving your room. I don't want to cause drama surrounding this important event. Holt and Serena deserve better than that."

"Wait, what does that mean, exactly? You're done?"

She shrugs. "For now, maybe. I feel like maybe that's best until this blows over."

"Hannah, Holt, and Serena's marriage isn't a storm that's going to blow over. I've been more than understanding since you said you didn't want to cause any extra stress for either of them right now, but you're really going to let that determine what you can and can't have? You deserve better too, you know." *I do too*, I want to add, but there's no way I'll play games and guilt Hannah into anything.

"The way I see it is, we'll get our time if it's meant to be. But right now it's their time, and they deserve it to be uninterrupted. I'm not going to take that away from them. I'll see you tomorrow, Miles."

And I watch her walk out my door as fast as she walked through it.

The next morning is filled with last-minute errands for the setup of the wedding ceremony, which will take place in the expansive yard at the cabin. I think Holt and Serena decided it was the perfect place for their wedding because when they were still not quite together, but definitely more than friends, Serena joined the Hawkins family on their summer trip. It's where Holt finally found the courage to tell her how he felt. They made it official, and the rest is history. Oddly similar to the story of Hannah and me that's unfolding in front of our eyes, come to think of it.

The cabin is big enough for all of us to share, but it only made sense for us to let Holt and Serena use it as a little getaway for themselves leading up to the wedding. It will also serve as the getting ready space for everyone on the day as well.

I've come to the cabin on many trips with the Hawkins

family, so I'm familiar with the home, and the beautiful sights that surround it where it's lost within the trees and hills that become mountains in the near proximity.

The girls have been out most of the day so far, getting pampered in town, which is okay by me. As if last night's one-eighty that Hannah made wasn't enough, she barely acknowledged my existence this morning—to the point that Bobby asked what the hell I did wrong after they left. I think I was correct, assuming her behavior was going to make things even more complicated than they need to be.

While they do their thing, us men are constructing things, like the altar they'll get married under—if we can get the damn thing right. It's currently leaning to one side —not the side I was in charge of, might I add. The groom doesn't have a builder's bone in his body, a fact made clear by the amount of times he's stood behind me "observing" as I make little updates around his home in the past. Despite that fact, he insisted on having a hand in making the props for their wedding, which I can understand. It's just frustrating. And in his defense, ninety percent of my frustration is a byproduct of whatever's happening between his sister and me, and I shouldn't be taking it out on him.

It's lunchtime, so we call for a break and the hope that we'll come back with the magical ability to fix the mess we've created. If it works, maybe they'll let me borrow it to fix the mistake I've made between Hannah and me, whatever it is. Because that bullshit excuse she gave last night wasn't good enough.

We were on the same page, or so I thought.

I'm walking around the property trying to find a cell phone signal (nearly impossible) to get ahold of Carolina at the bar, who left me a frantic voicemail sometime this morning that finally slipped through my terrible reception about twenty minutes ago. There were messages from my mom, but I scrolled past them. I don't have the mental capacity for her bullshit on top of everything today.

When I'm in the side yard, the Suburban pulls into the driveway. Jenn and Serena wave from the front seat, which I return between glances at the top corner of my phone screen, praying for a miracle.

"Hey, whatcha doin'?" Serena asks, the first one out of the vehicle.

I don't miss the way Hannah throws me a half-hearted wave and continues toward the door.

"Uh, trying to find enough signal to call the bar back."

"It's a bit spotty out here, isn't it?"

"Half the beauty of the place most of the time, but not for a newbie bar owner who's half convinced his bar won't make it through a short vacation."

"Miles, I'm sure they're competent enough to keep the place in one piece for a few days without you there. Don't worry so much." She reaches into her pocket, glances at her phone, and hands it to me. "But if it's important enough to you, I've got full bars for the moment. Use my phone."

"Thanks, Serena. I'll bring it right back, I promise."

"Good, and don't take too long. We brought food back for everyone."

"Thanks," I say, waiting impatiently for her to reach the house before finding Carolina's number and dialing. I never knew the sound of a simple ring could make a man want to weep, but here we are.

"Hello?" she answers.

"Carolina, it's Miles on a friend's phone. I got your message. What's going on?"

"Oh, Miles. Thank god. You know Edie had me half sure you were dead out there in the wilderness."

"Nope, just poor reception, which I warned everyone about before I left."

"You're right. Sorry I let her crazy stories go to my head. I just wanted to let you know that the new hire, Wyatt, from last week, was a no-show last night. Alicia covered his shift, but had to close up shop a bit early due to prior engagements."

"She's never supposed to close," I say, mostly to myself, frustration bubbling over in my tone. I promised Alicia—back when I hired her—that she'd have work-life balance, and never have to choose the bar over her child's extra-curricular activities.

She sighs, "I know. And I would have been there myself, but it was farmers market night and I missed her phone call. Please don't fire her for closing early. She did what she had to do."

"I understand. And firing her hadn't even crossed my mind." I rake my fingers through my beard. "Hey, can I ask you a favor?"

"Of course."

"Would you mind being the main contact until I'm back in town? I don't have consistent reception, and I'm afraid I won't be reachable if anything goes awry."

"Yes, I'll send out a message as soon as we're done here. And Miles?"

"Yeah?"

"You deserve a break. You don't have to explain yourself."

"Thanks, Carolina. I knew I could trust you."

"Well, if you can trust me, tell me how things are going with the girl now that you're in each other's hair all day. Around her whole family, no less. Have you and Holt gotten into a fistfight yet?"

"I don't trust you *that* much. And if you have no further questions about *work*, I should probably go give this phone back to its owner."

When I make it to the dining room, everyone else is already seated and eating. Hannah's gaze bounces to me, but doesn't stick.

I hand Serena's phone back to her. "Thanks for letting me borrow it."

"Everything okay back home?" Serena asks, and suddenly, everyone's attention is on me, presumably wondering what happened.

"Yep, just Carolina giving me shit, more than anything."

"Good, you need someone who keeps you on your toes. Say, is she single?" Holt breaks in.

"Nope, she's happily married, Holt."

"Damn, thought maybe there was something there."

I can't help it. My gaze flicks to Hannah, who's staring pointedly at her plate.

"There's food on the counter in the kitchen. Help yourself, then come join us."

"Will do," I say, turning toward the doorway that leads to the expansive kitchen—Jenn and Bobby's favorite room in the entire house. They've got it filled with all the bells and whistles a baking and cooking pair could ever need. They'll be preparing the food for tomorrow's small rehearsal. Then Bobby is smoking meat for the small wedding dinner with about twenty people in a couple of days.

I'm almost finished filling my plate with food when I hear footsteps on their way into the room. I turn at the noise to find Val smiling softly at me. She's known me long enough, she sees the invisible *Handle with Care* tattoo on my forehead that not everyone knows exists. She brushes her hands back and forth, setting her glass down on the counter across the island from me.

"Hey, Miles. Just here for a refill," she says, even though we both know better.

"Hey," I say skeptically.

"Need anything?" She asks, an array of drinks displayed at the front of the refrigerator she's holding open and showing off like Vanna White.

I laugh at her odd display. "Can you grab me a water, please?"

"Sure thing," she says, plucking two from their place and crossing the room to lean against the counter a few feet from me. She hands me my water. "Everything good between you and Hannah? She's been acting weird."

Ah, there it is. "You know, that would be a great question for her, since she's the one that knocked on my hotel room door last night, then ran out like it was on fire five minutes later with little explanation."

Val's brow furrows, her blonde curls bouncing as she shakes her head. "That makes no sense."

I can't help but laugh. "You've got that right."

Chapter Twenty-Five

"Let's go out tonight," Val says when we're shuffling around in our hotel room after a long day of being pampered, then getting minor details in order at the cabin. The suggestion is so far out of character for Val. I'm slightly taken aback. But I'm desperate to get out of my head. Maybe a night out on the town would do the trick.

"Seriously?"

She shrugs. "Why not? We've never had free rein of the town at a legal drinking age. It could be fun."

"Who are you, and what did you do with my best friend who would much rather sit here and read her romance book of the day on her Kindle than primp for an hour and go out in a somewhat unfamiliar town?"

She screws up her face. "Keep talking like that and you're gonna make me change my mind."

"Say no more. I'll jump in the shower and get ready, then by the time I'm done I'll be ready to get you beautified, just like I know you hate to let me do."

Her face says severe indigestion, but my heart says she'll let me do whatever I want.

"Can I try a smokey eye on you?" I ask Val over an hour later when we're sitting cross-legged on the bed facing each other and I have the lampshade turned toward her like a criminal in the hot seat of an interrogation room—but it's the best light we've got in here now that the sun is about to set.

She rolls her eyes. "Fine."

I should believe she's up to something, since she's being far too agreeable, but I give her the benefit of the doubt because she's my best friend. She's probably missing her day job as much as she's missing Brody.

"With everything that's going on, I forgot to ask, how'd that job end up going last weekend?"

"The Hartford Brothers? I can't believe I never told you. The party they threw was insane. It didn't even feel like I was working."

"So they made it worth the crap they put you through, leading up to the party, at least?"

"That and then some. They got me three referrals I need to call when I get back home and they handed me a hefty tip at the end of the night. They loved me, Han."

"I still don't know how you're surprised by this. Everyone loves you, Val. And if they don't, well, they don't fucking matter."

"Oh, how I've missed your pep talks."

"I've missed our face-to-face time like this. For being roommates, we don't see each other nearly enough." I wave my hand in front of her face. "Blink your eye a sec."

She does as she's told. "I know, and it's my fault. I'm sorry this living together thing isn't exactly what we expected when we made the plan to live together."

"You have a full-time job and a boyfriend who has a full-time job. I get it. Maybe we need to make a more conscious effort to see each other."

She puts her pinky up between us. "Okay, let's make it a deal. At least one night a week is for each other."

I link my pinky with hers. "Starting tonight."

Her face drops for a millisecond, barely long enough for me to be completely sure I saw it before she's smiling again. "Yes. Starting tonight."

Durango is a gorgeous mountain town that is a perfect mixture of new and old. Like the steam train that rolls through town, rattling the windows of our hotel room when the horn blows just down the block. There were many times growing up that we took that train to the neighboring town, Silverton. You'd never believe how incredible the views are unless you saw them yourself, especially when you see the bright yellow aspens in the fall. The *Welcome to Colorful Colorado* signs when you enter the state are no joke, folks.

But the nightlife perfectly juxtaposes the old-timey charm. The old little strips of shops turned new by their owners, carrying everything from books to cannabis dispensaries. Everything is within walking distance of our accommodations, so it makes our night out even easier to navigate by foot.

"Wait, where are we going?" I ask, realizing Val is moving with a purpose, rather than taking it all in like I am.

Val points down the street. "I saw a bar I thought would be good when we pulled through town. Do you care if we head there first for drinks? Maybe see if they have appetizers or something?"

I shake my head. "That sounds good to me."

We walk so far, I'm breathing heavily by the time we walk through the door. And not even one step inside, my gaze slides over a familiar figure sitting at a small high-top table in the corner of the room.

He looks taken aback at first, then the corners of his mouth turn up as he waves.

I wave back, dumbfounded. Then it all comes together. The agreeableness, the idea to go out, it was all Val. She set me up.

I swivel my gaze back to her. "Why'd you do this?"

She loops my arm through hers, pulling me toward his table. "I could sense something was off between you two. When I asked what he was up to tonight, he told me he'd be sampling some local beers and I told him we might show up. I'm sorry I went behind your back, but you would have done the same for me if I was self-sabotaging with Brody."

I open my mouth to argue, but can't because I know she's right. But hell if she's getting a thank you right now.

"Ladies," Miles says, his gaze bouncing between us, probably sensing the tension. He has a flight of beers of all different colors sitting in front of him.

"Hey," we both say at the same time with a completely different inflection. Val's is upbeat, like she's trying to overcompensate for the shift in my mood.

"Everything okay?" He doesn't ask either of us specifically, but it's clear we're at odds here.

Val grimaces. "I didn't exactly tell Hannah why we were here. She's still coming to terms with it."

"Oh," Miles' face drops, and I kind of feel like an asshole now that he knows I'm not happy because of his presence.

"It's not your fault," I hear myself say. "And I'm not mad you're here. I just don't like being lied to." I turn to Val and glare at her as I say those last several words.

"Noted. I really am sorry, but it felt like it was necessary. I messed up. I see that now." She grabs the beer menu off the table and stands next to me so we can both look at it. "Anything look good to you?"

"Ooh, pear cider for me," I say.

Miles holds out one of his small glasses, still focused on the beer menu in front of him. "Here, try it. It's one that I got in my flight because I thought you'd like it."

His thoughtfulness sets my chest alight. Our fingers brush when I take it. And I hate the way it has nerves tingling all the way up my arm. My life would be so much easier if this man didn't make me feel this way about him so effortlessly.

"Alright, first round's on me. I'll grab it, you sit," Val says.

We fire a million fighting words back and forth with just our eyes, but I ultimately end up staying at the table with Miles. I even sling my purse around the chair beside his and sit.

He's still pretending to be preoccupied with his little taste-testing experiment so he doesn't have to look at me.

That's one difference between the two of us. He hates confrontation so much, he avoids it at all costs. I'd rather face problems head on. I feel my feelings, and let them be known, if applicable, then resolve the problem (also if applicable). Last night, I went against my own rules, running from him rather than letting him know my reasons. Even worse, I avoided him today and I can tell it hurt him. I regret it all.

I tap the toe of my Keds against his boot. "Hey."

He glances up like he's just now noticing my presence. I try not to be offended since I have no business feeling that way. "Yeah?"

"I'm really sorry, Miles."

He purses his lips, tipping them downward, and shakes his head. "You don't have to apologize for not wanting me here."

"Okay, I'm sorry for that too, but I actually meant I'm sorry for the shit I pulled last night. And for making you feel like shit because of it."

He tips up his chin, finally leaning back in his chair to look at me as he crosses his arms. "Yeah, some explanation on that would be nice."

Damn, this man is turning over a new leaf. That was some great defense.

"I just got scared."

He turns more in his seat so he can look at me head-on. "Hannah. Do you truly believe that I'm not scared, too?"

I finally meet his eyes, his pleading with me to understand everything he's saying.

When I don't answer, he continues. "Hannah, I'm terrified. Terrified to trip up and show your brother how I feel before I can sit down and talk to him like a man. I'm scared to get a glimpse of being with you for real after all these years, dreaming of what it could be like, only to watch you walk out of my life, much like you did last night. My life has been one comprehensive collection of losses, and I'm not looking for another. Especially not from the two people who have gotten me through them. But, Hannah, you're worth the fear of that unknown. And it's like a stab to the chest to find I'm not even worth a simple explanation to you."

"Fuck," my inner thoughts fall right out of my mouth because that fucking hurt. Enough that I can feel my eyes turning watery. "I'm sorry I made you feel that way, Miles. And you're well worth the explanation, and more."

"Drinks," Val says, coming up with two glasses of cider, pulling out her chair at the worst time. She realizes it as soon as she sits, looking between the two of us. "Crap, I always have terrible timing. I can—"

She moves to get up, but I clutch her forearm to hold her in place. "Stay. And thanks for the drink."

"Okay," she whispers into her glass before she takes a sip. "So, bar owner man, how's the research going? Has it gotten you drunk yet?"

He chuckles. "Not in the slightest. One flight barely equates to one large beer from the tap, and I'm still on my first." He brings one to his mouth, and I hate myself for watching his lips as he licks a small drop from his mustache after he swallows. "Say, do you guys think having beer flights at the bar would be worth it?"

"Depends how many beers you have on tap," Val says. "Are there enough to choose from that it would actually be necessary?"

"Once the second collection of taps we had installed in the remodel is filled, we will. I need to write that down." He lifts a few inches from his chair to reach into his back pocket, where he finds the same slim black notebook I saw the other week.

"Wait, do you carry that everywhere with you?" Val asks.

"Yeah," he says, like it shouldn't be surprising. But it's the most surprising thing about him.

"I've known you forever, yet I feel like there's so much I still don't know about you," Val says.

"Welcome to the club," I say under my breath.

Miles pretends not to hear either of us as he scribbles in his little notebook. I already knew this about him, but it's still shocking to see how nice his handwriting looks. All wide spaces between words, a mix between print and script, and it all slants a little to the left.

Val slams her glass onto the table, stealing my attention. I'm only a few sips into my cider, so I'm surprised to find hers is completely gone. "What the hell?"

"My ride is here. See you back at the hotel."

I stand from my chair at the same time she does. "What? I'll go with you."

She waves off that idea. "Why? I'm only going to go back there and call Brody, then probably go to bed. You should stay," she says, glancing at Miles pointedly.

I look back at him. He's inspecting his notes and pretending not to hear our conversation, but I know him better than to believe that for a second. He hears everything.

"Okay, well, if you're sure," I say, suddenly nervous to be alone with him.

"Positive. You two have fun."

Miles finally tunes back into the conversation in time to wave at Val as she walks out the door.

"Did you know that was going to happen?" I ask, the accusation falling flat because I know the truth. We just got swindled by my best friend.

"We should have known she'd do that."

"The brat."

"You'd do the same to her, I think," Miles says, lifting to stuff his notebook back in his pocket.

I laugh. "Yeah, I guess you're right."

"Can I get anything for you here?" A bartender says, coming up to our table.

I look around and realize Miles' flight is nearly empty. We both pick some food off the menu and Miles buys two more flights. He waits until the bartender is gone to inform me I'll be helping him drink one of them.

Chapter Twenty-Six

"Ooh, this one's good. Try it," Hannah says, handing me the sour she had on her flight. If you'd told me this morning, this is how my night would turn out, I wouldn't even see how that would be possible. To say I'm thankful for Val's interference is an understatement. It may have been an underhanded way to force us into talking to each other, but I'm still grateful.

Our fingers brush as I take the glass from Hannah. Our gazes stay connected as I sip, and she watches with excitement as that first burst of sour flavor lights up my tongue. The fact that she knows me so well, she can even pick out a beer I'll like says a lot about our relationship. I knew I'd been paying attention to her all these years, jotting little notes in my imaginary Hannah notebook to shove in my back pocket and remember for later, but I was too naïve—too stuck in my own pit of loneliness to realize she's been doing the same.

"I'm glad you're here," I say without even thinking, but it feels necessary to not hold back my thoughts and feelings for Hannah right now. Especially if I'm right in my assumption that she ran off last night because I hadn't been doing this enough before.

She smiles. Another glass paused in front of her mouth. "So am I." I watch as she sips, the way her brows jump at the surprising taste. "Okay, this is another good one."

She hands it to me; her smile breaking open wide when she realizes I'm smiling at her, too. Her nose crinkles when she asks, "What?" In that whiny way that doesn't sound whiny at all.

"Nothing, just looking at you, thinking about how fucking lucky I am to have you sitting here with me."

She smiles down at the table, letting her hair fall and hide her reaction away from me.

I take a deep breath and extend an olive branch, hoping like hell she'll accept it. I use one finger to push that curtain of hair away from her face. She glances up, embarrassed.

"You're beautiful, especially when you blush. Don't hide it away."

She laughs, "Shut up, Miles."

And I lean in, a piece of my mosaic heart sliding back into place when she leans in too, meeting my mouth with hers. For a moment, it's only us in this bar, being serenaded by the eighties ballad, about wanting to know what love is. The irony.

"What do you say we chug these beers and get out of here?" Hannah challenges, bouncing her brows and being altogether adorable.

I look down at our flights and picked-over food. Instead of an answer, I pick up the fullest beer sample and chug, never taking my eyes off her.

She laughs, then does the same.

I'm a pretty quick chugger, but she surprises the hell out of me by holding her own. And when she slams her last glass back into its slot, she lets out the most unladylike belch without an ounce of embarrassment.

I fall a little harder as I laugh with abandon and pull her in for another kiss. I suck a rogue drop of beer from her top lip, then stand to give me leverage. She tips her head back to let me in, pulling at my shirt.

A very private noise rumbles from the back of her throat, and it reminds me we're in a very public place. She realizes it too, because she sighs, "Miles, let's go. Now."

I toss a wad of money from my wallet on the table and we're off. There's a pleasant breeze that cools the sweat on my skin as soon as we walk out into the pitch black night lit by the streetlights.

I intertwine Hannah's fingers with my own, walking on the road side of the sidewalk. I just can't stop looking at her. She smiles as she skips along the street. There are noises bursting from businesses as we go, but few people are out in the street. A fact that is fine by me. I'm perfectly content for it to be the two of us and the stars hanging above our heads.

I look up to see if I can catch them. They're there, but not as powerful as they'd be if we were on the outskirts of town—or better yet, in the middle of nowhere. Either way, the mountains are the best place to stargaze.

Hannah gasps, tearing my attention from the sky as she pulls me into a small alcove between two buildings. There are picnic tables and tons of flowers, but I can't make out much else in the dark.

But when Hannah jumps into my arms, wraps her legs around me, and leans against the wall behind her, my whole body stands at attention.

"Touch me, Miles."

We're hidden from the street by a small bush, and I'm thankful, because I can't hold myself back from doing so any longer.

I took in her barely there outfit the moment she walked in that bar tonight, and with her body wrapped around me, I realize just how little she's covered. I loop my finger underneath the strap of her cropped tank top as my lips find hers from memory, because I can hardly see anything from where we are.

She takes a sharp inhale through her nose as my fingertips graze the top of her shirt. My other hand finds her ass, sliding down the fabric of her short skirt until there's nothing but the hot skin of her thigh beneath my palm.

Her fingers fist in the hair at the back of my head as she deepens our kiss, letting out a moan that has a direct connection to the bulge growing under the zipper of my jeans.

I pull away, pressing my forehead against hers as we catch our breath—a terrible plan, because I'm now surrounded by the scent of her. "If you don't stop making noises like that, I'm going to—"

"Do it," she says against my lips. "I don't care, Miles. Do your worst. I swear I can take it."

"Christ." All my blood rushes south at the dirty words coming from such a pretty fucking mouth. I grip her hips, grinding myself against the space her spread legs reveals to me. I can feel the heat of her through my jeans.

"Miles," she holds onto the back of my head, whimpering my name into my ear, and it's nearly my undoing.

With one hand holding the weight of her against me, the other has the freedom to slide up her soft thigh. "Hannah, tell me what you want."

"You," is her only response.

Fuck. My palm glides higher on her thigh, my entire body aware that I'm about to pass the point of no return. As my mind and body war with each other, Hannah puts the final nail in my coffin, settling my hand over her and pressing me against the place she wants me most. I have no choice but to feel the pulse of her beneath my fingers.

When I swipe two fingers over her center, her hands find my face, her mouth landing hot and heavy on mine. She moans into my mouth as my thumb finds the exact spot she wants me most.

I take a deep breath, my retreating hand finding the hem of her panties at the top of her thigh, where her leg folds into her hip.

She presses her pelvis against me impatiently. I hook my finger into the material, slowly moving closer to her center. When I finally make contact with her heat, she bites my lip with a moan, and hell if it doesn't feel amazing.

My thumb grazes her bundle of nerves, and an involuntary noise leaves Hannah's mouth, so I cover it with my own in case anyone might be near enough to hear her. My finger finds the wetness pooled in her center, swirling to coat my fingers. Her hand fists my shirt in anticipation and I dip one finger in her heat until it can go no further. She exhales, sucking in air as I find the pace she likes. When her legs spread wider involuntarily, I add another finger to her wetness, pressing my palm in just the right place, finding a circular motion. She adds to the heady sensation by swiveling her hips against my hand.

"That's it, Hannah. You look so good riding my hand like that."

My praise only seems to help her take what she wants.

I pull my head back, detaching our mouths. I find my vision has acclimated to the lack of light here, because she's looking at me like she needs something more to get her there. My lips tip up in a smirk at the same time my fingers bottom out inside her. Her mouth drops open in a silent scream. I pull down at the cup of her tank top with my teeth until she spills out over top of it. My mouth lowers to find the peak of her nipple, swirling my tongue at the same time my hand under her skirt rediscovers the pace that was driving her wild a moment ago.

Her hips work against my hand faster and faster until the circles she'd been making turn into free-form shapes. I choose that moment to clamp my teeth down lightly against her nipple. The surprise of it forces her hips to jerk against my hand, then she's pulling my mouth back to hers. The open-mouthed kisses she's giving me are languid, but I'm too focused on pinning her against the wall and using my thumb to help her orgasm break free. And I know the moment it does, because she lets out a moan against my mouth, her hips moving in sync with my hand to ride it out.

"I'd give anything to see you come apart for me right now," I whisper against her lips.

"Fuuuuuck," she says, along with the last few pumps of her hips, before she goes limp in my arms.

I kiss her hard as I remove my fingers and right her panties, then pull her top back into place. Then her hands are in my hair, keeping me as close as she can while her feet lock behind me now that there's nothing between us.

"You'll be the death of me," I say against her lips.

She laughs like I'm trying to be funny, but I've never been more serious. And I can't think of a better way to leave this world.

Chapter Twenty-Seven

Hannah

Miles and I have been sneaking secretive glances at each other all day today. As much as I want to be mad at Val for her conniving ways, I'm glad Miles and I got to clear the air last night—amongst other things. And to hear him say how he feels was exactly what I needed this week. I didn't realize how hard it would be to have no time to ourselves throughout this trip. That, mixed with the fact that we have to hide what's going on between us, I got a little too insecure and took it out on the most innocent and sweet person I've ever known.

I hate that I hurt Miles, but it did teach me something—I never want to do that to him again. Not if I can help it.

"Things seem to be going well," Serena says, walking up beside me.

"Yeah, I think we've got this place as ready as it'll ever be for your nuptials tomorrow. Not that it needed much added anyway, it's already gorgeous."

"Well, thank you, but that's not what I was talking about."

"Oh," I say in confusion, then peer in the direction of her gaze to find Miles.

"I meant you and Miles. You two have been tossing googly eyes at each other all day today."

"We have?"

She laughs. "Don't act like you haven't noticed."

I look back across the yard to where my brother is talking animatedly while Miles listens with the sober expression he normally wears. "Speaking of noticing—do you think Holt has?"

She shrugs instead of giving me a concrete answer. That is not a good sign.

"What do you know?" I demand, and Serena takes a step back.

"Hannah, I'm not doing this."

"Doing what? I'm your Maid of Honor. We're supposed to be each other's person, right? There's a certain amount of trust that should be shared between us, but I'm not feeling it right now," I say with a laugh, only half kidding.

"You know everything's going to be okay, right? You speak about trust, but you won't give it to me either. I'm just going to need you to trust me when I say that, yes, your brother may be onto something, but it's not exactly in the way you think."

"Speak English, woman! My brain is too fried for these riddles." The words come out in a rush. After what transpired last night, I'm afraid there's no turning back for me. Having to talk to my brother about this at some point just went from a probability to a promise, making my fear of the conversation all the more real.

She puts her hands up between us. "I refuse to be the middleman between you and Holt. You both have things you want to say to each other, but neither of you will say them outright. I won't be this person for you two, so if you respect me at all, you'll stop badgering me to get inside information. I said the same to your brother. The ball is in y'all's courts. I'm just a spectator."

"I'm sorry, Serena. Badgering you wasn't my intention at

all," I say, biting my lip and looking across the lawn again. "So what you're saying is, he knows?"

"I thought I made it clear I'm done with this conversation."

She looks at me for a long moment, then sighs, shaking her head as she walks away.

I was so worried about hurting my brother that I inadvertently hurt my future sister-in-law instead. This secretive crap is not for me. Thank god this wedding happens tomorrow. I need to get this off my chest soon before I spontaneously combust with the stress of it. And I really need to make things right with Serena, because she deserves better from me.

Later that evening, we're all gathered in the cabin dining room, following the quick instruction of how things will go tomorrow in the backyard. There are twelve of us seated at the large table, and as far as I know, this is the group that will witness my brother marrying his best friend tomorrow afternoon. They kept the guest list extremely small. My dad's mother and my mom's parents all showed up today. My aunt and uncle, who only live about three hours away from here, also joined us, since they won't be able to make the reception back home.

I'm sitting across from Miles, with Val and Serena on each side of me. It's been a pretty great day, minus the little hiccup I had with Serena earlier, which we both apologized for even though hers was completely unnecessary. All her points were valid.

I have made awkward eye contact with my brother a few times since that conversation, though. It's beginning to make me nervous, what he knows.

There's a sudden noise throughout the house, and everyone looks at each other. As far as I know, everyone is accounted for inside this room. Could it be a bear breaking into the house? An elk slamming through a window, perhaps?

But my anxiety slows a bit when Holt hops up from his seat like he'd been expecting someone. And when he reaches the doorway, I figure out exactly why.

"Brody!" Dad yells in greeting from the corner of the room. "You were able to make it. Great!"

Yeah, great.

Don't get me wrong, I love the guy, but where am I meant to sleep now that he's here? With my parents? On the floor?

I look at Val, trying to figure out if she knew and hid it from me, but she somehow appears even more shocked than I am.

"Babe, how the hell are you here?" She asks, standing to round the table and hug him.

As far as I know, they talked last night, so I have no clue how he pulled off this surprise without any of us knowing.

"I gave him a call about something this morning," Holt says, rounding the table to smack Brody's shoulder in a brotherly way. "He told me he no longer needed to work, so we made some travel arrangements, and now he's here!"

"Well, let's get you some food," my mom says, pushing Val and Brody back toward the kitchen.

When they return a few minutes later, everyone gives Brody a warm welcome. I try to be excited that he's here, but I'm too busy calculating the ways this will screw me over in the long run, like paying for a hotel room I will no longer be staying in.

Someone has already shoved a chair in next to Val's, so they sit down next to me. Val won't meet my eye, but she looks around the table sheepishly as the guys shoot the shit with her boyfriend.

"Glad to see you could make it, Brody," I say, pushing my disappointment to the wayside. I mean, I love Brody, so I don't want to make him feel bad for surprising his girl. Because Val deserves to be happy.

He looks a little worse for wear after a long day of travel. But despite tired eyes behind his black-rimmed glasses, and his rumpled clothes, he smiles. "Surprise?"

"Surprise is right. I guess I've been replaced, because I won't be cuddling you both to sleep tonight in a queen size bed."

His cheeks turn pink. "I'll take the floor, no problem."

"No, I can't let you do that. I'm already the third wheel back at home. You guys take the room."

"But you paid for it," Val says. "If anyone leaves, it should be Brody and I."

"We'll figure all that out later. I'll just get another room, it's no biggie."

With my camera bag strapped to my back, I head for the mountains. As much as I tried to improve my mood in front of everyone at the table after Brody arrived, this day just has me in a funk I can't get out of. Thankfully, I had a change of clothes in my camera bag and some of my favorite hiking boots in one of the closets upstairs. When I walk back through the busy dining room, no one seems to notice, exactly how I like it.

"Han, where you going?" Miles—of course—asks as I reach for the door handle. Why does he have to have a sixth sense of every move I make?

I force a smile and turn back. "I'm gonna go scout out a few spots for pictures tomorrow. Be back later."

I'm out the door before I hear my mom say, "Wait, someone needs to go with her!"

I pick up my pace, making my getaway before anyone can

bother to do so. I head through the yard to a well-used path we've been taking for years that gives great views of the lake.

In all honesty, I've known exactly where I'll shoot since my brother told me they were getting married here, and planned on getting here early tomorrow morning to do some scouting before I get ready with Serena, but this will give me the solitude I need and maybe I can even sleep in a bit tomorrow—that is, if I'm not out on the street by then.

"Hannah, wait up!" A familiar voice calls from the house.

I turn to find Miles at a full sprint in my direction. Damn him and his lumberjack wardrobe. He was ready for a hike without even trying. Hell, he's even wearing hiking boots.

"Dammit," I mutter to myself, coming to a stop and waiting for him to catch up. There's a familiar bag swinging along behind him as it bounces around on his shoulder—the hiking bag. Everything you'll ever need out on a stroll in the mountains. Snacks that I swear never expire, bear spray, headlamps, and collapsible hiking sticks, among other things.

It's the one thing I forgot to bring with, so hopefully he'll hand it off and let me go.

"Hey, thanks," I say, holding out my hand for it. Instead of handing it over, he flings it over his shoulder and continues walking. "Hey!"

He turns around, a smile already playing at his lips as he continues to walk backward toward my destination. "Yes?"

I start walking again. "What the hell do you think you're doing?"

"It's a nice night for a hike, so I'm joining you. What's it look like?"

I run to catch up to his sarcastic (and perfectly rounded) ass. "*It looks like* someone asked you to babysit me, and I don't like it."

We're under the canopy of trees now, and the house is out of view, which he knows and decides to take advantage of. His hands clasp my waist and he leans in close enough for his cedarwood scent to fill my nose. "I'm not babysitting, just using any excuse I can find to get you alone."

My breaths are coming harder by the second. "Is that right?" I lift to my toes until our noses touch and rejoice in the puff of breath that hits my cheek. Nice to know I have the same effect on him as he does on me.

"Yep."

"Well, the rule is," I say, dropping back on my heels as I play with buttons at his chest, pausing over his heart when I realize it's beating like mad as if trying to give itself to me. My eyes shoot back to his and I say, "If you come along, you have to be my model."

As soon as the words are out of my mouth, I'm moving again because I know for a fact that he'll protest my rule.

"Hannah," he says, picking up speed behind me, our pairs of footsteps intermingling as the perfect background music of crunching leaves and kicking rocks. "You know you're not gonna get rid of me that fast, right? I'll be the best damn model you've ever had."

You've got that right.

My surprise must show on my face, because his lips split into my favorite smile as he looks down to ensure his footing. The view has my fingers itching for my camera. God, I just want to hold proof of that smile in my hands forever.

I take a deep breath, facing forward again. I'm happy he's joining me, but I can't let him hold me back. The sunset will be popping through in no time, and I need to get to all my lookouts before that happens. I push forward.

As I'm focused on getting ahead, his fingertips graze my palm. I look down at our joined hands as his fingers thread through mine. And when my gaze finds his, he's already looking at me, trying to gauge my reaction. When I smile up at him, his mouth quirks in one corner before he squeezes my fingers and moves his attention to the surrounding trees. "I forgot how much I love it out here."

I look above us at the breaks in the trees that give way to a deep blue sky with fluffy clouds that are beginning to turn pink. "I know. I need to come out here more often, like we always used to."

"Me too. I looked it up the other day. We're only a quick day trip away from where my grandpa used to take me every summer. I wish I could go."

"You should."

He shakes his head. "Nah, after the wedding's over, I've got to get back to the bar. If these past few days have proven anything, it's that they can't make it long without me."

"So you make them," I say, squeezing his hand as I halt to a stop.

He finally turns back to me. "What?"

"It's pretty clear you've been burned out since you bought the place. And as much as that's expected by taking over, you can't let that bar take *you* over. Why do you think your grandpa escaped out here every summer? In a place where he could breathe in the intoxicating mountain air, and no one could get ahold of him?"

He nods, looking at the ground. "Probably because he needed a break. Some time to decompress."

"Exactly. I bet if you called the people you trust most back at the bar, they'd understand. They lean on you all the damn time, lean on them for help for once. And when you get back, make it clear you're looking for someone who's willing to step up when you're not around, because you can't keep living the way you are right now, Miles. It'll send you to an early grave, and you're mistaken if you think I'll sit back and watch that happen."

We start walking again. After a few moments of silence, Miles turns to me and says, "Yes, ma'am."

When we reach the first clearing, I walk toward the edge first, taking in one of my favorite views on earth. Miles lets go of my hand, but only long enough to remove my bag from my back and set it at the root of a tree right next to us as he settles in behind me and wraps his arms around my waist. I feel his front press against my back as he rests his chin on the top of my head. A deep exhale leaves him. "Perfect," he whispers, almost like I'm not meant to hear. But I agree—this view, his arms around me, this is perfection.

After a moment of taking it all in, I lean sideways to look at him, and he shifts to look at me, a Miles smile stretching across his beard. I kiss his jaw, since it's all I can reach in this position, then turn back to our view, but it doesn't last long. Miles' hands find my hips and turn me toward him. He takes in every detail of my face, and I think he's about to kiss me until he asks, "What happened earlier with Val?"

I release a breath, sagging under the weight of it. "I don't want to talk about it."

Both of his hands push the hair back from my face as his fingers comb into my hair. "Hannah, I'm your self-appointed problem solver. You have to tell me."

"Oh, is that so?"

He rests his forehead against mine. "Yes. Now tell me, because we're not leaving this spot until you do. I'd hate for you to lose your light before we get to all your spots."

I sigh. He knows his way into Fortress Hannah far too well. My own personal dragon slayer. "I'm letting them have the room." I hold up my hands. "And before you come to my defense on that, I'm totally okay with it. It just…" I look out into the trees, but Miles moves a thumb and forefinger to my chin to bring my gaze back to his. "Every time something like this happens, I feel really insecure for some reason."

His voice is so soft and caring when he asks, "What are you feeling insecure about?" Like all I have to do is answer, and he'll move these mountains we're standing on to make it all better.

I take a deep breath, trying to prolong having to tell him. "I feel like I'm holding Val back. Specifically her and Brody."

His brow furrows. "Why is that?"

I shrug. "I love living with my best friend. It's like childhood on steroids because now we've got money, booze, and boys. But her and Brody are pretty serious, and I have this feeling that if I wasn't standing in their way, they'd be married. Or at the very least, living together."

"If I get my way, you'll be in your own serious relationship soon and you might realize that not everyone wants to rush the process. In fact, I'm sure Val was glad to have you instead of moving in with Brody so early in their relationship. I bet the distance—if you can even call ten miles that—is good for them."

My mouth is still hanging wide open like a faulty hinge at the first thing he said, but I snap it shut before he has a chance to say anything. "Is that really what you want?"

"What, a serious relationship? With you? Of course."

"But," I say, scrunching my brows, "You've never had a serious relationship before—at least, not since Eliza in high school, right?"

He bites his lip, measuring my reaction. "Yeah, Hannah. And I've realized recently it's because none of them were you."

"But—"

He cuts me off. "There are no buts. I've been alone long enough to feel the difference between the way I felt for everyone that came along in my past," he points behind him, then his pointer finger taps just above my heart, "and you."

My breath comes out in a sigh.

"For someone who doesn't talk much, you sure have a way with words."

"It's because I only say what really matters." His lips brush against mine as he says it, making me squirm in his arms. "And Hannah?"

"Yeah?" I ask, completely breathless.

"You fucking matter."

As soon as the words leave his lips, they land on mine in a crushing kiss. An involuntary moan escapes me and I feel his arm wind around my back like a crowbar as he tips my head back until I open for him to deepen it. His tongue brushes mine, then glides along my upper lip, leaving sparks of electricity in its wake.

When he pulls back, his brown eyes are practically black. We both work hard to settle our breathing until he takes my hand and bends to grab my camera bag.

Right, *that's* why we're here.

"Let's go," he growls, pulling me back to the walking path.

"But we didn't get any pictures!" I plead, even though I know I didn't actually need them.

"We'll get them at the next spot."

"You're kinda grouchy, you know that?"

He laughs, but there's no humor in it. "Try sexually frustrated," he murmurs under his breath. I assume I wasn't meant to hear that either.

"Well, the wedding's tomorrow," I say before I really know where I'm going with this. All I know is that kiss just flipped my libido switch.

Miles squeezes my hand as he turns that thunderstorm gaze in my direction. "And your point?"

I shrug. "I'm just saying, we're close to the day we said we'd wait for."

"And…" he trails off, clearly getting more frustrated by the moment.

"And…I don't know," I say, afraid to put myself out there in this way with someone who's clearly more experienced, more—everything than I am.

"Wait, so where are you staying tonight?" He asks, as if he finally realized I've been kicked out.

I shrug. "I plan on getting that answer from the front desk when we get back to the hotel."

"Stay with me."

I want to say yes, but know it's a terrible idea to act on these feelings that have been driving me crazy the past couple of months on the eve of my brother's wedding.

"As much as I'd like to say yes, I'm not sure it's a great idea."

"I'm not going to make you do anything you don't want to do, Hannah. I've got a king size bed. You can make a pillow wall between us if you want."

That makes me laugh. "I could always stay with my parents."

"Not to be gross, but watching them together the past two days has been enough to deduce that they're both here for the same thing as Val and Brody."

I halt, bringing my hands up to cover my eyes as if that'll help me get that visual out of my mind. "Disgusting, Miles."

"Sorry. I saw your dad grab your mom's ass today. They didn't realize I was there."

I playfully shove at his shoulder. "Miles, stop! You're gonna make me ralph."

"Would it help you forget if I grabbed your ass?"

Probably.

Chapter Twenty-Eight

Hannah

"Sorry ma'am, there's an event happening in town all weekend. We've been booked solid for weeks. We have a sister hotel down the road, but I'm sure you'll run into the same issue there."

I feel Miles' hand settle on my lower back. "Hannah, just stay with me," he whispers close enough to my ear for me to feel the warmth of his breath on my skin. Reminder enough that it wouldn't be a good idea.

I force a smile, looking at the woman behind the front desk. "Thanks for your help. We'll figure it out."

Miles pulls me by the arm toward the elevator bay and leans in close. "I'll sleep on the floor if that will make you trust me, but I'm not leaving you without a place to stay tonight."

"Miles, you're not sleeping on the floor in your own hotel room—I will."

He pulls me in close, unleashing a frustrated chuckle. I take advantage of his nearness, leaning my head on his shoulder as I wrap my arms around his waist. I hear—as well as feel—him release a long breath when he realizes what I'm doing. He wraps his arms around me too, the two of us clicking together like puzzle pieces. His hard planes against my soft ones. My head fits perfectly on his chest. Our bodies are one long seam from the knee to the top of my head. It's the best hug I've had in—forever.

"Well, you two look pretty cozy." A familiar voice comes from behind us. I shoot away from Miles like a rocket and turn just in time to see my mother hitting the up button for the elevator.

I share a quick glance with Miles, then it's damage control to the rescue.

Before I can form the right words to say, my mom cuts in with an excited, "So this is happening?" She asks, pointing a finger between the two of us. "Your father called it. Last night, he told me there was something going on between you two. So I paid attention today and saw it too. Your running after her into the trees was all I needed to know for certain." Then, as quickly as the words are out of her mouth, she leans away and says, "Wait, does Holt know?"

I take another step away from Miles and place my hands on her biceps. "Mom, breathe. Okay?" I wait until her crazy eyes get a little less crazy before continuing. "We aren't—"

Miles steps up beside me. "Mrs. Hawkins," he says, setting a hand on her shoulder. On top of my hand that's still there. My mom gives him the look that says 'you know better than to call me that'. He smiles and corrects himself. "Jenn, I have to be honest with you."

"Miles," I warn, but he keeps going.

"We were trying to wait until after the wedding for obvious reasons," he looks at me with such a caring expression, I forget to stop him from doing what happens next. "But I care about Hannah. A lot." He takes my hand and holds it between us as my mom stares at the connection. "We've been spending a lot of time together—because of the wedding, strangely enough —and it's kicked up some old feelings for both of us. We're planning to tell Holt after all the dust settles from the wedding, so we'd appreciate it if you could be discreet until we have a chance."

Mom looks between us, as shocked as I've ever seen her. She's quiet so long, I'm afraid we've broken her until she lets out the loudest screech I've ever heard in my life. She wiggles all her extremities, bouncing in place. "Oh, I could not be happier. I've been hoping you two would end up together. For *years*! Miles, you know I already love you like a son, so I approve. Oh, honey!"

She proceeds to throw herself into my arms with enough force to knock us both over, but thankfully Miles is there to set us right.

She doesn't let go until the ding of the elevator arriving breaks up our little group hug. She gives us one more excited little wiggle before entering the metal box.

Miles and I look each other up and down, then step on behind her. As soon as the doors close, I wish I'd taken the stairs.

My mom continues to gush in the corner of the elevator as Miles laces his fingers in mine. I flinch because it feels unnatural to flaunt our relationship in front of a family member, but there's nothing to hide now that she knows. I lean into his touch, even going as far as to rest my head on his shoulder.

I could get used to this not-having-to-hide business, and suddenly I realize I don't care how Holt feels about it as much as I thought I did. It feels like I'm flying, finally telling someone I love about it. Come what may, I'm ready to have this all out in the open.

"Gosh, you two are cute." The last word jumps two octaves.

Okay, I take it back. This is going to be torture.

We arrive at the third floor with a ding, and mom sets herself right after leaning against the wall. "Well, you two have a good night. I'll see you in the morning, okay?" She kisses my hair, then leaves.

I hold her in place. "Please remember, Mom, Holt doesn't know, and we'd like to keep it that way until after the wedding. Please."

She does another excited dance. "You got it. My lips are sealed." She does the lock 'em and throw away the key motion and I can't help but roll my eyes.

"Okay, Mom. Good night. Love you."

"Love you too, good night!"

Then she's gone and the elevator doors close behind her, but I'm still staring at the place she vacated.

"Hannah, breathe so I know you're alive, please," Miles says from behind me.

I whirl to face him. "What the hell was that? You do realize my mom is one of the biggest gossips I know, right? Her only son gets married tomorrow, and she's gonna be itching to tell everyone some juicy gossip. We're fucked."

He's grimacing by the time I'm done talking, but he pulls me in anyway. "Hannah, what's done is done. We can't take it back now, so whatever happens, I'm ready to weather the storm. You know why?"

I take a deep breath, savoring his words before I meet his gaze. "Why?"

"Because I'll have you next to me," he squeezes my hand. "No matter what happens."

My eyes ping-pong back and forth between his before I finally rest my hands on his chest. "You're right," I plant a peck on his mouth, "You do have me. No matter what happens."

His grip on my hips gets tighter, more possessive. "Yeah?"

"Yeah."

"Was it just me, or was finally being able to tell someone like a weight off your shoulders?"

I smirk, nodding my head as I think about how it felt to tell all the girls about us weeks ago. "It does. I just held your hand in front of my mom. It felt awesome."

"Fuck yeah it did," he says with a blazing smile, his eyes burning with something I can't quite place.

Before I can prepare myself, his hand combs through my hair and pulls my mouth to his, and I go willingly. The kiss deepens as his hand trails to my ass, moving lower until his fingers hook at the back of my knee, pulling it toward his hip. My body moves of its own accord as the kiss turns hotter and the bulge below his waist causes the perfect amount of friction to graze my center, eliciting a moan from the back of my throat. The sound that has come as a surprise to me only spurs Miles on further as his arm latches behind my back, pulling me ever closer. I sigh as his mouth moves from my own to my neck to place wet, hot kisses down the length of it.

Then the ding of the elevator wrenches us apart, both breathing heavily.

Miles' eyes dilate as we stare at each other.

"Let's go," Miles finally says. "No way in hell am I letting you sleep anywhere else tonight." Then he takes my hand and pulls me out of the elevator.

In his haste to get behind closed doors, Miles fumbles with the room key, failing to make the little light turn green after three tries. I rip it out of his hand and get it after one try before he wiggles the handle and the door gives.

He smiles. "Well, aren't you in control of yourself?"

Not really.

The heavy door rattles on its hinges as I let it close behind me. "One of us has to be," I say, turning back to slide the lock chain home.

Miles left one of his room's side lights on while he was gone, so I can see him perfectly in the soft light when I turn back to him. His eyes, which have always been softer than the picture he paints of a rough exterior, are a richer brown than normal. His steps, closing the distance between us, are slow but sure. He pushes a strand of hair behind my ear when he's right in front of me. It's such a simple gesture, but that mixed with his proximity takes my breath away.

"You're so beautiful, Hannah."

His gaze is so intense, I have to look away, but it doesn't last long. He hooks his finger and thumb under my chin and asks, "Why do you do that?"

I meet his gaze. "Do what?"

"Avoid all compliments—act like you're not a fucking catch? Hannah, if you don't start seeing how amazing you truly are, I'll be forced to sit you down and tell you just what I think of you."

I shrug, a wicked smile playing at my lips. "That sounds fun. Will your shirt be on," I pull at the hem of his shirt, then dip my fingers below it, trailing them up his torso, "Or off?"

"Definitely off, if you'll be touching me like that," he says, his breathing out of control.

He leans in with a devilish grin as he wraps one hand around my waist and the other eases the hair tie from its place and drops it to the floor as my hair falls to my shoulders.

"You know, no matter how far and wide I look, I've never found hair quite like yours," he says, caressing a piece of it between his fingers. "The color is simply Hannah."

The line is so damn cheesy, I kinda want to give him crap about it, but tears build in my eyes instead, causing a blockage at the back of my throat. I clear it, then ask, "Why are you so good to me?"

Miles smiles before landing a chaste kiss on my lips. When he pulls away, he squints while taking in every inch of my face, like he's really trying to come up with a perfect answer. "Because, Hannah. Ever since we first met, I knew we were linked in a different way than I am with anyone else."

"We've always been kindred spirits, I think. When your

brother was off having a bitch fit, we were sitting next to each other, rolling our eyes."

"Mentioning my brother is literally the worst way to seduce me."

He laughs. "Yeah, you've got a point there." He rubs small circles on my lower back, looking at me like he's got more to say, so I wait. "Do you remember when I almost took you to prom?"

I take a deep breath, and look away before he can see the reaction his bringing that up does to me, but I must not do a good enough job.

I will never forget the afternoon I walked in the door to find Miles and Holt sitting at the kitchen table drumming their knuckles on the surface. As soon as I walked in, Miles popped up and said, "Hannah, there you are. We've been waiting for you forever."

I don't know if you've ever been the little sister who's dying to be included, but even my fifteen-year-old self was transported back to my younger days with just that statement. Especially when it came out of Miles' mouth.

"Really? What's going on?" I looked over Miles' shoulder to find my brother with a smirk on his face.

"Well, as you know, Eliza and I broke up."

"Yeah, I was sorry to hear that," I lied.

"No, you weren't," Miles said, calling me out.

Ever the dramatic teen, I rolled my eyes. "Anyway, what about it?"

"Well, prom is Saturday. I was going to stay home, but Holt won't let me. So," Miles looked at Holt, then back to me before continuing, "well, I was wondering if you'd like to go with me."

I accepted, and the next forty-eight hours were spent preparing to stand beside the one person I admired the most in this world. Miles O'Harrow.

But the afternoon of the event, my dreams were crushed.

I'd spend the entire day with mom and Val by my side as I got ready for my first huge school dance.

"You look beautiful, baby girl," Mom said on her way out my bedroom door to leave Val and I to talk until it was time to get picked up in the limo Holt, Miles, and all their friends were sharing.

But while the door was open, my brother—all dressed in his tuxedo—halted at the sight of me in my dress.

At first I thought he was speechless. I even remember laughing at the sight of him in my doorway with his jaw like a wide open hinge. But the next words from his mouth sobered me real quick.

"Hannah, what are you doing? Did Miles not talk to you?"

I ran my hands down the bodice of my emerald green dress. "What? No, I haven't talked to him since the other night. Why?"

"Shit," he whispered under his breath, then guided me to sit on my bed as he followed.

"Eliza and Miles got back together yesterday. She still wanted to go together, so he no longer needs a date. Hannah, I'm so sorry. I offered to tell you, but he was adamant that he wanted to tell you himself. He was going to come over to the house and explain everything. Wasn't he here?"

My view of my brother's almost manly features blurred as tears started swimming in my eyes. "No. I was out all night preparing for today. Why didn't you tell me, Holt? Why?"

He set a hand on my shoulder and took a deep breath. "I'm so sorry. I should have told you. I misplaced my phone and just got it back. I'm so sorry, Han. He was excited to go with you."

"Just go. I didn't feel like wearing this itchy thing, anyway. I need to change."

"I really am sorry, Hannah. And I know Miles is, too. Hey at least now you'll still get to take your camera out for a spin now, right?"

"No," I said, my tears finally rolling down my cheeks. "I'm not going. I'll stay home instead. Have fun."

"Hannah, don't be like this, please. I know it sucks, but we'll make it up to you. I promise."

"No, just go Holt. And don't tell Miles about any of this, please. Just let him think you told me, okay?"

"Hannah," Holt said.

"Please, just go. Now." And he listened.

To this day, I still don't think Miles knows what really happened. Part of me wants to know what my brother said when Miles asked about me that night. Or maybe he didn't even think twice about me.

It's fine though, because they broke up right afterwards. That summer, he and Holt were trying to make the most of what time they had left in their hometowns before everything changed. I got to see him a lot before they both went off to college and left Val and me behind.

"Hey, where'd you go?" His hand cupping the side of my face brings my gaze back to his.

"Back in time, I guess." I laugh it off, but he doesn't buy it.

"Why do I get the sense that we have two completely different recollections of that time?"

I shrug, shifting back and forth on my feet nervously under his probing gaze. "Probably because we do."

"You wanna tell me yours first, then?"

I huff out a laugh, although there's no humor in it. "Which part? The one where I was excited that the guy I'd had a huge crush on my entire life asked me to prom? Or the one where I went out and found the perfect dress at the absolute last minute." I hold a hand out between us, "No wait, my favorite is the fact that I spent the entire day getting ready, and had just gotten into my dress when Holt walked past my doorway and looked completely devastated for me before he had to break the news to me that you and Eliza had reconciled and that you didn't need your last-minute date anymore."

His mouth is hanging open, the textbook definition of shocked, and my inner fifteen-year-old is filled with glee at the remorse written all over his face, at least for the moment.

"What?" he finally asks when his brain unfreezes. "Hannah I called—"

"My brother?" I interrupt. "Yeah, you called Holt when you found out. But I was young and had a curfew, so I was sitting at home, blissfully unaware that you were back with her, Miles." I look away and laugh at the memory of it. "I woke up at the ass-crack of dawn to get *beautified*," I punctuate the word with air quotes. "My mom did my hair and makeup, and I remember Val sitting on my bed watching the entire thing with envy, because I was that freshman girl going to prom with a hot senior." I rub my forehead for a moment to hide. "It was humiliating, to say the least."

When I finally look at him, his brows are scrunched as if he's still processing. The news is almost ten years old, so I guess it's understandable that he needs a minute to rewrite the memories he thought he had.

"So that's why you didn't show up at pictures with your camera like every other time? Because of *me*?"

I feel tears forming anew at the recollection of that day. "Yeah, I couldn't exactly let you see me with a full face of makeup and a fresh updo. That ensemble didn't really pair well with my high top Converse and t-shirt."

He takes my hand, his legs give out as he drops into a sitting position on the bed. The move yanks me down with him and I nearly land on top of him. I put a few inches between us and he definitely notices.

"Why would you protect me in that way, Hannah?" He asks, running his hand through his hair like he does when he's processing. "You should've shown up fully dressed to put me in my place."

That makes me laugh. "Unfortunately, I didn't have the

balls to do such a thing back then. I'd definitely do it now, though. Fair warning."

"God, I swear, Hannah." He says, leaning over with his head in his hands, "I swear I remember calling you and apologizing. Why didn't you ever tell me? Hell, why didn't Holt ream my ass for it?"

I look up slowly, suddenly uncomfortable. "Because I forced him to promise he wouldn't."

Miles sets our intertwined hands on his knees. "You know the worst part about it, besides the fact that I hurt you?"

"What?"

"I had a terrible time with her and we ended up breaking up the morning after. I know if I'd just told her we were over and gone with you instead, I would've had the time of my life."

"Guess you owe me a dance."

"What are you doing two weeks from Saturday?" He asks.

I laugh, because we both know it's the night of Holt and Serena's reception. "Dancing with you, hopefully."

"Not hopefully. Definitely." His forehead falls to mine. "I'm so sorry I did that to you, Hannah."

"Thank you," I say, feeling my inner child heal a little at the apology.

Then my mouth dips to find his, initiating a desperate kiss that ends too soon when he pulls away suddenly.

My eyes flutter open to see what's the matter, and his eyes are intense, boring into mine. He looks down at our hands, linking his fingers with mine before he looks at me and says, "It wasn't my intention, but either way, what I did was careless and hurtful. I can't imagine what something like that could do to a young girl's confidence. I promise to make it up to you now. Just tell me how."

I nod and hope that's enough of an answer for the moment, because I know I won't get words out if I try. And the best part about Miles? He notices and pulls me into his lap for a full body hug.

I don't even care that I'm straddling him—I take that back, I definitely care. And so do the parts of me that have never gotten to touch him like this, but I try not to think about it as I squeeze my arms tighter around him as he does the same.

"I'm so sorry," he whispers. "I feel like such an asshole."

"I'd say I'm sorry, but my past self feels better knowing you feel like shit about it."

He laughs, and not only does the timbre of it come from next to my ear, but I can physically feel his chest rumble against my own. It sends a spike of heat straight to my core. Damn.

I lean away, just enough to meet his gaze before I go in for the kill. After only a whisper of contact, it's like a flip has been switched on. Neither of us can get enough. My hand weaves into his hair, pulling him closer. His hand explores the curve of my waist from underneath my shirt, then slowly creeps up until his fingertips rest under the clasp of my bra.

I knew sharing this space with him tonight would come with its own pressures, given last night's festivities. It was the reason I was hesitant to take his offer, but now that I'm here in his arms, I feel safe.

Miles moves us until I'm lying on my back on the mattress, the weight of him deliciously heavy on top of me. I've been in this position with other men in the past, and I always remember being nervous—scared I'd do something wrong. But with Miles, I'm surprised to find that part of my brain has shut off completely. All I can think about is how much I want this. How much I want to know what it feels like to be pressed into the mattress beneath him with no barriers between us.

But before that fantasy has a chance to become reality, Miles grumbles into our kiss and pulls away. "Cold shower."

I pop up into a sitting position so fast, it's a miracle I don't have whiplash. "What?"

He dips his face to mine for one more quick kiss. "I'm gonna jump into the shower and use the coldest setting possible."

"No," I say, fisting my hands in his t-shirt to keep him in place. "Stay here. Let me touch you."

His exhale is so forced, he sounds like he's in physical pain. "I can't believe I'm about to turn down that offer, but I am, Hannah. I want you, more than I have ever wanted anything. But I'm not rushing this. I want to do it correctly."

I look him up and down. "You look like the type who knows how to do it correctly. I'm not worried about that."

His hands find mine, prying them away from his shirt and pulling until I'm standing. Our faces are only inches apart. His lips are swollen from our kisses, and that fact delights me to no end.

"Hannah," he says with a sigh.

"Miles," I say, matching his tone. "Come on, let me make you feel as good as you made me feel last night."

He brushes a few loose strands away from my face, his hand nestling under my jaw and behind my ear. "Let's get one thing straight. I did that last night to make you feel good, period. No other expectations. I don't need reciprocation, and it was no favor. It was simply giving you what you wanted, and me enjoying every minute." He flips the covers on the only bed in the room and pats the mattress where I was lying on top of him only a few short moments ago.

Before I obey, I flip my shirt over my head and slide my pants down my legs. With a smirk in his direction, I climb into the sheets, wiggling around until I'm comfortable. Miles tosses the covers over my half-naked body like he's offended by the sight, although the way his teeth are sunken into his bottom lip tells a different story.

He turns on the television, then hands me the remote. "Need anything else, Princess?"

"Not unless you've changed your mind about coming under here with me."

He chuckles, dropping a kiss to my forehead. And I watch him in wonder as he crosses the room, stacking clothes into a pile in his arms. Then, after one last glance and a smirk to match, he disappears into the bathroom.

Chapter Twenty-Nine

Miles

The next morning, I wake to the sound of my phone ringing. The shrill noise makes me jump to grab it, but my arm snags on something and I open my eyes.

I turn to find Hannah's wide green eyes on me from where she lies on my shoulder.

When I came out of the bathroom last night, she was sleeping peacefully. I left her where she was, taking up two-thirds of the bed, and tried my best to fall asleep on the sliver of the bed that was left for me. Apparently, she found me in her sleep.

"Hey," she says. "You gonna get that?"

I shake my head clear and turn to shut off the damn thing. "Yeah, sorry." I barely get a glance of Holt's name before the call goes to voicemail. "Shit," I say, flopping back onto my pillow. "It was Holt."

She settles a hand on my chest, and there's no way she doesn't feel the way my heart is pounding underneath it. "Call him back. I'll be quiet."

I do, and the call connects on the first ring. "Hey, best man!"

The sound of those words mixed with the view I have of his sister makes the title feel like a lie. I'm a bad, bad man—the worst man, but I try to hide the shame from my voice. "Hey, groom. I'm planning on being there within the next couple of hours. What's up?"

"Oh, no need. I'm on my way to you right now."

My earpiece must be loud enough, because despite her promise to be quiet, Hannah squeals, detaching herself from me and scrambles around the room like a wild banshee, the bathroom door slamming behind her just before the water turns on.

I wonder if she realizes she doesn't have any of her things back from her room yet, but there's no time for that.

"What the hell was that?"

"What was what?"

"That sound. Did you just squeal into the phone?"

I laugh, sounding extra husky after a night of deep sleep with Hannah in my arms. "Yeah, sorry. I was surprised. I thought I could catch another hour of sleep or something."

"Well, get your ass in the shower, because I'm only about five minutes away."

"Shit, okay. Go slow, I literally just woke up."

"Fine, but I'm not waiting forever."

"Okaybyyye." I hang up so fast, I don't even wait to hear him return the parting phrase.

"Hannah?" I call from the outside of the bathroom door.

"Yeah?" she whines, and I hate that a great couple of days have to be overshadowed by this predicament.

"You okay in there?"

I hear the toilet flush, the water running immediately after. Then, a few moments later, the door unlatches. "Yes," she says, but it's not close to believable.

"Would you mind calling Val to see if she'll let you squat in there until I can get him out of here?"

As soon as the words are out of my mouth, there's a knock

at the door. I'd think Hannah's bug-eyed look was comical if I weren't so worried about what's about to happen.

I thought he said five minutes! Hannah mouths.

"So did I," I say, slipping into shorts and a t-shirt. "Get in the bathroom and we'll figure it out."

She closes the door carefully, and I wait for the sound of the lock clicking before I move to unlock the main door. I look in the peephole, but no one is standing in front of it. I open it slowly, unsure of what to expect on the other side.

"Hey," Val steps into the doorway with Hannah's duffle bag slung over her arm.

My body sags with relief. "Oh thank god." I step back into the room. "Hannah, it's just Val."

She steps into the room and sets the bag on the floor as the bathroom door flies open. "Val, you almost gave both of us a heart attack! Why the hell didn't you text me? We thought you were my brother!" I don't know if she realizes it, but she's still only clothed in her sports bra and thong from last night.

"One, I did text you. And two, nice outfit, Hannah."

Hannah looks down, and quickly hides behind the door, peeking around it to say, "My brother's on his way to the hotel, and everything we worked so hard to hide from him goes up in smoke if he finds me in here. Can I take a shower in your room?"

She grimaces. "Sorry, Brody was just getting in there when I walked out. My guess is he's probably on the toilet at the moment. If you want to bask in that smell, be my guest, but…"

"Okay, that's enough. I'll go to my parents' room."

"And risk walking in on them doing it? That's a terrible idea," I say.

But Hannah doesn't hear me. "Shit, you forgot my toiletry bag."

"Shit," Val says. "I'll go get it right now and bring it back."

Hannah's panic-stricken face moves between her best friend and I. "I'm so fucked."

All this panicking is doing us no good, so I attempt to put a stop to it. "Hannah, you shower so you don't get caught out here with your brother at any time. Val, you take this," I say, handing her my room key. "I'm going to try to run interference downstairs. Thank you so much for your help and please pray for us."

A smug smile crosses her lips. "I must say, I truly love what's happening here."

"Valerie! Get your ass out of this room before I kick it. You know all of this is on you, right?" Hannah yells, slamming the bathroom door.

Val grimaces, "Sorry."

I wave off her worry. "It's all going to be fine," but even I barely believe the words as they come out of my mouth.

When Val is gone, I knock on the bathroom door. It unlocks and Hannah peeks out at me, this time wrapped in a plush white towel.

"What?" she asks, but the fire from before is missing from her tone.

I step closer and wrap my arms around her as tight as they'll possibly go. "No matter what happens from here on out, I've got you, alright?"

"I'm so scared to come between you two, Miles. I don't want to hurt anyone."

I brush a hand over her hair and kiss her forehead before pulling her back into my chest. "I know. Neither do I. I'm going to do everything within my power to do this right. Please don't forget how much I care about you. Okay?"

She swipes a tear away from her eye. "Okay, you either."

I smile, despite the fact that it feels like I'm unraveling. "I won't."

She lifts on her toes, pulling me down to her for one last quick kiss. "See you when I see you. I just know you're going to be so damn beautiful today. Not sure how I'm going to hold myself back from you."

She gives me the first smile I've seen all morning, and it helps me believe everything will be okay.

I run into the bedroom and throw on a change of clothes. I'm tossing on my favorite black hoodie when there's a knock at the door. I freeze, then cross the room and throw it open, expecting Val to be on the other side. Instead, Holt pushes past me into the room. My gaze slides to the bathroom door, knowing it's the worst thing I could do, but I can't help it.

"Holt, you're early." With his back turned, I scan the room for any lingering items belonging to Hannah. I shove her hiking boots into my bag, then lift to find Holt looking at me, suspicious as ever.

"Who's in your shower?"

"Brody," I say. "He had to stay here last night with the last-minute changes. So what's up? Why the hell aren't you still in bed at the cabin?"

"Oh, I don't know, man. Maybe because it's my fucking wedding day, and I was burning a hole in the rugs at the cabin from pacing too much. My bride's getting pampered all morning, so I was going stir crazy." He turns suddenly from his spot at the window and the look on his face makes the contents of my stomach bubble uncomfortably.

"I need coffee, bad," I blurt before he can talk, even though I know it's the worst thing for my nerves right now. It's the first thing I can think of to get him out of here. "Can we head down to breakfast and grab some, please?"

Before he can answer, the lock on the door clicks and the front door gets thrown open. Val sees us both staring in her direction. "Hey, guys. Sorry, uh," I notice the hiccup and hope Holt doesn't. "Brody forgot toiletries, so I'm just gonna slip in here quick." She disappears behind the door and I can't believe how well that worked. I could faint right now.

I take a deep breath to calm my nerves. "So, how about that coffee?"

He jumps to attention, heading for the door without a fight. I thank my lucky stars, following him to the elevator bay.

The doors open and I lean back against the wall with a loud sigh.

Holt clears his throat and I pop one eye open to find him looking at me expectantly.

"You're quieter than usual."

I shrug. "I'm a pretty quiet guy. Now tell me what's got you so nervous," I say, hoping it will help take my mind off my own.

He runs a hand through his hair, a telltale sign that he's not lying about the nerves. "It's not so much that I'm nervous about marrying Serena. I love her more than I can put into words—trust me, I tried to finish my vows last night." He rolls his eyes. "It's hard as fuck to put it into words," he chuckles to himself. "But I don't know. I'm just being my usual high-strung self, I guess. I'm nervous about the day and all it entails."

"A little advice from someone who has no business doling out advice pertaining to relationships?" I ask and he nods, giving me the go ahead. "You two are perfect together, and you're having a small ceremony with all the best people in your lives. Every single person you invited was hand-picked for a reason. It's going to be intimate and special. There shouldn't be anyone on the guest list you don't feel comfortable around. And even so, this day isn't about the people who show up, it's about the two of you. We're all here to witness your love and celebrate the rest of your lives together. It's not about the food getting spoiled—"

"The food's spoiled?" he shrieks as the elevator dings, letting us know it's on the ground floor.

I laugh as we exit, slapping a hand on his shoulder. "No, I just mean that, if something does go wrong, that's not what this day is about, you know? I want you to live your day in such a way that all you remember is the loving looks you and Serena shared. Not all the bullshit that *could* happen. So when something happens because surely it will—I want you to look at her, take a deep breath, and remember everything I just said, okay?"

We're nearly across the expansive lodge when Holt suddenly stops to swivel in my direction. "Okay, who are you, and what the hell did you do with my cynical best friend?"

I laugh it off and continue walking, but he's on my ass in an instant.

"Seriously, Miles. Something's going on with you. I've noticed a change in you these past several weeks." He pats my shoulder as I reach for a coffee cup. "And it's fine. You don't have to tell me yet. I've got other things to keep me busy today, but you can bet your ass that when I get back from my honeymoon, I'm gonna be expecting a full explanation for why you just gave the best man pep talk of a lifetime."

"Not much has changed, man," I say, realizing the lie as it rolls off my tongue. Because everything *has* changed. I may have always felt...something for Hannah, but what's happening between us has shot my feelings straight into the stratosphere. If I'm not careful, my head and my heart will be floating in space before I know it, and the thought of that drop back down to Earth after things go awry scares the hell out of me.

I usually go for black coffee, but this morning, like many of my afternoons spent with Hannah, I add a little flavor. Milk first, then a packet of sugar, and the last addition is a couple of those small cups of vanilla creamer. It won't be comparable to the ones I get at Brew & Bean, but at least it's something. I turn to throw all my trash down the receptacle, only to find Holt staring at me wide-eyed.

"What?"

"I've only ever seen you drink it black. What the hell happened?"

I shrug and go for honesty with this one. "Hannah made me try her drink one time while we were wedding planning, and I actually kinda liked them." I poke a finger into his chest. "This is your fault."

He raises his eyebrows at me. "Don't tell her how much you enjoy it, she'll end up with a bloated self-esteem."

"She already knows."

"Hey guys," I hear from behind us to find an oblivious Brody and a visibly nervous Val behind us.

"Hey," I say with wide eyes, hoping it will convey my need for discretion.

"Hey," Holt repeats. "Damn, Brody. Your hair dried fast. What's your secret?"

"Huh?" He asks, looking between us all in the half-circle.

"Oh, Holt was in the room when you were showering earlier," she says. Brody looks like he's about to spill the beans due to his confusion, but Val sets a hand on his shoulder and says, "Yeah, I taught him how to use my blow dryer. It's been a game changer. Hasn't it, babe?" She gives a pointed look that, luckily, Holt is on the wrong side to see.

"Oh yeah, definitely," Brody says, still looking a little confused, but game to go along with whatever his girl says.

Good man.

"Where's Hannah? Figured she'd be tagging along with you two," Holt says.

Val waves a hand behind her, "Oh, she was still upstairs showering, so I left her to it. She said she'd meet us down here."

Holt looks like he wants to say something, but spots his parents at a back table and heads in their direction. Thank fuck.

Val and I share a mutually exhausted look and a deep sigh before we follow him to Jenn and Bobby.

Chapter Thirty

HANNAH

I'd been hoping for a reprieve from the craziness that started this morning, but it never came. It's been full speed ahead since I woke to the sound of Holt's phone call.

I hired a local photographer to help with group shots I knew I'd need to be in, and she's been a dream to work with. I got most of the shots of Holt and Serena done before she showed up, then I stood next to Miles for the pictures of the group of us. Standing so close to him but being unable to touch him the way I wanted made me envious toward my future self, whose feelings for him will no longer need to hide.

I'm standing off to the side of the altar the guys made the other day—it's covered in a beautiful, draping floral arrangement, with the beautiful lake background. I know their photos are going to be gorgeous. Despite the fear and imposter syndrome I've been battling with for months, I can't wait to edit these pictures. I think the mountainous backdrop will be a nice change from the usual. I turn to the side to find my brother and his wet eyes (they've been like that for a majority of the day because he's kind of adorable) looking toward the space Serena will walk through shortly. In the front row, next to my mom, Miles gives me a soft smile that makes my heart do impressive flips in my chest, trying to show off for him, the flirtatious little shit. He's wearing the uncharacteristically blue pants Serena and I gave him shit for weeks ago when the guys went clothes shopping. He fills them out perfectly, along with his white button-down shirt with a dusty blue tie hanging from his neck. He looks delectable. My camera clicks, taking a candid of the moment.

It may not end up in the final wedding album, but at least I'll always have it for myself.

The music starts, tearing my attention away from Miles to the end of the aisle, where Serena stands smiling alongside my father, who she asked to escort her on her big day.

I snap several pictures as they move through the intimate crowd toward the altar. I was there for her dress appointment, but have only seen it post-alterations in pictures. So seeing her in this peaceful, outdoor environment with full makeup and hair, and a dress that fits her like a glove, it took my breath away when she walked out for her and Holt's first look. I can only imagine what he thought when he turned toward her for the first time.

Between trying to get all the money shots and trying not to cry as Holt and Serena said their vows to each other, the cere-mony flies by. It was more beautiful than I could have imag-ined, and exactly what I'd hoped for the two of them.

And as the shutter clicks, my lens following them down the aisle, a single tear drops down my cheek because the end of the ceremony marks a new beginning. It marks nearing a life where Miles and I will no longer feel the need to sneak around. Soon, I'll finally be able to hold Miles' hand in front of my family. That is, if everything goes as planned.

"Let's have a toast," Dad says later in the evening while everyone is seated in the dining room, a full champagne flute sitting next to their plate.

Serena's fidgety in her seat next to mine, and when Holt's gaze finds hers, I watch them have a complete conversation together before Holt bolts upright out of his seat.

"Before we do that, Dad," he interrupts, waving Serena over to his side.

She goes to him, ducking under his arm and wrapping hers around his waist. Holt kisses her forehead and looks out at their guests sitting at the table hanging on his every word.

"Serena and I have been holding onto a bit of a secret," and I'm not sure why, but the choice of words makes me look across the table at Miles. He senses it and looks at me, too. Given the look on his face, I think his mind went in the same direction. Surely Holt didn't catch onto us and decide to call us out in front of everyone?

Holt's eyes turn misty for the millionth time today before he smiles and says, "We weren't sure we were going to tell everyone yet or not, but my beautiful wife is pregnant!"

The room full of family, both biological and chosen, cheers at the news. As for me, I turn hysterical. I've somehow kept my composure throughout the day, and I think that's mostly due to the fact that I've been hiding behind my camera. But not now. Now, the tears are streaming down my face as I watch my parents hug Holt and Serena, and Miles slaps his best friend on the back.

"Congrats, auntie," Val says, wrapping her arms around me from behind, and I squeeze her back as well as I can from this position.

She lets me go, and I realize why when Miles walks up in front of me.

"You're going to be an aunt," he says, his dimples popping with his smirk. "Don't cry. It's a good thing," he says, and I think he surprises the both of us when he rests both hands on either side of my face and uses his thumbs to wipe away my tears.

It's such an intimate gesture. I should be worried about who's witnessing it, but I'm fully in the moment with him. My head is bent backward to see him this close, and his eyes haven't left mine either.

"Congrats," he says, pulling me in, where I go willingly. I savor his embrace, my hands fisting the back of his shirt.

"Thank you," I say into his chest.

When we pull apart, the first person I make eye contact with is Holt. The smile on his face changes somehow. Instead of joy over his news, it's almost knowing, and I feel my own drop off my face at the realization. Did he just see that? Could he see the longing written all over my face?

"You should get over there," Miles says.

"Does he know?" I whisper.

"If you're asking if I told him on his wedding day, the answer is no. But I have a feeling he might be onto us."

"Shit," I mutter under my breath. Miles hears me and squeezes my hand discreetly enough that I don't think anyone can see.

"It'll be okay, I promise. Now go."

I nod, rounding the table, but getting stopped by my parents, then grandparents, on the way.

Finally, I reach Serena, who looks guilty as she grabs me by the biceps. "I swear I almost told you a thousand times. I'm sorry I didn't."

I hug her. "You have no reason to apologize, Serena. I'm so happy for you. I have a million questions, though!"

"I found out the day after girl's night. I woke up feeling way more hungover than I ever have, and I had no clue what was wrong with me. I took a pregnancy test, and I guess that's the full reason I've been so stressed and emotional lately. I'm nine weeks today, so it's still pretty early."

"Hannah," Holt comes up beside us and wraps us both up in a bear hug.

I get an arm around him too. And lean my head into his chest. "I love you both so much. Congratulations. I'm so happy, my heart could burst, I swear."

"Thank you. We're so excited to tell everyone. It's been so hard to keep this secret with everything going on."

"I can understand that," I say, and realize how incriminating it sounds as soon as it's out of my mouth. I immediately wish I could take it back.

Given the way Holt's looking at me, he knows there's something I'm holding back from him, and I hate it. We've always been honest with each other. "Yeah, secrets can really eat at you, if you're not careful," his perma-smile is still fixed on his face when he looks over my shoulder, which only makes me feel worse. I know he just found Miles out in the crowd. He knows, and I want to be strong and tell him, but I'm torn. I would never forgive myself if I ruined this moment for all of us.

I'm saved by my uncle, who walks up behind Holt and claps him on the shoulder. "Well, we've got more than one reason to celebrate now."

When Holt turns to him, I walk away, back to where Val and Brody are still standing.

I find Miles' gaze in the crowd, and it says the same thing I'm thinking—we need to tell him.

Chapter Thirty-One

MILES

Everyone's exhausted by the time our vehicle reaches our hotel. It wasn't long after the toast Bobby made post-baby news that everyone started going in their own directions.

Hannah and I stuck around to help clean up, and are now among the last of us to return to the hotel. I'm beyond done caring what anyone thinks, and take her hand as we walk through the automatic doors and into the lobby. She smiles up at me, exhaustion making her lids droop. "You did amazing today, Hannah," I say, repositioning her camera bag that's on my back. "Every time I get to watch you with that camera in your hands, I grow even more proud of you."

She hits the up button on the elevator, then smiles up at me before she leans into my shoulder. "That's the sweetest compliment I've ever gotten."

I kiss her forehead. "I meant every word."

The elevator dings, and we step inside, the only two here. I lean against the back wall of the elevator and she leans back against me, her eyes closing as soon as her head finds my chest.

I set my hands on her hips, and stare at our reflection in the mirrored side wall. I love the way we fit together.

"You know, I never realized I gave you your first camera," I say, breaking the silence in our tiny metal box. "Val reminded me of it when we ran into them at the bar during Holt's bachelor party."

Hannah's movements are lazy, like she's already half-asleep, but she turns in my arms until she's facing me. "I think about that all the time. If it weren't for you, I might not have found what I love to do. I never told you how thankful I am for that. For you."

She lies on my chest, hugging me around the waist. I kiss the crown of her head.

A moment later, the elevator dings, announcing our arrival on our floor. I hold most of Hannah's body weight, ushering her down the hallway to my room. As the door unlocks, I pull her up into my arms and she links her legs around my waist, taking the free ride across the room like we've done this a million times.

I place her camera bag down on the side table, then carefully set her on the bed. I move to head across the room, but Hannah pulls me by the damn tie I can't believe I'm still wearing.

"Come back here," she says playfully, apparently finding her second wind.

I press my hands into the mattress on each side of her head, smiling down at her as she peeks up at me with one squinting eye, and one closed. "Did I mention how beautiful you looked today?"

"Maybe once or twice. Feel free to do it again. I won't mind."

I pull back, taking in the full image of her. The auburn curls, the long lashes and painted lips. Her dusty blue dress that hugs every single one of her curves and kept my attention on her all day today. "You're so beautiful. It takes my breath away, honey." I trace the contours of her face, continue down her neck, and follow the strap of her dress until it connects with the bodice. I pause, watching her chest heave under my touch. Her eyes are heavy, for different reasons than exhaustion this time.

She arches into my touch until I finally trace the edge of the neckline of her dress with my finger.

I hook into the V of her bodice, lowering it a couple of inches. She lays her head back, elongating her neck, the smooth skin calling out to me.

I lower my mouth, exploring the freckles there with my tongue, swirling it over her pulse, then place a kiss lower. A third brings me to her chest, where I can feel her heart flutter under my lips. I lift only slightly to look at her, running my lower lip along the hem of her bodice, my palm sliding over her breast, her beaded nipple pushing against the fabric.

I pull down on the dress, my mouth moving quickly in its wake. Just before my mouth clamps down on the raised pink bud, her hands fist into my hair, pulling me closer.

When I finally make contact, a gasp falls out of her mouth.

"God, that feels good," she says, spurring me on. One quick maneuver by her, and both sides of her dress fall away, leaving her chest bared to me. I switch to the other side as Hannah's hands work at my neck. I don't realize how restricting the tie has been all day until it's loosened and falls away.

My mouth continues to work as she loosens the buttons of my shirt and pulls it from the waistband of my pants and shoves it down my shoulders.

I sit her up on the bed until I can reach the zipper at her back. She stands and lets it fall to the ground, leaving her in nothing but her black panties.

"Beautiful," I repeat, lowering her to the bed until she's lying down.

Her eyes sparkle back at me as I hook my fingers in both sides of her underwear and pull. She lifts her hips to help.

I grab her thighs, lowering to kneel between them. She squirms with each kiss I trail up her inner thigh, unable to sit still in the anticipation of what's to come.

As my mouth hovers over her center, she lifts to glare at me, only making the fire in my chest burn brighter for her.

"Dammit, Miles. Stop teasing me."

Our gazes stay locked as I slide one finger down her center, testing how ready she is. "Not sure you're ready quite yet, honey," I say, even though she's soaked.

She groans, dropping her head back to the mattress.

I chuckle, small puffs of air hitting her as I lean in closer, making her squirm under my touch yet again. And when my mouth makes contact, a satisfied moan falls right out of her. Once I find what she likes, I add one finger, then two.

She's much more vocal than she was in the alleyway the other night, given the privacy we now have. It's like discovering a whole new side of her. I know she's almost there when she grips the hair at the back of my head, keeping me in place. She pulses around my fingers, but I don't stop wringing out what's left of her orgasm until she pulls me up and on top of her.

She kisses me hard, wrapping her legs around my hips.

While she's got me good and distracted, she uses strength I didn't realize she had to flip us around until she's straddling me.

She smiles down at me as she reaches for my belt and begins to unbuckle it. Although I'd love to see where this could go, I set my hand over hers to stop her.

"What?" she asks with a devious look.

"Not so fast."

"Okay," she sets her palms on my chest, running her hands over my arms, then back up and down my torso. It feels better than I could have ever imagined. "What else did you have in mind?"

"I'd love to push this further, but I meant it when I said we're taking this slow."

"Your mouth tastes like me. You call that taking it slow?"

"I call that losing control and making you feel good while going as slow as I possibly can."

We've had years of foreplay. Pretty sure that's as slow as it gets.

"Let me make you feel good."

I set my hands on her waist, rubbing my calloused palms all over her torso and back. "This does feel good, having you here."

"You know that's not what I mean."

I sit up, pressing my lips against her forehead. "Not yet."

"Ugh," she sighs dramatically and falls back onto the bed.

"Besides, didn't you say you needed to do something with your camera before we went to sleep tonight?"

Her eyebrows lift and she jumps off of me quicker than I thought possible. "Shit!"

She tosses the first thing she can find—my shirt—on and starts digging in her camera bag.

Well, that got her mind off things. Unfortunately, I can't say the same.

I watch in fascination as she goes to work, sliding each memory card into the reader and loading them onto her computer.

"What are you doing when you get home?" I ask after observing her process for a while.

"I don't have anything but editing to do for about a week. Why?"

I pull her by the hips and spread my legs so she's sitting between them, resting her back on my chest. "Well, I've been thinking about what you said the other day."

"What, exactly, did I say?"

"That I should take a few more days off for an actual vacation. I think I'm going to," I run a hand through her hair. "And I want you to join me."

Her lips turn up in a smile. "You do?"

"Yeah, I was thinking it could be the cure for what ails both of us. I could show you the hike my Grandpa Lyle took me on when I was young, and you can take your camera. It's beautiful this time of year. Wildflowers, everywhere."

"Sounds beautiful."

I lean to kiss her forehead. "It is. What do you say?"

She bites her lip, trying to hide the smile spreading across her face. "I say, I'm in."

I can't help my smile. She sets down her computer and turns in my arms. Before I know it, she's straddling my hips, her hands slipping behind my head to pull me in for a kiss. This one doesn't last long before she leans in to lie on my chest.

From her place there, she mumbles into my chest, "Why does this feel so right, being in your arms?"

That is a question I hope I have years to find the answer to.

Chapter Thirty-Two

Miles

We'll return to the cabin one more time this morning to join Holt and Serena for brunch as they open the presents they've been given this week.

Hannah's scrambling around the room to get ready, and all I need to do is hop into the shower and change my clothes, so I'm letting her do her thing. I can't complain, because being surrounded by the coconut cloud—the scent of her hair products and body lotion I've recently found out—she's always walking around in is a great way to start my day.

I'm still lying on the bed watching her because I put in some hours last night staring up at the ceiling, thanks to my guilty conscience. Hannah slept cuddled right into my side a majority of the night and, by all means, I should have gotten the best night's sleep of my life. But the happenings of the past several days were on my mind, forcing my mind into overdrive, rather than resting mode. While I've never made it a habit to gab with Holt about the details of my sex life, it still feels wrong to feel this strongly for someone I've been hiding from him.

It's not that I have any regrets about Hannah specifically.

Learning her in a brand new way has been the highlight of my year, and nothing can take that away from us. It's that I've had years to come clean about my feelings for her, and I'm still keeping it from my best friend. It makes me feel like shit.

It doesn't help that I woke up to a million questions from my employees at the bar, and another dreaded missed call from my mother. Despite the clusterfuck of outside forces trying to make me implode, I'm trying not to let them take up space on my mental plate.

"Hey," Hannah says, the hem of her purple sundress hiking up her thigh as she sets a knee on the bed next to me, leaning down to kiss me. "You've been over here brooding all morning. What's up?"

Her hand rests on my chest and I set mine on top of it. The other finds her exposed thigh. "Just in dire need of some coffee," I say, and at least it's a half-truth.

She laughs. "Me too, but I can tell that's not the full story. Tell me what's going on, Miles."

I pull her on top of me and twist to the side until we're both lying on the pillows, looking at each other. "I'm going to tell him today."

She takes a deep breath. "Yeah?"

"Yeah. I'm still trying to think of the best way to go about it, but do you mind if I tell him on my own?"

She bites her bottom lip. "Are you sure that doesn't make me look like a coward?"

"If you want to be there, you can be. I know I owe it to him to stop hiding this from him. It's eating away at me and taking away my ability to be completely present in this. I feel like shit."

"Me too," she says, taking my hand. "The way he looked at me last night when he saw you hug me, I think he knows."

There were several openings yesterday when it was just Holt and I. I should have said something then, but I was scared of the repercussions, and didn't want to do anything that would jeopardize his wedding day.

"I'm excited to no longer have this little rain cloud following us around anymore," I say.

"Don't get too ahead of yourself. He still might not be happy for us," she says.

Of course, that thought had occurred to me, but I refuse to believe he'd actually disapprove of us being together. "You really think he'd do that?"

Hannah lets out a sigh. "I sincerely hope not, but I know there's a possibility. What would we do if that's the case?"

"We'll take it one day at a time, together," I say, squeezing her hand.

She squeezes it back and kisses me. "That will work for me."

The cabin looks different in the light of day. The flowers are still beautiful, if not a day old. Almost everything has been disassembled, and I'm out in the backyard working on the rest with Holt. The intense urge to talk to him takes over and I finally give into it. "Hey, Holt?"

"Yeah?"

"I was wondering if we could talk."

"Oh. Yeah, of course. What's up?" He asks, but before I can find the right segue into the conversation we need to have, Jenn calls out from the back door of the house where it opens into the backyard.

"Holt, Miles. We need your muscles in the house. Come quick!"

Holt's already halfway to the house when I sigh and follow. So much for getting that over with.

When we walk into the house, I find Hannah's nervous gaze, and I know exactly what she's wondering. *Did you two talk?* her gaze asks. I shake my head discreetly, and she looks about as disappointed as I feel.

We help move all the furniture back into its rightful place, then we move right into brunch, where Holt and Serena sit at the head of the table opening gifts as we eat. Thankfully, the family mostly left it to cards and money, since there will be a reception at a later date, and they're going to be traveling.

By the time we finish brunch, it's almost time for Holt and Serena to leave for their flight. My chances of getting Holt alone to talk to him are dwindling.

To drive the point home, Holt lifts to his feet. "Well, should we get ready to go, wife?"

Serena smiles, setting her hand in his, "We should."

They step away from the table. But Holt stops when we make eye contact. "Oh, wait. What was it you wanted to tell me earlier?" Holt asks, suddenly remembering our time outside.

I wave it off. "Nothing that can't wait until after your honeymoon. Have fun, man."

His smile doesn't quite reach his eyes. "Thanks, Miles."

And when they leave the room, I can feel everyone's eyes on me and I hate it. I hate that I got so lost in something great that I tricked myself into believing it was a good idea to keep it from him. Everyone in this room knows what I'm hiding but him.

An overwhelming sense of dread washes over me as my heart begins to pound overtime in my chest, and I recognize it immediately for what it is.

I need to get out of here.

"Excuse me," I say to the room. Standing from the table, my breaths come heavier as I feel sweat coat my forehead. My hands are shaking when I reach for the door handle, and it takes a couple of tries to get it slid open. When I step out onto the veranda, I trip, but steady myself on the nearest pillar for a moment, taking a few deep breaths before trying again.

Everyone in the dining room can still see me where I stand. I need to move. I need to get away from this cabin for long enough to breathe.

I walk further into the backyard on unsteady feet until I reach the fire pit that's secluded from the house by a few towering evergreens. As my vision morphs into something unrecognizable, it's like staring out of one of Hannah's special camera lenses.

I choose calm, I think to myself. *I choose calm*. I take a deep breath, and try to remember all the coping mechanisms I worked on with my therapist for moments like this.

A tree swaying in the mountain breeze, a bird in flight overhead. The fire pit in front of me. A Jeep driving a mountain road in the distance. The small shed in the backyard. I move on from objects to sounds. The birds chirping all around me. The trees swishing in the breeze. My deep breaths—

"Miles?" I faintly hear Hannah's voice from near the house, but can't bring myself to call back to her when I'm not back in control. "Miles, where are you?"

I take several deep breaths in and out, desperate to feel better before Hannah finds me.

I'm sitting forward with my face in my hands when her footsteps approach.

"Miles," she says as her footsteps pick up speed. "Are you okay?"

I focus on the way her hands and feet move toward me. The worried line of her brows.

I'm thankful for the way she gives me space, finding a seat on the concrete fire pit in front of me instead of shoving her way onto my lap, like she knows how to handle me in all the different ways that matter.

"I'm sorry," I finally whisper. "I just started panicking. I needed to get away for a minute."

She watches me before saying anything. "Can I help?"

I reach out, taking her hand and squeezing it like she's my lifeline. I guess she kind of is in this moment.

"Yeah. I'm exhausted. Will you just sit here with me for a minute?"

She nods, and I pull her onto my lap, wrapping my arms around her, a solid reminder that she's here with me, and no matter what, everything's going to be okay.

I lay my head back against the chair a little harder than necessary, but the bite of the wood against my scalp helps me return fully to the present moment. "Thank you," I whisper as Hannah clutches onto me like she's trying to reassure me with her presence. It surprises me by how well it works.

"I'm always here for you, Miles," she says, rubbing circles on my arm. "If it helps to talk it out, I'm here to listen."

My instinct is to tell her no, but my therapist's words ring in my ears. *It's okay to let people in, Miles. You don't have to fight everything on your own.*

"I think everything's finally catching up with me," I finally say, easing into it.

"Like what?"

"The bar, the wedding planning…us," as soon as I say it, I clutch onto Hannah's hand. "And please don't take that the wrong way. I can't get past feeling like I went about it all poorly. I was hellbent on telling your brother today, and I was looking forward to having that off my chest, and for us to finally have some normalcy, no matter what repercussions I had to face. So when it didn't happen, I think it sent me into a bit of a spiral."

"Do you want to go tell him now? We could force him to listen before he leaves."

I chuckle. "Thank you, but I'm not sure I have the energy to run up to the house right now."

"Then I'll go get him," she says, moving to get off my lap.

"I think I'll just stay right here and cuddle you until the

feeling goes away." I squeeze her in my grip until she's laughing. The sound helps me believe it'll all be okay, eventually.

"Hello?"

"Carolina, hey. It's Miles," I say into the phone later that afternoon when we're back in the hotel room.

"Hey, boss. How was the wedding?"

I look across the room at Hannah, who's packing and clearly pretending not to hear my conversation. "It went well. How are things back home?"

"They've been running smoothly since we talked last, but some people have been complaining they're bored. Do you have anything we could work on for you in the slow hours?"

Everything. I could use the help.

I could name ten things to get them started, but I refuse to assign them work that I don't even want to do myself. My uncle used to do that to me, and I despised him for it. "You could always deep clean the place."

She clicks her tongue, "Already did that. Isn't there some sort of inventory you usually do? We'd be happy to get that off your plate before you get back."

I glance across the room at Hannah as I contemplate how to answer her. She straightens, catching me looking, and smiles. What she's been drilling into my head for a while echoes in my mind.

Take a break.

"Actually, that would be great," I say. "Call me when you're at the bar and I'll tell you how you can find it. But back to the reason I called."

Chapter Thirty-Three

Hannah

I'm giddy, sitting in the passenger's seat of the Subaru Miles somehow found at a rental company near Durango. Well, giddy, but as Miles navigates yet another switchback, it's not the only feeling that comes to mind.

"I don't understand how a highway can be both terrifying and so fucking gorgeous at the same time," I tell him, white knuckling my seat as I stare out the window.

"Do you know why they call it the Million Dollar Highway?"

"I assume it's because of the million dollar views you get while driving it? Actually, I take that back. You get the million dollar view as a passenger. Ain't no way I'm looking around when I'm driving this death trap."

He snorts out a laugh through his nose. "That's one theory. Another is, *you'd have to pay me a million dollars to drive that road*," he says.

"Ah, I should've guessed that one because it's definitely me."

"And some say it's because of the hefty bill they were left with when they built it. I'd say all are true in their own way."

229

I gasp as we come around a curve, a flawless view of a mountain peak straight ahead. "Wow, that's beautiful." I've only said it twenty times so far on the drive and it makes us both laugh. "Yep, I guess you're right. It's definitely all three."

Telling my parents about this trip was nerve-wracking, although my mom already knew about us—and my dad had an inkling. Either way, I still felt like I was fifteen again, asking my parents if I could go on my first date.

I should have known they'd be excited, but I overthink things to the point that I settle on the worst-case scenario in my head and gaslight myself into believing it will happen. You could also blame my messed up dating history for thinking that good things don't happen to people like me, because they generally don't.

I turn in my seat to get a peek at Miles as he navigates the mountain road. A pair of black wayfarer sunglasses hide his eyes. The trimming he did to his beard for Holt's wedding has grown out a bit already, concealing his dimples when he smiles. But it's his half-revealed forearms that really have my attention.

The last time we had to slow down, he rubbed his hands on his pants and slid the cuffs of his light gray henley up his arm.

Hot.

"You have full control of the dash," he told me as soon as traffic was rolling again. "Can you make it a little cooler in here?"

I changed the dial further into the blue. "Is that better?"

He smiled but didn't dare turn his head. "Is my sweating at the thought of plunging over a road set in the middle of a mountain range making you second-guess your attraction to me?"

"Not in the slightest."

"Then I'm good," he'd said.

I've been sneaking glances at his forearms ever since.

"So, are you going to tell me where we're headed, or do I have to guess?" I ask, fully aware of the white-knuckle grip he has on the steering wheel.

He pauses, full attention on the curve he's navigating. "You could guess, but I'm still not telling you. Because I know you."

"What's that supposed to mean?"

"Little miss photographer will immediately look up where we're going because she wants to know what it looks like, and plan what pictures she can take. But this isn't a paid job. I want you to go in blind and enjoy yourself."

That message takes the express route straight to my heart. I sit there in the passenger's seat, contemplating what I could have done to deserve a guy like Miles.

When I don't answer, he glances my way. "That okay with you?"

I feel tears threatening, but blink them away. "Yes, Miles. It's perfect."

Chapter Thirty-Four

Miles

"Wow, this is beautiful." Hannah says as we're nearing Crested Butte, the place we'll be staying overnight. I'm getting far too much enjoyment out of watching her crane her neck in an attempt to take it all in. There's a lot to see, I'll say that.

"Could you imagine living here, and having this all within driving distance?" I ask, taking it in as much as I can from behind the wheel.

"I feel like you'd get desensitized by it before too long. I'd never want to lose that magic."

"Yeah, I guess you're right."

I didn't tell Hannah where we were going, besides how long of a drive it was when we left Durango. But she ended up guessing from the signs on the side of the road, and I finally told her.

With just over a four-hour drive, we covered so many things we haven't talked about in a while. She told me more about the wedding couples she'll be photographing the rest of the summer. We even shared memories long forgotten. It was a great way to decompress after the stress of driving the Million Dollar Highway with precious cargo in the vehicle alongside me. I hadn't been anticipating how intense that would be.

We stopped along the road for Hannah to take pictures in a few spots, as well as the tourist sign that reads *Switzerland of America*, where we posed like idiots. Then there's the waterfall you'd never guess streams right out from underneath the road. It's already been an incredible trip, and we haven't even gotten to our destination.

Thankfully, I was able to snag a reservation at a bed-and-breakfast in town that had a last-minute cancellation. Then, after our hike tomorrow, we'll likely start making our trek back home.

"I know you've made plans for us, but I swear I could just explore this cute little town and be content. It's so cool here."

I don't say it aloud, for fear of freaking her out, but I have a feeling this will be the type of trip we'll want to make again someday. "We can do whatever you want," I say, and mean it. I could spend our time in this town staring at the back of my eyelids and be happy as long as she's in my arms.

She reaches for my hand, something I've noticed her getting more comfortable doing. "No, I want to see where you have memories with your grandpa and make some new ones."

I squeeze her hand, my chest aching at the thought of him. He'd be smiling ear-to-ear if he knew I'd made the trip out here to see it all again—and give me endless shit about the girl I'd brought with me. I smile at the thought.

"What are you smiling about over there?"

I look at her, then back to the road. "Just thinking."

"About your grandpa?" She asks, her voice suddenly softer.

"And you," I say, going against my own rules about going too much into detail, but I've been finding it easier to do where Hannah is concerned.

"Yeah?"

"Yeah." I say, thumbs tapping the steering wheel as I wait

for the light to turn green. "He used to always go on and on about you and Holt. How I needed to keep you two close. Then, as I got older, I think he started to notice things I didn't even know myself. I could always tell you had a thing for me growing up, but I was oblivious to my own feelings until he knocked me over the head with the information."

"Really? When was this?"

I laugh at the memory. "Do you remember when Holt was still on his pre-Serena bender?" I ask, referencing the time where Holt had just gotten blindsided by his ex, who he caught cheating while we were in college. I'd help out at the bar when I was home, and this particular night he was drowning his feelings in hard liquor.

The thing about Holt is, you don't usually know he's drunk until the moment it takes effect. He appears sober for ages, then all of a sudden, he's done for. This particular night that had materialized in the form of Holt all but passing out on the bar top. Not knowing what else to do, I called Hannah, who was eighteen, and about to graduate from high school. I was so not in the right mindset to think of Hannah in any other capacity than being my best friend's sister.

She helped me shovel him into the backseat of my car—much like the night of his bachelor party. And we had such an easy rapport when we talked. I didn't really think anything of it, other than we'd known each other forever. But unbeknownst to either of us, my grandpa was taking his nightly break in a rickety old chair out back when I walked her to her car. I remember it all like it was yesterday, thanks to him pointing it out to me.

She'd laughed at whatever I'd said before I opened her car door. On the drive back, I'd listened to her drone on about whatever guy was taking her to the prom and how she thought he was a great guy. All I could think about was how I wanted to find a way to warn the guy he'd have me to answer to if even a lock of that gorgeous auburn hair was out of place when he brought her home.

Before she dipped into her driver's seat, she slammed into me with a hug that damn near stole my breath. It was the first time that the coconut scent of her hair stuck with me, and when I took notice of how well she fit in the circle of my arms. I grew up with barely an ounce of affection unless it came from my grandpa, and it was the moment I realized how good it felt to feel affection given away so freely.

I knew I'd cared about her before that moment, but something about that specific night had things clicking into place in a way they never had before.

I still remember walking toward the back door of the bar a little rattled about the storm of emotions brewing in my chest when Grandpa spoke up. "You're going to have to make a choice, you know."

The sudden appearance of his voice on what I thought had been a private moment had me jumping out of my skin. "Grandpa, I didn't see you there," I said, my heart rattling in my chest under my palm, where I placed it. "And what are you talking about?"

"You'll either go all your days trying to pretend you don't feel something for that girl, or you'll find the courage to have an honest conversation with that friend of yours and see it might be the best decision you've ever made."

"Grandpa, what are you going on about?"

"Hannah, of course. You telling me you can't see what's right in front of your face? You're half in love with the girl and completely blind to the fact."

"I'm not—"

"Ah, ah," he said, holding up a hand to stop my anxious babble. "Don't waste your breath. I've seen it before. Out my own eyes when I was young and too dumb to court your grandmother."

My ears perked at the mention of her. It took Grandpa a

lot to bring her up after the pain of losing her. He still kept her picture in his wallet decades after she was gone. I'd seen it a million times, weathered with age, and front and center every time he opened it.

But I lost him only a year later, and even thoughts of Hannah weren't enough to escape my grief back then.

Oh, what he'd do now if he saw us together. I think *told you so* would be the first words out of his mouth. I hate that I was both too much of a coward to make a move earlier, and that Grandpa didn't make it far enough to see how it all pans out.

"Of course I do. I had to change my shoes after Holt puked on his way into the house. Thank God Serena saved him from himself."

I chuckle at the memory. "Well, my grandpa was outside when you got in your car. He scared the daylights out of me when I was headed back inside, and well," I pause. "He kinda spelled it out right there in front of my face."

"Miles, that was ages ago."

I lift her hand that's still resting in mine up to my mouth, kissing the back of it. "I know. Stupid, now that I know better."

"Well, you weren't the only one. I'd crushed on you so long, I half-believed you were a figment of my imagination."

"And now?"

She squeezes my hand. "You feel pretty damn real to me."

Chapter Thirty-Five

Hannah

Somehow, amidst our reminiscing, we showed up at a quaint little house with a bed-and-breakfast sign out front.

"I'd usually camp out as close to our trailhead as possible, but it wasn't an option on such short notice. I hope you don't mind this?" Miles asks.

"A bed-and-breakfast over a piece of polyester between me and the wilderness out in Bear Country? Yeah, don't mind if I do."

Don't get me wrong, I love Colorado, but I've also visited enough times in my life to know the dangers that come along with the beauty. One bear sighting when I was ten was enough for me.

"Just so you know, when we come back out here again someday, we'll definitely be camping," Miles grumbles. "It's a non-negotiable."

"It seems you've underestimated my will to live."

"I'll strap you to my back and bring you along for the ride. It's proven easy enough this far."

"And I'll go kicking and screaming into that tent if you

make me. Pretty sure loud noises would attract those bears, so probably in your best interest not to try it."

"Actually," he says with such confidence, I know he's about to annihilate me with wilderness facts. "Loud noises are said to make bears aware of your presence. And since they'd like to steer clear of you as much as you want to steer clear of them, they'll usually mind their business. Any other myths you'd like debunked? I could do this all day."

I furrow my brows, trying to act mad, but it's hard when I've finally managed to get Miles to be this open and fun around me. "No, Chatty Kathy. I think that'll be all for today."

Then I toss open the passenger door and round the back of the vehicle for my bags.

When I'm back there, I realize I'm on Miles' time right now, and so does he. He waits a dreadfully long time before finally unlocking the back hatch and I retrieve my suitcase.

He appears behind me as I lug the brute out of the vehicle.

"Here, let me help," he says with open arms, but I'm feeling too stubborn to take his help.

"I've got it," I say, dropping it to the sidewalk with a thunk that sounds suspiciously like plastic cracking.

I find out why when I try to roll it behind me. The whole suitcase is leaning to the left, the sad, broken wheel still covered in dirt several inches away.

"Shit," I say under my breath.

Miles pretends not to notice my side show, but he can't quite seem to hide the twitch that happens at the corner of his mouth.

With his own suitcase hanging at his side, he takes it from me and presses down until the telescopic handle is put away and carries it on his other side.

I stare after him, shaking my head, but after watching him

take a few steps, I grab the broken wheel from the ground and run to catch up with him.

"Good afternoon, welcome to Precipice Bed-and-Breakfast. How can I help you?" A graying lady asks from behind the counter once we're in the door.

Miles steps forward, turning on the same persona I see in him while he's at the bar. He may be a quiet guy, socially. But he knows how to be charming and outgoing when it's needed. "Hi, yes, we have a reservation under Miles O'Harrow that was made yesterday."

"Ah, Miles. Yes, I see you right here," she says, pointing down at the clunky appointment booklet on the desk. This place is so old school and I love it.

She types a few things into the computer and trades a few things with Miles before she grabs a key from the hook behind her marked *Summit Sunset*.

"If you two are ready, I'll show you the way."

We follow her up the stairs and down a long hallway with three doors. She leads us to the lone one on the left side. "This is the only room in the place with a summit view," she says, unlocking it and stepping inside. "You'll understand why we called it the Summit Sunset room once you see it." She proceeds to lead us to the window, tossing open the sheer curtains to reveal the view of the expansive backyard that rolls into hills, then finally, behind that, a mountain. "That right there is Crested Butte, the mountain the town is named for. I'm sure you can understand why this is my favorite room in the whole place. Not only for the views out the window, but the room itself."

I turn to look back at everything I'd passed on my way to the window. A king-sized bed with a plush sunset orange comforter flanked by two bedside tables that are the same off-white as the bedframe. A majority of the room is painted white except for the wall behind the bed, which is a deep orange. There are accents all around the room that range in each color a sunset transitions to in the sky.

"As I'm sure you could guess from its name, this room was inspired by the sunsets that can be viewed from it. They're different every night, of course, but the palette is from my favorites."

"It's gorgeous," I say, mesmerized by the artwork on the wall, showing what I assume to be the sunsets she's talking about.

"Then we go in here," she says, leading us to a door across the room.

It's a surprisingly modern bathroom that is ninety-nine percent tiles, and one percent mirror. It's bright, well-lit, and adorned with a jacuzzi off to one side. My mouth goes dry, imagining Miles reclined in it, his chest glistening with water.

I look over to find him staring in the direction of it, too. I wish I knew what he was thinking.

Our host claps, making me jump to attention. "Well, that's about the end of the tour. I'll let you two get settled. Feel free to come find me if you're interested in a tour of the rest of the house, or have questions on places to go while you enjoy your visit."

"Thank you so much," Miles says, closing the door behind her. When we can hear her retreating footsteps disappear down the stairs, he meets me halfway. "We're finally alone," he says.

"We've been alone for like four hours, Miles."

He leans his forehead against mine, wrapping his arms around me. "I know, but this feels different."

I look around the room and feel it, too. "You're right. What are we going to do with all this privacy?"

His thumb tips my chin up until our gazes meet. "Well, I was hoping," his mouth inches closer to my own until I can feel his words brush against my lips, "we could start with something like this."

His kiss is soft and unhurried, like we've got forever to explore each other. And even though we have matters needing addressed looming in the near future, I give myself over to the moment and forget my problems completely.

"I saw a small grocery store on our way in that should be within walking distance. Want to go explore the town with me and pick some things we'll need for the morning?"

I hop up off the bed, excited to stretch my legs after a long day in the car. "Yes, please!"

We're greeted by the same woman who showed us our room on the way out the door, and she helps point us in the right direction for what Miles is looking for.

Even after spending a handful of days in the mountains, the view everywhere I look takes my breath away. Add having Miles' hand in mine as we walk, and it's a miracle I'm breathing at all.

This small mountain town is definitely pedestrian friendly with large sidewalks lined with old colorful buildings and crosswalks everywhere. Miles leads the way back to the grocery store he saw on our way in and find that I love doing mundane things, like strolling through aisles in stores in new places with him.

"You want anything?" Miles asks after I've been eyeing the candy aisle for a moment.

I look up and see he's been watching me and laugh, trying to hide my pink cheeks.

He grabs an overpriced bag of LifeSavers Wild Berries flavored gummies and tosses them in the cart.

"My reputation precedes me," I say, lacing my fingers between his as we continue through the store.

When we're finished, Miles tosses everything inside the

backpack he was smart enough to bring with him so we have a hands-free trip back through town.

"It smells good," I say as we're walking down the main area of town. "What is that?"

"Looks like pizza," he says, halting us outside the door. "Want pizza for dinner tonight?"

I nod so fast, Miles chuckles as we walk through the door. Ten minutes later, we're carrying a pizza back to our bed-and-breakfast.

When we return to the Summit Sunset room, there's limited seating, so Miles set a towel in the middle of the bed, placing the greasy pizza box on top of it and flipping open the lid.

He pulls the big curtains on the big window with a view open wide so we can watch the sky turn colors outside while we eat. We're both sitting cross-legged on either side of the pizza box, taking turns leaning over it so we don't spill any toppings on the comforter.

It's nothing fancy whatsoever, but the intimate setting makes it feel like a gourmet meal.

After the pizza box is shoved haphazardly into the room's mini fridge, we settle on the bed to watch the finale of the sunset. We're both lying on our stomachs when I notice Miles keeps turning his head this way and that, rubbing at his shoulders.

"You okay?" I ask.

"Yeah, I'm fine. My shoulders and neck are just sore. Probably from driving with my shoulders at my ears down the Million Dollar Highway."

"Can I help?" I say, raising to my knees.

"Would you mind?"

Would I mind getting my hands on this fine man?

Ha! Hell no, I wouldn't mind. "Not at all," I say, moving to straddle his hips for the perfect angle.

"Right here?" I ask, squeezing his shoulders lightly.

He groans at the contact, and that's the exact moment I realize just how sensual an experience this will be. "Hannah, that feels amazing," he says, as I continue kneading his shoulders and biceps.

Christ, a deep, aching need pools low in my belly as he continues reacting to each touch.

"You know, I could probably do a better job if you took your shirt off." It's a true statement, but I say it just to tease him. He's been so buttoned up when it comes to our interactions recently.

"Lift up," he says, raising his body underneath me and fisting his shirt at the back of his neck and pulls. In a flash, his bare back is exposed to me.

I'm in a trance when he settles back into the mattress. "You still back there?" he asks when I don't immediately move.

"Yes, sorry," I say, my hands hovering over the freckles on the tops of his shoulders, then I move, pressing my hands tentatively into his skin. He groans again, and I catch myself breathing hard and snap my mouth shut.

Once I get back into a rhythm, his sounds seem to get more and more sensual. I think he's trying to kill me here.

I *tap, tap* his shoulder with finality. And lift on my knees in preparation for moving off his hips and far, far away. But before I can, he flips to his back underneath the V of my legs, settling his hands on my hips to place me back on top of him.

I can feel the hard length of him, perfectly lined up with my center.

"Oh, god," I say when he grinds his hips against me.

"Do you see what you do to me?" he asks, showing me his proof once more in case I missed it the first time.

"And what do you plan on doing about it?" I ask.

The crinkle in his brow is prominent as his dark, half-lidded eyes take me in.

Then on a sigh, he palms the back of my head, pulling me

in for a kiss. His hands explore me everywhere as we make out on the bed.

His tongue tangles with mine, and I moan because it just feels so damn good.

"Maybe the jacuzzi would be good for your sore muscles," I say, and the next thing I know, he's on his feet, crossing the room and carrying me like it's nothing.

He turns on the tub's faucet, checking the water temperature a few times with his hand until he's satisfied. Then his mouth returns, this time trailing kisses down my neck and across my chest. The sound of the water drowns out our heavy breathing, but when Miles leans in to nibble on my earlobe, there's no way he misses the whimper that escapes me.

"Damn, Hannah. You taste so good," he says, his mouth on my neck.

I wish I could read his thoughts, because in the next moment, he's hauling me into his arms again, and stepping into the jacuzzi, with both of us fully clothed.

I squeal as we drop into the water. And Miles' smile is wide and brilliant, standing out against his sun kissed face.

I stare at it in awe until his expression changes, and re-situates in the tub until I can feel him underneath me like I did out on the bed. I reach behind his head to shut the water off, because if we let it go much further, we'll overflow.

"Fuck," he says, fighting against his inner turmoil as he removes my tank top, letting it drop to the tile floor with a wet *thwack*. My sports bra is soaked, but he uses that fact to his advantage, scraping his teeth against it until my nipple is raised through the thick material.

His gaze snaps to mine as his tongue reaches out to flick against it. But the restraint he's displaying by keeping me covered doesn't last long. With a thumb under the band, he pulls off my bra in one swift motion. Then he's lapping his tongue against the raised pink bud before his hand falls under the water, sneaking up my shorts to work my bundle of nerves.

I'm bucking against his hand in no time, the movement causing friction for both of us with his hand wedged between us. His hips begin to move and he groans when I lift to standing, taking away the pressure he'd been enjoying.

I hold his shoulder with one hand, stepping out of my shorts and letting them fall outside the tub with the rest of my discarded layers.

"You're so fucking beautiful," Miles says, pulling me back down on top of him, the friction there elevated without the extra layer between us.

Soon, we're both panting against each other's skin, and I can feel my orgasm on the horizon. "This feels so good, Miles."

"Fuck," he says, lifting to his feet suddenly, still holding me against him.

The water pours down our bodies in one wild rush.

"Wait, what are you doing?" I ask with desperation. If he ruins this impending orgasm by trying to be a gentleman again, I just might scream.

"I'm taking you to the bed, because I need inside you. Now."

"But I thought you said—"

"I know what I said, Hannah," he says, stepping out onto the oversized bath rug. Then continues through the room, his wet footsteps leaving a trail behind us. "But unless you don't want this, I'm done thinking for the foreseeable future," he says, lowering me to the mattress. "So, what's it going to be?"

In lieu of an answer, I sneak my fingertips under his waistband and pull.

Chapter Thirty-Six

I'm frenzied trying to remove Hannah's clothing until she's completely bared to me. Somewhere in the back of my mind, my conscience is screaming for me to stop and think rationally about what I'm doing. But I have thought about it, more times that I can count.

This is inevitable, and we have the room to ourselves. We're miles from anyone who can stand between us. If Hannah wants this too, who am I to deny her?

I find the just-in-case condoms I'd stashed in my bag for this trip. I told myself I'd hold myself back, that I wouldn't use them. That I could handle waiting until we were back home, and the dust had settled to take this relationship with Hannah to the next step. But recent events prove I'd been lying to myself the whole damn time.

Hannah's hair is plastered to the sides of her face from the humidity of the tub. I brush it away, admiring the truth I can see in her eyes as she leans into my touch. She wants this too.

I swipe my thumb against her bottom lip and she pulls it into her mouth. I pull back with a groan. I'm already close to diving head first over the edge, so there's no way I could handle her sucking on my thumb.

I rip open the small square, watching Hannah watch me roll the condom on. That hungry look on its own could end it all right here.

I pull her hips toward the edge of the bed, leaning down to kiss her mouth as I slide one finger against her center to test how ready she is for me. She's swollen with need and more than ready. But I still take my time, watching the way she reacts to my touch.

Her eyes watch my every move, though they're half-lidded with lust. "I want you, Miles," she whines, her words springing me into action.

I position myself at her entrance, each of us gasping when I slide home. She feels tight around me, but she's slick enough that I'm able to move with ease.

My hand finds her breast, tweaking her nipple because I've noticed how much she likes it when I do. I pinch it a little harder than I had before, and she moans against the flood of sensation.

I drive my hips into her, already feeling the first sign of my orgasms ready to detonate.

I focus on what Hannah needs, trying and failing to forget how good it feels to be inside her for the first time.

"I'm so close," she says, moving her hips in unison with mine, meeting me in the middle.

Just as her innermost muscles begin contracting, I drive into her deeper until her moans become less controlled.

I continue pumping my hips through my own release as she writhes underneath me in satisfaction.

And when we've rung out everything we can, I drop onto her chest, absolutely spent.

"Rise and shine, honey," I whisper, brushing Hannah's auburn hair out of her face.

She was attached to my side like a barnacle when my alarm went off ten minutes ago. Between the still-darkness of the ungodly early morning, and the warmth of her body pressed against mine, I would have been happy to spend the rest of the day right here in this bed with her. Especially after last night.

But I've been looking forward to revisiting the place I haven't seen in almost twenty years, and I know Hannah will love it too. That thought got me on my feet and into the bathroom. I decided it was safe to let Hannah get the extra minutes of shut-eye, but now she needs to get up or our entire schedule will be off-kilter. And I want to give her the best possible experience.

"How am I supposed to shine before the sun comes up?"

"You shine no matter what time of day."

That gets her to pop one eye open. "Stop being sweet. It makes me feel bad for being grumpy."

I chuckle, leaning down to press a kiss to her forehead. When I lift to stand, she catches my hand and pulls me on top of her. Hannah's hands slide up my back until they're at the back of my head, pulling me closer. Her mouth lands on mine and she kicks her leg free of the sheets to wrap it around my hips. I give into her, letting her take what she wants. It's all hers, as far as I'm concerned.

When her hips buck underneath me, my thoughts flood back into my consciousness. "If you keep up with this, we aren't going to make our hike today."

"That's fine," she says on an exhale against my mouth.

I finally pull away, putting some space between us. "No, we really should go. It will be worth it, I promise."

Her hands fist in my shirt as she groans. "Fine," she says, drawing out the word as I pull on her hands to lift her into a sitting position. She's a wet noodle as I lift her, but malleable enough to wrap her legs around my waist as I carry her to the bathroom. My gaze snags on the bathtub, memories from last night rushing back.

She shrieks like Winifred in Hocus Pocus when I turn on the light. I chuckle, depositing her onto the counter, where she finally decides to peek up at me. She looks so damn adorable. I land a peck on her lips, but don't linger, because we're seriously short on time.

While Hannah gets ready in the bathroom, I put our pack together—one good thing about using my small backpack as my carry-on for our flight out here. I'm already half prepared.

We picked up snacks for the hike on the drive yesterday, and I already filled a few large water bottles and stashed them away.

"Need some help?" Hannah asks, coming up beside me in a maroon long sleeve shirt and navy blue leggings, looking far more awake than she did ten minutes ago.

I've already rolled up our extra layers for us in my bag, leaving our coats out for the cool morning as we travel to the trailhead.

"Do you think you'll have any room for these in your camera bag?" I ask, handing her the small packages of trail mix and granola bars that we grabbed last night.

She crosses the room, lifting her bag from its place by the bed, unzipping it on her way back to me. "Yeah, I've got plenty of room if you need me to carry more, too."

"That's all," I say because I refuse to make her carry as much as me. "Will you be ready to get out of here soon?"

"Yeah, just let me grab my things and we'll go."

It's odd, being up here after so long. Especially when things start looking familiar. We left town early enough, the sky is just barely taking on that hazy blue-gray glow of morning. Not the best way to navigate the last stretch of the dirt road that leads to our trailhead, but it will have to do.

"I can't wait to see this view in the light of day on our way back down," Hannah says, looking out the passenger's side window as lights have started turning on out in the distance, a sign that some people actually start their day this early. There hasn't been too much traffic on our way, but there were a few cars where the pavement turned to dirt.

"Wait until the sunrise casts some light on what we're about to see. You charged your camera batteries, right?"

"Sure did."

"Good, because I have a feeling this place is going to give you plenty of inspiration."

Her hand finds my thigh. "Thanks for this, Miles." I glance at her for a quick smile. "For the invitation, and for thinking of me when you made the plans. You sure know how to make a girl feel special."

I snag her hand from her lap and kiss the back of it, the action articulating my feelings for her better than my words could right now. "You're special to me."

She squeezes my hand as we ride the last expanse of road in comfortable silence.

Once we're parked, I bend to look out at the sky through the windshield. "I think we got here at the perfect time for the sun to rise."

The sky is still a deep blue, a pale yellow-orange glow has appeared at the horizon in the past couple minutes.

"Okayletsgo!" Hannah says the three words as if they're one and is out of the car an instant later, her bag slung over one shoulder.

I laugh, tossing open my own door, removing the keys from the ignition and attaching them to a carabiner hanging on the inside of my bag. When we meet in the front of the car,

Hannah's making that teasing face she probably never realizes she wears while she makes a joke, and makes exaggerated movements of her limbs as she stretches.

"Come on, join me," she says.

I shake my head at her, hiding my smile as I dig into the front compartment of my bag. When I find what I'm looking for, I pull it over my head and switch it on.

Hannah's boisterous laugh as she points at my headlamp is all I need to know getting her to wear one will be difficult.

"Okay, this might be my favorite Miles look yet," she says, the words oozing sarcasm.

Little does she know I'm wearing one of these each time I go camping. Once you get past feeling like a dumbass, they're extremely handy. A light strapped to your head beats holding a regular flashlight any day.

"Don't knock it until you try it. I promise you'll want it at least until the sun is up."

She sighs, holding out a hand and I hang the black band from her fingers, getting deep satisfaction out of the disappointment on her face as she puts it over her head.

Just as I thought it would be, the strap is a bit too loose. "May I?" I ask, stepping closer, my hands suspended in the air between us.

She nods and the whole thing wobbles, making us both laugh. I tighten the strap enough for it to stay in place, then we fasten our bags to our backs and get on our way.

The trees are tall, dark shadows in the distance as we approach the head of the trail. For the most part, the hiking trail sprawls in front of us like two tire marks cut through what is otherwise a lush and beautiful prairie of tall grass and wildflowers. I can't wait until the sun rises, unveiling the beauty of the place. I can't wait to see Hannah's reaction when she can finally see it.

I look up to the sky, which seems to be gaining color

behind a few of the mountains that stand before us in the distance.

"Okay, I can hardly see the view, but I'm already loving it. I can tell my camera's about to get a workout."

I smile, knowing she's right.

Chapter Thirty-Seven

Hannah

My camera has been poised in front of my face since the sun started coming up this morning. This hike is even more beautiful than I imagined it in my head. I'm glad Miles didn't give me any details beforehand, because he's right. I would have spent the entire drive yesterday scouring every photo of it I could find on the internet. I would have walked in here with a game plan.

This way, I'm surprised by every little twist and turn I encounter. Instead of having a list of photos I wanted, I'm forced to do what I loved to do all those years ago with my first camera—inspect the surrounding space with a careful eye, and find the tiniest details I think deserve to be frozen in time to refer to for years to come.

I've even found myself getting out of my step-by-step processes I use in my everyday shoots, flipping my dial to completely different settings than I usually gravitate to. I'm out here in the wild, breaking every rule I've ever made for myself and my camera. It's a glorious feeling.

After getting up close and personal with a patch of maroon bells to my left, I turn back toward the direction we're walking. There's something about the light, the scenery, and the broad-shouldered man I'm following through this dreamland that's too perfect not to capture. I snap a few photos, and Miles must have some sort of sixth sense that tells him my lens is pointed in his direction because he turns around.

At first, his expression is inquisitive, but it transforms to amusement and quickly into bashfulness, and I get every single emotion on camera.

I pull back from the viewfinder and click a button to see the photos I took as Miles starts to walk away.

"Hey wait," I say.

He turns back with his hand in front of his face. "No more photos of me. I don't want to be held accountable when your lens cracks."

"Not even if it's a picture with me?" I ask, already connecting my tripod to my camera.

He steps closer until his face is hovering just above mine. "I'm finding that the list of things I won't do for you is quite short these days," he says, his gaze looking deep down into my soul. His beard brushes my cheek as he pulls me into his chest. I enjoy the momentary shelter of his warmth away from the relentless breeze, but it doesn't last long enough. Not that I'm complaining, because he bends to kiss me. Between the sunshine warming my cheeks, his hands around my waist grounding me, and the sweet scent of wildflowers dancing through the air, it feels like I'm lost in a movie.

I hope I'm never found.

"How about that picture?" He asks when we separate.

"Right," I say, trying to make something of my scrambled brain. I turn around, hitting a couple buttons to set up my tiny handheld shutter button that Bluetooths to my camera.

"What's that?" Miles asks, looking at the little pill-shaped thing with a large button on it.

"Look," I say, pointing at the camera.

When he does, I hit the button. We're close enough to the setup that you can hear the shutter.

"Really?"

I smile at his childlike wonder. "Yeah. You didn't think I'd made it this far without all the fun little gadgets, did you?"

"So that's how you take all those sexy little headshots you sprinkle all over your social media, then," he says, leaning in to hold me.

I spring back when his words register. "I thought you didn't use social media, Miles?"

His laugh is guttural. "Yeah, well, I learned the basics when I saw the photos you were sharing."

I feel my cheeks heat under his gaze. "You're kidding," I say, a little embarrassed despite being proud of those photos.

It was a little challenge I gave myself in the downtime between Christmas shoots and spring blooms—to find new ways to take self portraits. I really enjoyed the project. My backdrops changed almost each time. Some on my bedroom fluffy white rug. One in front of a sheet. The olive green wall in our living room. Out in the snow. It was that first little spark that lit a fire for more inside of me.

"Alright, hop up," Miles says, looking at me over his shoulder as he's crouched in front of me.

"There are people watching us."

"Guess we better give them something to look at. Come on."

He holds out his hand and I take it. I jump and he bounces me up on his hips. I accidentally hit the button for my shutter. He twirls us around until my hair is blowing in front of my face and we're both laughing. I've lost count of how many photos I've accidentally taken. Hopefully, one or two turn out. He finally slows down enough for us to get some good ones, then I'm sliding down his backside to the ground. He pulls me into his arms and we take a few more. Then he dips to kiss me and I forget anything exists but the two of us.

We start our drive toward home after finishing our hike. I'm disgusting and sweaty, but exhilarated from the fresh mountain air. The quality time with Miles both yesterday and today, and using my camera for fun, rather than necessity, has added to this high I'm riding on the trip home.

Although I wouldn't mind a shower, I know Miles is running out of vacation time. I'm just proud he took this time out for himself. Especially after his panic attack the other day. I think today was good for both of us.

Listening to him retell all the things he learned about this place the last time he was here with his grandpa was so sweet. When we made it to the end of the hike, there was a waterfall. We found a large rock to sit for a while we ate granola bars. I laid back against his chest, content feeling it rumble against my back as he told me as much as he could remember.

The only person close to me I've lost was my grandpa, so I can't imagine what it feels like for Miles to have lost the people he has. Then there's his little brother he lost in childhood. I've seen the repercussions of that loss throughout his life. I think it's why he bonded with Holt the way he did at such a young age, and probably why he feels like us being together in secret is such a betrayal. He doesn't talk about his little brother, but I've learned enough to know he blames himself for what happened. He's always been protective of Holt—and of Val and me since we were kids. Not a day goes by that I take his quiet love for granted.

That's what it is, too. I think to myself as I watch him drive us down the interstate. When that word crosses my mind, it surprises me how right it feels. There's no shock to my system, more like a puzzle piece clicking into place.

I've always loved him, and as much as I'd like to say those feelings were romantic, they weren't. I had a crush on him, sure. But I loved him somewhere between familiar and affectionate love—like that of a friend or family member. And now I can feel it morphing into something different, entirely.

The thing about your love for someone changing like that is it doesn't take a lot for it to make the switch. And after the night we shared in a quaint little bed-and-breakfast, I'm afraid I'll never be able to part from the idea of us.

I think there's been a part of Miles that has always loved me a little bit. But that love was a lot different than what I feel now. It's not just protection, but affection and safety. And I know this throbbing I've felt in my chest is about as close as I'll ever get to feeling what love feels like.

It's something I've searched high and low for since I was in high school, believing the first boy who gave me a lick of attention was the one. I didn't know anything back then.

This mutual longing was a stoking of a fire not long ago when Miles all but admitted his feelings in the parking lot of a home decor store. That ignited a spark in both of us, and now I feel like the heat radiating between us could burn down an entire countryside, especially after last night.

"Thanks for bringing me on your little getaway," I say, breaking the comfortable silence we've been keeping for miles while we listen to a playlist of soft alternative rock that Miles has put me onto the past few days.

"It wouldn't have been a true getaway without you along," he glances at me between lane changes.

"Oh yeah? What would it have been exactly?"

He shrugs. "Just a trip, I guess."

A guitar strums in the speakers of the Subaru, then Miles adds, "I don't use my words enough to know exactly how to articulate this, but having you along with me the past couple days meant more to me than you'll ever know." He stares at the road, refusing to make eye contact as he says the most beautiful words I've ever had directed at me. "No matter what lies in front of us, I'm going to treasure that experience for the rest of my life. I hope you know that."

I can't speak, for fear of the tears in my eyes falling, but it's no use. Miles notices when he finally turns to me.

He reaches out, cupping my face while he keeps his eyes on the road as he swipes one away with his thumb. "I didn't mean to make you cry, honey."

"It's okay, they're good tears."

I lose track of our time on the road once he takes my hand. All I know is I don't want this to end, and like Miles said, I'll treasure this time forever.

Chapter Thirty-Eight

MILES

I've only been at the bar for twenty minutes, and I'm already dreaming of Hannah, a hotel room, and not much else. I can't get her off my mind, it's true. But it's clear this place wasn't ready for me to leave it for any period of time, and I know I'm partly to blame.

Carolina did a great job on late notice. And I'm quickly realizing I need to be more trusting and delegate more so they aren't completely clueless when I can't be here. It's just hard, letting go. I worked really hard to get here, and I refuse to put my entire life savings into hands I can't trust. I won't let this bar turn into something resembling what it was when my uncle owned it ever again.

"Hey, boss man," I hear from behind me and turn to find Carolina. "Hope you had a great getaway with your girl."

My brow furrows. "Who told you that?"

"Edie, of course."

How the hell did she know?

"And between me and you—and maybe Edie—it's about damn time."

"You and Edith really need to mind your own damn business if you want to keep your jobs."

She laughs a big, boisterous thing. "As if. This place wouldn't survive without us, especially if you make leaving more of a habit."

I nod. "You're right. Thanks for the hard work you've put in lately. It hasn't gone unnoticed. Speaking of, are you still in a place where you could handle more hours?"

If her wide-eyed expression is any indication, she's taken aback. The only thing is I'm not sure if it's because I thanked her—something I know my uncle wasn't great at or my actual question. Maybe it's both.

"Seriously?"

"Yes. Recent events have made me realize I need to let go of the reins a bit. You take a couple days to think it over, and if it seems like a good fit, we'll talk it over. Sound good?"

She sighs, breaking into a smile. "It sounds great, Miles. Thank you."

"No, thank you."

And because I can't handle the way she's looking at me all excited, I retreat to my office to find something I can do there instead.

My inbox tray in my office is halfway full of unpaid invoices and the inventory report I requested to be finished while I was gone. I look it over and am pleasantly surprised to find it filled out correctly.

I almost didn't ask Carolina to divvy it up amongst the staff, because I feel a responsibility to do it myself. In fact, I feel a responsibility to do a lot of things around here on my own because of the stack of responsibilities Uncle Stu had given me when he was in charge.

"Here, you do my bitch work. I don't want to do it anyway," he'd say.

That memory has always held me back from asking it of anyone else. But there's been a negative connotation between those odd jobs and how much time I spend in my office after hours.

I'm coming to find out that one of the best things a boss can give their employees is trust. Trust they'll do the job they've been given, and trust that things will get done without always having a hand in it.

My phone vibrates from my desk. It's Hannah replying to me asking what she's up to later.

HANNAH

Val and I are heading over to Ella and Lainey's for girl's night. You?

I imagine she'll spill all there is to know about us to her girlfriends tonight. It feels good to be a big enough piece of her life to be the subject of these conversations. But that familiar wave of guilt crashes against me like it always does when I think about the fact that I haven't done the same with my best friend.

MILES

It's looking like I'll be spending most of it in my office again tonight.

And before I can overthink whether it's a good idea, I type out a second message.

MILES

I miss you, though.

I watch the bubbles bounce as she types a reply, my heart in my throat as they disappear. My heartbeat thrums in my ears when they start again, and a new message appears.

HANNAH

I'd give anything to go back to our time in Colorado right now.

HANNAH

I miss you, too.

Instead of replying, I hit the button to call her. She answers on the first ring.

"Hey. Did you mean to call me, or is this one of your infamous butt dials?"

I laugh because I've been known to be all thumbs with all things technology. It is what it is. "No, this time it was on purpose."

"Can you hear that?"

I don't hear anything out of the ordinary in the background. "No, what is it?"

"I'm smiling so hard, I figured it would transfer through somehow. I'm glad it wasn't a butt dial, Miles."

"I'm glad you're glad."

"So what's up?"

"Well, you miss me. I miss you. There's a good chance we won't get to see much of each other this week. What do you say we go out on Friday night? I know you're busy most of the week, and so am I. I know scheduling each other in isn't the sexiest thing—"

"Absolutely, yes."

"Yeah?" I ask, little ridiculous bubbles popping in my stomach.

"Yes."

I smile at how quickly her answer came. "Perfect. I have some ideas, but let me know if there's anything in particular you'd like to do."

"I actually like the idea of you planning it. I'll leave it up to you."

"Okay, I know you're going to love it."

"If it's with you, I already know that's a given."

I tap the end of my pen on the table. "Listen, I should

probably get back to work, but if I'm not stuck here too long tonight, would you mind if I called you before we fall asleep?"

"I'd really like that. And Miles?"

"Yeah?"

"Just because you're back doesn't mean you have to kill yourself to catch up at the bar. You know that, right?"

I scratch my beard, eyes darting to the pile of papers again. "I know, but it would be nice to knock it all out and get back to normal again faster."

"That's the thing, though. There will always be things you can do if you're willing to devote your life to long days. But you can ask for help, too. More people working toward the same goal still gets the job done, and in less time."

She has a point. "You're right. And you'll be glad to know, I just had a conversation with one of my bartenders about the possibility of more hours. She sounded interested."

"Oh, Miles. I'm so proud of you. Good job."

"It could still fall through, but the possibility of help feels really good."

"Good, keep it going. I've had to have this same conversation with Val. She tends to bury herself in her work and burrow in there all comfortable. I keep her in check, and I'm going to do the same for you."

"Thanks, honey. I like having you in my life, you know that?"

"Ditto, Miles. Have a good day. I'm looking forward to hearing your voice and making sure you don't fall asleep at your desk. I hope you know that."

"Ruin my plans, I beg of you."

She laughs and we both say our goodbyes.

I'm not proud of how long I sit there smiling down at my phone—and the photo I set as my background of Hannah smiling in the middle of a wildflower field.

Chapter Thirty-Nine

Hannah

"Alright, Hannah. Time to spill! Val already told us about your little detour you took with Miles," Lainey says when we've found our lounging positions later that night in Ella and Lainey's living room.

I have a mocktail in my hand because I'm driving Val and me home. It's so flavorful that if I didn't know the truth, I'd think it had alcohol in it.

"Yeah, and how did your brother take the news?" Ella asks. "Was there drama?"

I grimace at that. "He still doesn't know." I watch as both sisters' faces fall. "They were in a huge rush to leave for their flight. And my mom, of all people, interrupted Miles and Holt as Miles was working up the courage to bring it up." I refuse to tell anyone about Miles' panic attack, because that's his story to tell, not mine. "I know Miles feels pretty shitty about it, because Holt is his best friend. I can't imagine something as drastic as them never speaking again, but I can see my brother having a very dramatic reaction to it, as he does with everything."

"Or you never know, maybe he can already see how

perfect you two would be together, and he'll be totally okay with it."

I panic laugh at that. "Right, one can hope." And as I sit there retelling the highlights of my detour with Miles, I realize just how badly I need everything to be okay when this gets out, because I know I can already feel myself falling for him. And I don't want to go back to that place in the past where I stayed away from him out of spite.

Later, we're in the back of the house where Ella and Lainey have turned an entire room into their own little library.

"So wait, this doesn't consist of your own personal library at all?"

Ella doesn't smile much, but she is as she nods at Val's question. "Yep. What was it, a few years ago?" She looks at her sister, who nods. "I started collecting books I knew people wanted. First editions, special edition covers, popular series sets and stuff like that."

She straightens a book on the shelf. I haven't known Ella long, but I know her well enough by now to she doesn't enjoy attention. All the signs are there as she talks. The inability to make eye contact, drawing attention away from herself. With her tattoos, immaculate makeup, and badass attitude, I wish she could see how cool I think she is.

She stands up for anyone who needs it, and she has this hilarious deadpan personality that I absolutely adore. The night I met her over a year ago, I was intimidated by the way she seemed so comfortable in her own shoes—black high-top Converse that night, to be specific.

"She started selling them on this book-selling site, but switched over to her own website when she started generating a following. It got so big that she had people asking for certain books. I was in college at the time, and even I was trying to help her find what she was looking for."

Ella laughs. "I kind of pulled Lainey into it against her will."

"So what's the endgame for you?" I ask, curious to hear about another female building her business from the ground up. Hell, I could probably sit here all night and talk to her about it.

She grins at Lainey, "My dream is to own a bookstore with Lainey. I'd be in charge of the books, and she's the one with a business degree, so she'd essentially run the place. I even have a dream spot in mind." She laughs nervously, as if catching herself getting a little too passionate about her dreams, although there's no such thing. "Sorry I get a little carried away when I get asked that question sometimes."

"Don't apologize to me," I say. "I could talk about this all freaking day."

"She really could," Val cuts in. "I can't tell you the amount of times I've been out with her somewhere and she talks relentlessly with another female business owner. I'm talking boutique owners, coffee shops, restaurants. So many places."

I just shrug because we both know it's a part of me. "I love learning from people, and I love teaching them things that I've learned along the way, too."

"Okay, we might have to schedule a time to chat about business then, because I've always wanted to find people that understand."

"Oh my gosh, I'm so excited to know about this!"

When I pull into the driveway after we get back from Freeport, I put the car in park, but don't get out. Val collects her things, and reaches for the door, but when she realizes I haven't moved, she turns back to me.

"Are we going into the house?"

"You know what? I think I'm going to go."

"Where?"

"To see Miles. He was going to call me before bed, but I miss him, and I think I'm going to surprise him at his door instead."

She smiles. "I think you should."

I bite my lip, but my smile shows through, anyway. "Okay, don't wait up for me. I'm not sure when I'll be home."

"I say stay out all night," she says.

"If I do, you'll know things went well."

Val leans over the center console to wrap me in her arms. "I'm so proud of you for putting yourself out there and taking what you want, Han. Have fun tonight."

"Thanks," I say, saving that morsel for later so I don't get emotional.

She gets out of the car and I wait until she disappears into the house before backing out and heading the couple blocks to Miles' alley.

I send him a text that I'm ready whenever he is, and by the time I reach the top of his stairs, he's calling.

I answer quietly, "Hello?"

His voice is deep when he says, "Hey, Han. How was girls' night?"

"Good, I had a fun time," then I cover the microphone and hold my phone as far away from me as possible as I knock on the door.

"Shit," he says. "Someone's at my door."

"You should probably answer it."

"Nah, if I ignore it long enough, they should go away."

I knock louder, this time not trying to mask the sound from the phone. "I think you should definitely go to the door."

"Wait," he says, and I can hear shuffling on his end, then the sounds I'm hearing start echoing on the other side of the door, and I know he's on his way to me.

A lock unlatches, then the door swings wide open.

He's still got his phone to his ear, and so do I.

"Hi," I say, finally lowering it and ending the call.

He doesn't say a word, dumbfounded at the luck of finding me at his door. "Hannah," he sighs, against my hair as he brings me into his arms and pulls me in past the threshold.

He pulls the door shut, locking it behind us. Then he kisses me, hauling me up until my legs wrap around his hips instinctively. "I can't believe you're here," he says, the disbelief in his eyes making his words ring true. "This is the best surprise. Will you stay?"

My heart is mush inside my chest with the way he's looking at me right now. Like he can't believe someone would do this for him. And all I had to do was drive two blocks.

"Of course I will," I say, pulling his mouth back to mine.

Chapter Forty

Miles

"Thanks for coming in on such short notice," I tell my staff the next afternoon at the last-minute meeting I threw together this morning.

It's a miracle I was even able to focus after Hannah spent the night. We stayed up later than we would have had it been the phone call we had planned, but I'm glad she surprised me. It was intense, how much I missed her after only a day apart.

I even let her talk me into sleeping in. For the first time in ages, I felt well-rested by the time I showed up in my office. Probably has something to do with my ability to accomplish so much today, too.

We're in the back room an hour before opening time and I'm about to get everything I've been overthinking during the past several days off my chest for good and I'm going to hope like hell they listen.

I look around the room and find Carolina, who called this morning after I sent out the mass message about our meeting tonight. She wanted to talk beforehand. I was a bit nervous she was about to tell me to go to hell, but instead, we worked on negotiating the terms of her promotion to manager. I'm feeling great about my decision to take a chance on her.

"As you know, I was out of town for a few days. In that time, I realized some changes needed to be made around here when I returned. I'd like to start by inviting everyone to congratulate Carolina, who, as of today, has been promoted to a management position. She will now be overseeing the bar as a whole five days a week."

"'Bout time you let some slack into the reins, boss," Edith says from where she sits, front and center of the group, making everyone laugh at my expense. "And there's no one more deserving of the promotion," she says, smacking Carolina on the thigh with her paper of the day she's using to cool herself off. She's always claiming the bar isn't too hot, but she runs warm, and doesn't want all her makeup to melt off.

The rest of the staff becomes a collection of claps and voices of agreement as Carolina tries her best not to blush under all the attention.

"I didn't take making this decision lightly. In fact, I've been thinking about it for a while. I'll be the first to admit that I've been avoiding having to delegate many things to my employees, but that will be changing from now on." I look around, "Carolina will now be doing many important daily tasks, releasing me to focus on the business aspect of everything and focus on reclaiming our clientele that was lost in the last several years of my uncle's ownership. If you worked here during that time, you're most likely aware of what I mean by that. That being said, I'd like to open the floor to anyone who might have some money-generating ideas that we could start implementing into the bar. For instance, a good friend of mine had the idea of hosting a trivia night. Possibly once a month, or even once a week, depending on interest." Calling Hannah a good friend doesn't feel right, and I realize that technically we haven't had the right conversation to label anything, but I want to.

"Oh, I love that idea!" Edith says. "I call bartending those nights!" She adds, giggling as the rest of the bartenders try to fight her for the job, dollar signs dancing in their heads, I'm sure.

"No need to fight over the opportunity. We'll probably need to be doubled up those nights, anyway. But I'm glad you're all excited."

"I have an idea!" A college-aged girl says, raising her hand like she's in class.

"Andi, thank you. Let's hear it."

"Maybe I'm wrong, but I've looked for the bar's social media channels when I'm telling people to come visit me for a drink, but have never been able to find them. Could we make some?"

"Yes! We've got that in the works, actually. I'm clueless when it comes to these things, so maybe we could appoint a few people to help keep things relevant. Any takers?"

A few hands shoot up around the room, including Andi's. I point to Carolina who I armed with a notebook and pen to test her new managerial skills during the meeting. "You got those names?"

She nods. "Way ahead of you, boss."

"Don't even know why I asked," I chuckle. "Let's also write down which places we need to create an account." The group rattles off at least half a dozen social platforms to consider. To no one's surprise, I only recognize two of them. "Okay, this is good. Any other ideas?"

"I worked at a place back in college that had different microbreweries come in on Sundays. I don't know the legality of everything, so it would need checking into, but you wouldn't believe the crowds those days would generate," says Phillip, a thirty-something who's working on a tech startup and only needs this job to help pay the bills until it starts to take off.

"Good, thank you, Phillip. Let's write it down."

"To go along with the social media thing, we need to make things more Instagrammable," Victor, another one of my college students, says, looking up from his phone.

I expect him to elaborate, but apparently the blank look on my face isn't enough proof that I need an explanation.

"He basically means photographable, boss," Carolina says. "Like some businesses have very cohesive branding, a logo or brand colors that are recognizable, even from photos with no context."

"I don't know how it works, but my friend was telling me about branding. I'm still learning, but please, write it down. Just out of curiosity, what would make this place more inflammable?"

"Instagrammable," Victor corrects. "But things like a logo on the glasses, or a mural that everyone wants a photo in front of to post online. People eat that shit up, Miles. Then they post it and their friends get FOMO, and want to go take a picture in front of it too. It's a great marketing tactic."

What the fuck is FOMO?

I don't dare ask, because I refuse to keep my employees longer than necessary to answer all my clueless questions. "Okay, I think a mural is out of the question. I spent too much on this paint job to ruin it within a few months of changing it."

"Not necessarily. You've got a huge stretch of brick out front. That would be a great place for it. Might even attract people driving by, too."

"Now there's an idea. Carolina, write that down. I might even know an artist we could hire." I have a buddy from high school that is a literal artist, and he works with every medium imaginable.

The rest of the meeting goes much the same. They toss out ideas I hadn't even thought of, and I tell Carolina to make sure it's written down. But by the end of the hour, I'm filled with a new sense of purpose. I thank everyone profusely, then send everyone besides my opening bartender and Carolina home.

"I think that went pretty well, boss," Carolina says.

I smirk. "Yeah, I think it did too."

The first thing I do when I get to my office later that evening is pick up my phone to send a message to Hannah. Both because I've had a question on my mind all day, and because I want to talk to her.

MILES

Do you know what FOMO means?

HANNAH

Fear of missing out. Why?

MILES

I had a meeting with my employees today. I was clueless about half the things they said, so I was afraid to ask another question.

HANNAH

Oh! What was the meeting about?

MILES

Well, I have a lot to fill you in on, but I officially promoted Carolina to manager today, then we went over ideas for the future of the bar. One of my college students said that.

HANNAH

You're such an old man at heart.

HANNAH

I love it.

Chapter Forty-One

Miles

I spent my entire Friday staring at the clock, wishing for seven o'clock to roll around. It's a few minutes before, and I just parked my truck in Hannah's driveway.

That familiar wave of nerves rolls through my belly on my walk up to the door, even after all the time we've spent together lately. I look down and immediately realize I'm cradling the bouquet in my hands like a baby. I re-situate and step in front of the door, my free hand poised to knock. I barely rap my knuckles twice before the door is thrown open wide and Hannah jumps straight into my arms.

There's an audible snap as she wraps herself around me, but I barely register it.

"Hey, you," I whisper into her neck as I squeeze her back, basking in the feel of her against me. Remind me again why I went so long without this in my life?

"Hi," Hannah whimpers into my chest, where her face is buried. "I really missed you."

I lean back, smoothing a palm over her hair. "I missed you too, honey."

Her eyes are glistening with tears when she finally looks at me.

"You okay?" I ask, wiping at the corner of her eye with my thumb.

Her face contorts as she nods. "Just happy."

I drop my forehead to hers. "Me too."

I slide her down my body until her feet touch the ground.

"These are for you," I say, bringing the bouquet between us. The momentum of the movement causes the entire thing to flop to the side like a broken neck.

"Uh," Hannah says, pushing them back upright and making a show of admiring and smelling them. "They're beautiful."

"I think we broke them during our hug, but I picked this bouquet because they reminded me of our hike."

She drops the hand that was propping them up and they sag back down.

She takes my hand, leading me into the house. "Let's see what we're working with."

Like a surgeon with the finest skills, she peels back the Kraft paper wrapping and carefully pulls each piece from the sleeve. Some are broken too high up to be salvageable, but she puts them behind her ear while she goes through the rest. With a pair of shears, she trims each one in a diagonal line.

"Can you grab that and fill it with water?" She asks, pointing at a huge Mason jar above the fridge.

I fill it about a third of the way full with lukewarm water, and sidle up behind her, reaching around her to set it on the counter.

She's arranging the bouquet just so in her hands. I push her hair behind her shoulder and kiss her on the cheek. She leans her head to the side, elongating her neck and letting me in. I continue planting slow kisses down her neck, inhaling the coconut scent of her skin. She drops the stems into the jar and turns around in my arms.

My hands move to her waist, slippery against the satin tank top she's wearing.

I look into her green eyes, rimmed in black and accentuated with light purple eyeshadow. "Have I told you yet how beautiful you look tonight?"

"Not really," she says, leaning up to kiss my neck. "But I did kind of maul you as soon as you walked through the door, so I think that might be my fault."

"Well," I say, stepping back and grabbing her hands to hold them off to her sides as I make a show of looking her up and down. I take in her low-cut black satin tank top, flowy, olive green shorts that tie in the front, and strappy sandals with her magenta-painted toes. She's biting one of those pink lips—something I don't think she realizes she does while nervous—when my gaze meets hers again. "You're so beautiful. Whether you're all done up like this, or lying on my chest with sleepy eyes, you're the most beautiful girl I've ever seen."

"Shut up," she says with a chuckle.

"I will not do that. I'll keep saying it until you finally believe me. Then I'll keep telling you for as long as you'll have me."

"God," she sighs, then lifts on her toes to kiss me like she doesn't have a choice.

I prop her up and set her on the kitchen counter and she squeals when the back of her thighs connect with the cool granite, but it's quickly forgotten as we deepen our kiss.

Before I know it, her pink lip gloss is all over my mouth. I know because it's slick against my skin and tastes like vanilla. My hands also have a mind of their own, because one is on her thigh, the other has snuck under the hem of her shirt, pressing against her lower back.

"If we don't go do what I had planned for us tonight, we won't be leaving," I say against her lips.

She doesn't move a muscle when she asks, "And what would we be doing instead, Miles?"

I brush my hand higher against her back to find it bare where I expected to find the clasp of her bra. "It would start with your clothes on the floor—"

She pulls back, a huge smile rearranging the freckles on her face. "You promise?"

I groan. "Dammit, woman," I say, planting a chaste kiss on her mouth before pulling her into my arms and setting her feet back on the floor. "There are perishables in the bed of my truck, so as much as I'd like to see where this could go, we're going on our date, damn it."

"Fine," she rolls her eyes, teasing me. "But only because I'm intrigued by these plans you speak of."

We roll up to the lake just before the sun reaches that point in the sky that turns the whole world into honey. Which is perfect, because that still gives us plenty of time for what I've got planned.

"My favorite place," Hannah says, smiling from the passenger's seat.

I unbuckle and sprint around the front to open her door. She's absolutely giddy about the gesture, and that fact weasels its way into my heart, right past every one of my defenses that was useless against her.

I hold out my hand and she takes it, stepping out onto the running board, then jumping into my arms. I assist her to the ground and take her hand. From the back seat, I pull out a blanket and small cooler and we're off to a secret, secluded spot I know.

"It's gorgeous out tonight," Hannah says, staring out at the lake and pretending she's not curious about where we're headed.

The lake glitters with sunlight and there are boats galore out there, enjoying the night in their own ways. I wouldn't mind owning a boat someday, but I'm glad we've got privacy for our official first date.

"Sure is." I stand on a rock and lead Hannah up to higher, steadier ground. "How was your day today?" I ask once we finish climbing the rock wall and have reached the area well above lake level.

"Oh good, I helped mom with some last-minute reception things. She's obsessing over the event, but she did this all to herself." She leans against me a moment before saying, "She asked about you."

"Yeah? What did you tell her?"

Her dimple pops in her cheek as she skips a few times. It's like she's so happy, she can't help it. And that's just one of the many things I love about her. She's never shied away from letting her heightened emotions seep out her pores and into everything she does.

"I told her you make me really happy." I look up at her after she says it, my smile already big. She stares at my mouth. "God, you can't do that when the sun's out, Miles. You'll blind me for good."

"What on earth are you talking about?"

"Your smiles. They're always catching me off guard."

"Good, I've been saving them up for you."

She stops, yanking me back before I even realize she did. "Is that why you've avoided smiling all these years? Saving them for your *one true love*?"

Those three last words come out teasing, but they feel like the truth.

"For you, yeah," I say, looking down at her. The way she's looking at me, my feelings must be written all over my face.

"Are you this way with all the girls, Miles? I've never seen this side of you before."

"What girls, exactly? And that's because there's never *been* this side of me. You've brought it out in me, Hannah. I don't even recognize myself these days."

"Oh," she says, suddenly shy.

"Here we are," I say, as we veer off the path through a tiny clearing in the trees where there's a flat rock cliff that overlooks the lake.

"I've been to this lake a million times, but I've never been here," Hannah says, looking around with that photographer's eye, taking in everything this spot has to give, I'm sure of it. "This is perfect, and we'll have a great view of the sunset here in a bit," she says, confirming my suspicions.

And that's exactly why I brought her here tonight. Because I wanted something that could be just for the two of us, and I knew she'd love it. "Yeah, I've been coming here for years."

"Really?"

I throw the blanket out for us to sit on, then set down the cooler. Hannah kicks off her shoes and finds herself a spot. I sit down next to her, staring out at the view.

"Yeah, it all started when we used to camp down the trail from here when I was young. I was on my bike and probably had no business being here on my own, but it solidified it as my favorite place to escape to for solitude. But that ends right now. I knew you'd love it, so it just made sense to show you."

"I'm the first person you've brought out here?" She asks incredulously.

I pull her closer and let her lean into me as we both look out at the view. "Yeah, of course you are."

"You better be careful, Miles. Or I just might fall in love with you."

"That's the goal, so I will not be careful. Thank you very much." She leans into me harder, and I wrap my arms around her, rubbing my hand up and down her arm. "Want to see what's in the cooler?"

"Yes please."

I flip open the top and pull out glass containers full of meat, cheese, and fruit.

"Yum," Hannah says, going straight for the strawberries,

driving me mad with the noises she makes as she enjoys one after another.

"I wasn't sure what to drink, but I brought a few options," I say, pulling out bottled water, canned wine spritzer, and a beer.

She plucks a wine spritzer out of my hand with an exaggerated smile.

"How does this feel like our first date and our hundredth all at once?" Hannah asks after we've been sitting here snacking for a while. She's snuck her way into the space between my thighs, leaning back against my chest. I've become transfixed by the smattering of freckles on her shoulder. I swear I've kissed it a hundred times, and I can't wait to kiss her a million more times, every single place my lips can reach.

I plant a kiss there before I say, "I'm not sure about you, but for me, there was always a part of me that knew you were it for me. In my head, we've shared so many looks, so many innocent touches, that we've had a chance not many people have to know each other long before we were ever together. So it's familiar and comfortable, but new and exciting all at once. Now we're learning the more intimate parts of each other." I brush my thumb back and forth at the top of her biceps.

She turns around in my arms, placing her knees on each side of my hips and wrapping her arms around my neck. My breaths are shallow, but my heart is pounding inside my chest, having her this close.

"You say some of the sweetest things, Miles," she says, smiling up at me.

"Yeah? Are they workin' on ya?"

She laughs into my lips on her way to kiss me. "Yes," she says, then proves it with her kiss.

We sit there, entwined in the solitude of the trees, learning each other, and exploring each other with tongues, teeth, and fingertips. It isn't until we finally come up for air that I notice the sunset in all its colorful glory behind Hannah's shoulder.

"Honey, you're missing the show going on behind you."

"What if I'm too interested in the *smoke* show in front of me to care?"

"But your favorite color is out there. The one stuck somewhere between pink and orange. You sure you don't want to see?"

Her thumb brushes my bearded cheek. "How do you know my favorite color, Miles?"

"Years of listening."

She laughs like I just told her a joke. "You're unreal, I swear."

"I'm one-hundred percent real, honey. Let me know if you need more proof." She laughs. I play with a tendril of her hair that's turned copper in the golden light. "Come on, look. It's what we came out here for."

She moves to the side, but her gaze stays locked with mine. She brushes her fingers through my beard and into the back of my hair. "I can see it in your eyes. That's good enough for me."

"Yeah? What else do you see there?"

She smirks and says, "Too soon to know for sure, but I think you might like me just a little."

"Yeah, maybe just a little."

She leans in for another kiss, the sky behind her forgotten completely.

Chapter Forty-Two

HANNAH

I spent all week trying to imagine what a first date with Miles would be like. It's been nothing I expected and absolutely perfect.

It's the last glow of twilight when we're walking back to his truck. My lips and cheeks are still tingling from friction with his mouth and beard, my cheeks hurt from smiling, and my heart is so damn full. I'm carrying our blanket and leaning into Miles' side, smiling to myself again, thinking about how blessed I am to even be in this situation.

The looming promise of trouble that lies ahead for us is still there in the back of my mind, but I refuse to let it ruin our night. I'll plan for that tomorrow.

As we reach the truck, my phone vibrates in my back pocket. I pull it out as I wait for him to stash the cooler.

VAL

I'm at Brody's for the night. Just for your information.

There's a winky face at the end. I roll my eyes as I pocket my phone and toss the blanket into the backseat.

"Where to next?" I ask when we're back on the road.

"Well," Miles says, "We could go back to mine, but I have a feeling that I'll get called down to the bar if they see my truck sitting there."

"We wouldn't want that, would we?" I bite my lip, then finally say, "Val will be at Brody's tonight, so we'd have the place to ourselves."

"Yeah?"

"Yeah."

"Sounds perfect. Is that okay with you?"

I nod, scooting across the bench seat and leaning into him for the rest of the drive.

When we're finally back at the house, it takes me three tries with my seat belt until I'm finally free. Miles opens my door, and I jump out, pulling him by the hand toward the porch, and fumbling with my keys on their way to the lock. Miles sets a steadying hand on mine and the key finally slides home, unlocking with a click.

Once I lock the door behind us, I'm pushing Miles back against it. He anticipates the move and has me by the hips before his back makes contact. He lifts me, my feet tangling behind his waist like it's muscle memory. And when he's got me pressed back against the kitchen wall, the entire move feels reminiscent of that night in Durango. The same swarm of feelings is buzzing deep inside of me tonight.

Miles takes his time trailing kisses up my neck, his fingers locking into my hair and pulling down until the long line of my neck is exposed. He's hard against me, his chest, abs and the arms that envelop me. And if I wasn't so high on his hips, I'd probably feel the hard length of him against me, too.

"Bedroom," I sigh against his beard. Then he's carrying me to the back of the house.

When we're past the threshold, he sets my feet back on the ground, our bodies sliding against each other. The bulge in his jeans is prominent against my stomach as we stand there, taking each other in.

There's not a light on in the room, but in the window's glow, I can see the desperation written all over his face. Can he see it in mine?

I raise to my toes to kiss him, his hands finding my ass as he pulls me against him. He trails kisses down my neck, one hand palming my breast.

"Please tell me you're mine, Hannah," he pleads against my mouth.

"Yes, I'm yours, and you're mine."

"That's right honey," he says, moving my hair away from my face to kiss me on the forehead.

"Make love to me, Miles," I say.

He lifts me, depositing me onto the bed as I lie back on my elbows. He takes one leg in his large hands. After exploring the length of it with his fingertips, he unbuckles my sandal and tosses it on the floor. The other follows as he steps out of his boots. He presses me to my back, his hand grasping my neck, then sliding down my chest and stomach slowly as goose-bumps form in the wake of his touch.

"So beautiful," he says as his fingertips dance above the waistband of my shorts. Then his fingers dip inside and peel them off me slowly, never looking away.

He lifts me to sit, and does the same with my shirt, sliding his palms along my skin, the material pooling around his wrists until I'm fully uncovered. I didn't wear a bra tonight, and as he gives each breast the attention it deserves, I work at removing his shirt and tossing it on the floor.

I run my hands all over the expanse of his chest and back, in love with the way his hot skin feels against mine. I work at his belt next, the furthest he's let me go with undressing him. I rejoice when I hear the belt and shorts hit the floor.

He slides me back on the bed, making room for himself to lie on top of me, my touch turning frenzied the moment our chests make contact. His warm skin against mine, and the heady scent of his cologne taking up my space, is intoxicating.

His kisses are hot and slow, taking his time.

I shove his boxers down his hips and he looks up at me briefly, lifting from where he'd been peppering kisses all across my chest.

With my toe, I pry open my bedside table where I stashed the condoms I bought for the occasion.

He takes the hint, and lifts to standing, and I don't even pretend not to check him out as he lets his boxers fall to the ground, fisting his length in his hand. He rips open a packet and I watch as he puts it on.

I wiggle out of my underwear, watching him as he watches me. I spread my legs, finding my clit and working myself as he watches. His chest heaves as he steps closer to me, touching me everywhere, driving me crazy in the best way.

"That's so sexy, Hannah," he says, leaning in to find my mouth. The way he's touching me only turns me on more. When I know I'm more than ready for him, I grab his hips and he looks between us as I guide him in.

He pumps his hips until he's fully seated, resting his forehead on mine. "Fuck," he says, as I pause, still getting used to the feel of him inside me. Then, with his mouth on mine, and my legs wrapped around his waist, we find our pace together.

"You feel so good," he says breathlessly, his fingers tweaking my nipple.

"So good," I agree, savoring the feeling of his mouth on my chest.

I bite my lip, trying to hold back the urge to ask for what I want. It hasn't always gone well with partners in the past. But I push past the fear of it, because I feel safe with Miles.

"Can I get on top?" I ask breathlessly.

He releases my nipple with an audible pop, his eyes hungry. "Absolutely, honey." In a quick maneuver, he moves us so he's lying on his back with me straddling his hips. The position makes me feel so powerful.

His hands hold me up by the hips as we find a tantalizing rhythm together in this new dynamic.

With my fingers splayed and palms pressed to his chest, I swirl my hips, finding exactly how good he feels in this position. And by the heavy breathing coming through Miles' nose, I'm pretty sure he doesn't mind my exploration.

When I lean forward, moving my hands to either side of his head, and it brings my chest closer to his face. He leans up to clamp his mouth around one nipple, rolling his palm in circles against the other.

I roll my hips against his pelvis, the friction of each thrust sending closer to the edge of my orgasm. "Shit, I'm almost there," I say, and Miles pushes my hips down, making him reach a depth I didn't know was possible. My hips jerk involuntarily with each movement as my release overpowers all of my senses. I lean in, taking Miles' face in my hands and kiss him until our tongues are tangling as I ride out the pleasure I know we're both feeling. He drives up into me hard once, twice, and a third time until his release breaks free right after mine.

"Christ, Hannah. You're really trying to kill me, aren't you?" he asks. His fingers clench in my hair at the back of my head as he pulls my mouth back down to his. He tells me everything he hasn't voiced out loud with the sweet pressure of his mouth and his strong arms holding me in place.

I hope he never lets me go.

Chapter Forty-Three

HANNAH

"What was that?" Are the words that wake me the next morning.

"Huh?" I ask, my head popping up from its place on Miles' chest. That's when I hear it, someone pounding against the front door. "Shit, it's probably Val. She always forgets her key at Brody's."

I pop out of bed, fully prepared to run out and let her in real quick, but Miles catches my arm before I can.

"Are you sure? Maybe I should go check that it's not someone scary trying to maim you."

I smile at his protectiveness. "I'm sure," I say, standing again, but he pulls me back a second time. I figure it's a ploy to get me to kiss him, so I play along, leaning over to give him what he was looking for.

But when I pull away, he looks me up and down. "I'm not complaining about the view, but whether it's Val, or anyone else at your door, I think you might want to put some clothes on, honey."

I look down, suddenly remembering my nakedness—a

product of the things we did in this room last night until I simply passed out due to exhaustion.

"Shit," I say, running back to my closet as the knocks at the door get louder.

I toss on a mismatched outfit, blow Miles a kiss, then run to the front door. I unlock it, not bothering to pull back the lace curtain to see who could be on the other side.

"Christ, can't a girl get some sleep around here—" I say, fully intending to give Val an earful about how I could use the beauty rest after arguably the best night of my life, but I stop abruptly. "Holt? Serena! You guys are back early. It is only Saturday, right?"

"Well, good morning to you too. We appreciate the warm welcome home, and I'll overlook the outfit. And the hairdo."

I pull up the hood on my sweatshirt because I can only imagine the way my hair looks at the moment, and my brother, of all people, does not need to see my sex hair.

Oh, shit. Miles.

"Are you going to let us in?" He asks, a wide-eyed Serena looks over his shoulder at me. I have no doubt that she's at least partially aware of what they just walked in on, and it only makes me feel worse.

"Oh, right. Of course," I step back, hand outstretched like a butler letting in important guests. "Please, come in, *Holt and Serena*," I practically yell their names, hoping it will act as a beacon for Miles lying in my bed in the back room not to come out. This coast is not clear—it's littered with empty cans of sparkling wine and bad decisions and possibly Miles' shoes. Shit, where did he put his shoes?

I can't even look my brother in the eye right now, so I do the first thing I can think of and start a pot of coffee. "Well, how was it?" I ask, hoping small talk will carry us through the moment and get them out the door.

The two of them ramble sweet nothings about their honeymoon, and if the circumstances were different, I know

I'd be asking a million questions and hang on their every word. But right now, all I want is to get them out of here.

"That's great," I say, delivering coffee cups to the table as soon as it's finished brewing. I'm already aware they both take their coffee black, but I slather mine in sugar before I find a seat at the table right next to my brother.

"Yeah, what have you been up to while we were out of town?" And am I seeing things, or did my brother's eye just twitch? What does he know?

"Not a whole lot. I have started on your wedding pictures. I can't wait for you to see them all. I thought the sneak peeks I sent you were my favorites, but I've found even more that I love."

"Why not grab your computer and show us right now?" He asks.

My eyebrows shoot up, taken aback. "I mean, I guess I could. They're not all finished, though. I'd rather show you the finished product, if you don't mind."

"Lay off, babe." Serena says, coming to my defense. "You know we woke her up, coming over here. Maybe we should take our coffee to-go."

I love that idea, but don't want to offend them by saying so. Instead, I smile like nothing is amiss. Which I'm sure is conveying anything but that.

Holt looks at me, then back at his wife, his shoulders slumping. "Yeah, okay. Sorry. I was just excited to tell you everything about our trip."

"Okay, well, we could still get breakfast at the diner, if you want. Just give me an hour to get showered?"

Holt smiles, and I know I've placated him for now. "Okay, yeah. Let's do that." And it's like he knows I'm antsy for him to go, because he lies back in his chair and takes another long sip from his cup. Serena's chair scrapes the floor with a long screech as she stands.

"Sounds good. Holt, let's go, shall we?"

He looks up from his cup like he's surprised Serena's in such a hurry to leave.

"Okay," he says, still in disbelief as he stands and chugs what's left of his coffee before walking out of the house behind Serena with a small wave. Over his head, I see Miles' truck parked out on the street, my heart pounding in my chest as I wait for him to look at it and put two and two together. Thankfully, it's just far enough down the street that it doesn't look like he's visiting me. But it's still close enough he'd have to have some questions. But instead, he jumps into the driver's seat of Serena's small SUV. I lock the door behind them, just in case, and spring back to my bedroom.

When I burst through the door, I find a shirtless Miles sitting up in my bed looking like he'd been half expecting it to be Holt.

"What did you do out there, entertain them with a full English breakfast? Christ, I thought they would never leave. Wait—" he says, switching to a whisper. "They're gone, right?"

"Wow, you're cool as a cucumber, aren't ya? Thank god it wasn't *me* hiding in *your* bedroom. You would have broken and told him before he could even finish saying good morning."

"Sorry," he says, brushing his hand back and forth through his hair, leaving it sticking up all over the place. "I just thought I had one day of blissful ignorance before reality came knocking."

"Literally," I say, recalling the sound we woke up to.

Miles chuckles, but the humor doesn't stick around. "I was hoping we'd still have the day. What's your plan?"

"I agreed to breakfast in an hour at the diner. You could come with me?"

"Do you think a public confession is a good idea?"

I shrug, a reel of worst-case scenarios playing through in my mind. "Might keep you two from killing each other, at least."

"You really think he's going to react that badly?"

"I don't know. It feels like he knows something, though. I half expected him to walk back here and find you for himself. He was almost too calm and aloof."

"I think he knows, too. But why would he pretend not to?"

I sit on the side of the bed and Miles pulls me into him. "What if he's testing us, waiting for us to tell him?"

Miles kisses the side of my head, then leans against my shoulder. "Shit."

"Whatever, it's going to be fine. Let's jump in the shower for now, then we'll worry about that later."

Miles ran home for a change of clothes after we spent a little too much time in the shower, but he should still be able to make it on time. He asked if I wanted him to pick me up, but we decided that driving separately was probably smarter.

But when I park in front of the diner several minutes later, his truck is nowhere to be found. When I get inside, I spot Holt and Serena are already sitting at a table near the back. I bite back my nerves and wave at a few people I know sitting near the door. I head their way, checking my phone in case Miles canceled. But my phone has no notifications.

I shouldn't be worried that he hasn't checked in, given the fact that his phone was dead when he left my house, but with my brother back in town, I feel a black cloud following me around, and I can't get rid of that sensation.

We say our hellos, and I try not to act like anything's amiss, even when the waitress takes our order a few minutes later. It's not like I told anyone that Miles was coming to breakfast, but ordering in his absence doesn't feel right.

Maybe, even after all that insistence that he couldn't wait to have our relationship out in the open, he decided it wasn't a good time. And I can't figure out why.

"You okay?" Serena whispers as the waiter chats with Holt.

I fake a smile and nod, sipping on my water so I don't have to make eye contact. I know she wants to pry more, but the waiter leaves and Holt turns back to us.

"So tell me how the honeymoon was!" I say, mustering as much excitement as I can while trying not to look at my phone every five seconds.

They both fall into sync, finishing each other's sentences, as they recount their favorite stories of their tropical getaway. Then Serena admits the excitement of it all was rerouted a few times due to the morning sickness that has begun to kick in for her.

After being told about the baby at the end of their wedding night, and a quick departure the next day, I hadn't had much time to grasp onto the reality of my brother becoming a dad, or Serena carrying a life inside her tiny little belly. I find a renewed excitement in the news, and watch as they talk over each other, telling me about the morning they found out Serena was expecting and every new experience they've had since.

And it's somewhere within that conversation that I realize I want this too. This feeding-off-each-other, finishing-each-other's-sentences kind of love that I've been able to witness for the past few years between Serena and Holt. And it isn't just some abstract thing, but attached to a particular person. To Miles.

The guy who promised he'd see me here, that he'd show up for me—that he wanted this like I do. But he's not here now, and I'm trying to give him the benefit of the doubt, but it's easier said than done after years of giving away too much of myself, only to have no one willing to show up for me.

"Have you seen Miles since the wedding?" Holt asks well after I've finished my pancakes.

I'd been zoning out before he asked, so I'm not sure how

we got on the subject, but I've just been going through the motions since I sat down, worried sick about Miles, but also a little angry that I wasn't worth the time it takes to notify someone that your plans changed.

"Uh, yeah. I have a few times. You know what? I'm so sorry to have to do this, but I'm actually not feeling well. Would you hate me if I cut this short? I promise I'll be over at mom and dad's all week to prepare for the reception. I just— need to get home pronto." I hold my hands against my stomach, although the pain is radiating from a place about a foot higher than that.

Holt holds up his hands. "Please, say no more. Go."

I hug them both, and try to ignore Serena's knowing, worried look she's throwing at me.

"Again, I'm so sorry," I say, but turn and start speed walking toward the door. As soon as I'm out on the sidewalk, I sprint to my car. Thankfully, I'm able to hold it together until then, but once the first tear falls, I end up crying the whole way home.

Chapter Forty-Four

Miles

"Oh, there you are! Thank god you're finally here. I've been sitting out here all morning." A voice I know all too well, but haven't heard in months calls the moment I jump out of my truck at the bottom of my apartment stairs.

I squint against the morning sun, but I'd know that stature anywhere. She's thinned out a lot in recent years, and her hair is now almost completely gray. My mom is leaning against my door.

The high of the past several days leaves my body immediately upon the sight of her. Not only because she's here, but because I know I won't be going anywhere, anytime soon.

"Mom," I say, each step up the stairs feeling like I'm wearing shoes made of concrete. Dread fills me the moment I see her eyes are glistening with tears.

On a hunch, I grab my phone from my back pocket, but a click of the side button reminds me it's dead. But I don't need to see the calendar to know what day it is. My baby brother should have turned twenty-five today.

That realization is like a shock to the system. With everything going on, I'd forgotten to dread this day's approach like I do every other year. This year, I'd been happy. I'd been living, just like my therapist always reminds me that I should do. It's no good to drown myself in my feelings and bury them so deep that no one knows they exist.

Hell, I'd been proving those feelings existed, hadn't I? I like to think that Hannah saw that I was trying to be more than the silent grump she's always known me to be.

"My baby," Mom says, when I pull her into my chest. But I know from many years of our interactions that she isn't talking about me. She's weeping for my little brother. Her baby that she lost so many moons ago.

It was a freak accident in the backyard. I told him to wait for me, that I'd be there in a second, but he went out there without me. He'd fallen off his bike, out of a tree, or landed weirdly off the deck a million times. He'd even climbed the outside of that wooden swing set enough times that our family called him a little monkey. But that time, he fell and hit his head just right.

I was the one who found him lying there, unconscious. I can still see the gruesome scene laid out in front of me when I close my eyes.

Where some families take a lesson like that and advocate for it, trying to save others from going through the same thing, ours just fell apart. I've been learning how to live with the guilt of it since the moment it happened. I think a lot of that has to do with my parents' insistence that it was all my fault for several years after we lost him.

After a lifetime of leaving us to our own devices ninety percent of the time, they placed all the blame on me. And I held it like the world on my shoulders for years until I broke under the weight of it.

Therapy hasn't miraculously made me believe I'm innocent in all of it. But it's given me ways of coping with the feelings I've bottled up for so long they'd practically fossilized inside my heart.

But my mom doesn't believe in that sort of thing. I'd step foot on the moon long before I ever see her step foot in a therapist's office. She has a lot to unpack, not only from losing her son so young but also from what I've heard of her childhood, too. After therapy started working for me, I tried to suggest it for her too. Her reply was, "I'm alone in life, and I always will be. I don't need some shrink to tell me that."

I tried to fight her on it, but quickly gave up. Between losing my brother, my parents practically ignoring my existence from that day on, and my dad walking out of our lives when I was a teenager, I've realized people find it easier than I do to leave, and trying to help someone who refuses it is a waste of precious time, because we only get so much of it.

So I hate to admit it, but I tolerate her when she's here, but force myself not to get involved when she's on one of her stints of completely forgetting I exist.

I unlock the door and lead us inside. "Go ahead and sit," I say, heading to the cupboard for my tea kettle I haven't used in a while and get it on the stove. Digging into the back of another cupboard, I find an old box of English breakfast tea. One I bought to keep for emergencies (AKA the very infrequent visits my mother makes).

I pull my phone out of my pocket to warn Hannah about what's going on, but I'm once again reminded that it's dead. I toss it onto the counter with a loud clack.

"Please don't tell me you have your father's damn temper now too," Mom says under her breath. Just quiet enough to make me think I wasn't meant to hear, but loud enough she knows I *accidentally* did.

Losing my brother ripped my family apart, and although there was plenty of tension in our household, my father never hurt her, barely ever raised his voice. She was the one who yelled and became a bitter soul the day her baby died, and she's never recovered.

"Sugar?" I ask, although I know she'll decline.

"Gave it up again," she says from the couch.

I don't think giving up sugar is what dropped all that weight, I think, but don't say anything.

I let the tea steep and turn to lean against the counter. "So where have you been lately, Mom? It was like you suddenly fell off the planet. You didn't answer your phone, and mail bounced back too."

Her eyes go shifty as she shrugs, "Around."

I nod, knowing that's all I'll get out of her right now.

I sit at the opposite end of the couch when I bring her mug over to her, handling it with care even though I've seen her hold hot plates that would singe off my fingerprints if I ever attempted it.

I listen to her ramble on about her life's happenings for several minutes, but she still hasn't given any hints as to where she's been since I last saw her several months ago.

What are you doing here, Mom? Are the words I want to ask, but I know she'll come out swinging if I do. Instead, I bring up the subject I've always dreaded—not because I refuse to think about him, but because I've always had to think of him in private to not set off one of my parents. "I miss him too, you know?" I say, blatantly talking about my brother to her for the first time in years.

She immediately breaks into a sob. "I'll still never forgive you for that day," she says, and it breaks something inside of me.

If she blames me for it, then why does she come to me when she needs to talk to someone about it? I ask myself. It's a question I'll never have the answer to.

Almost like she can hear my thoughts, she asks. "But you're all I have left now that your father left me, too. And I don't think you even love me anymore. I'm not sure what I was thinking coming here."

She moves as if to stand, but I push down on her shoulders to make her sit. "Even if you feel that way, you're here, and you're not in any shape to drive back to wherever it is you came from. Just rest, and you can come and go as you please."

"I think I'll go lie down," she says, setting her tea down without taking so much as a sip.

She knows exactly where to go in my tiny apartment, because she's been here just enough to use me whenever she needs it.

I follow her into the bedroom, collecting a change of clothes.

From my pillow, she asks, "Have you realized yet how far over your head you are with that piece of shit bar yet?" I don't know how she found out I own it, and I don't care.

Just once, I wish she could talk to me without an insult coming out of her mouth, but that wishful thinking hasn't done a damn thing for me for almost two full decades, so I'm not sure why I even bother with it anymore.

"No, Mom. It's actually been pretty great," I say, but regret it as soon as I say it. I know she was fishing for information, and I just gave her exactly what she wanted. If I'm not careful, she'll strut her way into the bar and empty the cash register before she leaves later tonight.

But ever since I was a kid, I've always wanted to prove to my parents that I'm more than their fuck up son who's responsible for his little brother's death, so I can't hold myself back from trying. "I've got a great team I can actually count on in that bar. A lot better than what Uncle Stu did when he was the owner."

"You're still trying to live in your grandpa's world. You always did look up to him, but he was the only one too blind to see what you did to Silas. You don't deserve to be happy and successful. Your brother never got the chance *because of you*."

The words roll right off my back. They're nothing I haven't heard spew from her mouth before. I sometimes wonder if the words she's saying are really meant for me, or if she blames herself and says these things to take it out on me. After all, my parents frequently left Silas in the care of a minor. With the way we fended for ourselves growing up, it's a miracle I lived to tell the tale. Either way, I'm done with consoling her and I'm done with this conversation.

I have no idea what time it is, but maybe if I can get a change of clothes, I'll make it to breakfast with Hannah, Holt, and Serena. That's my focus now.

I slam my bedroom door a little harder than necessary, but I can't find it in me to care.

I change my clothes as fast as I can, and come out ready to speed across town to Hannah. But before I can swipe my keys and phone off the counter, my front door swings wide open, nearly hitting the wall on the other side with the force of it, leaving a raging Holt standing in my doorway.

He walks in, not bothering to shut the door.

I take it he knows about Hannah and I, by the way he looks ready to ring my neck.

"Holt, I know whatever you're here about, your anger is probably warranted. But please be quiet," I say, looking back toward my bedroom door.

"Why?" He bursts, "Who the hell's in there?" He takes two large steps across the space, like he's about to barge into my bedroom, but I rip him backward by a fist in the back of his shirt.

Holt turns like that was the last straw for him. He winds back, but I stop him with a hand to the shoulder.

"My mom's here. She got here this morning. It's Silas' birthday today, and she was inconsolable. She's sleeping in my bed."

He takes a deep breath to regroup.

"Shit, I'm sorry, man."

"Yeah, well, I need to get the hell out of here before she wakes up. Tell me why you're here."

Holt bites his cheek, still looking like he's ready to throttle me. "Really, Miles? You want to act all innocent here?"

I scratch at my beard, finding no way out of this but the truth. "Is this about Hannah?"

He pokes a finger at my chest. "Damn right it's about Hannah."

"I've been wanting to talk to you about that—" I start, unsure of exactly where I'm headed with it, but get cut off before I can figure it out.

"What the hell did you do to her?"

That gives me pause. The most recent thing I can think of is something I will not be giving him details on.

"She was distraught at breakfast and I couldn't figure out why."

"Shit, breakfast is already over?"

"Yes, it got cut short when Hannah left complaining that she wasn't feeling well. But I saw her checking her phone a million times and *your* name on the screen," he says, poking my chest. "That and the fact that I saw your truck parked down the street from her house this morning tells me just about all I need to know without straight up vomiting. Now what the fuck did you do?" He shoves at my chest, and I fall back against the counter in defeat.

"Distraught, how, exactly?"

"Like you did something to ruin her day. Now fucking tell me!"

"I was supposed to be at breakfast this morning, but then I got home and—" I throw up my hands. "This happened.

"Christ, you *were* in her house this morning, weren't you?" His eyes are like lasers. "I knew it! Damn it, Miles."

"I've been wanting to tell you, and I'm sorry I didn't. We were exploring the possibility of us being together, and I didn't know how to approach it. I didn't want to ruin our friendship before your wedding."

"How long has it been going on?" He asks incredulously.

"Actually, you know what? I don't want to know. But I swear if you hurt her, you're dead to me."

"I'm in love with her, Holt. If I hurt her, it was completely unintentional. So can I go tell her this, or do you need more of an explanation before I do?"

"No, go," he says, waving me away. "I just can't believe it worked," he says as soon as I pass him.

I stop and turn back to him. "What worked?"

He has the audacity to laugh. "You really didn't see it?"

"If you don't stop speaking in riddles, I can't be held accountable for what I end up doing to you, man. My patience is running so fucking thin. My phone's dead, and I can't call Hannah, so tell me what the hell you're talking about. Please."

Holt studies my face like he's suddenly afraid to admit whatever it is he has on his mind.

"Holt—"

"Yes, I know. I'm sorry, it's just, I think this is going to piss you off even more."

"What could possibly do that?"

"You and Hannah, spending all that time together while helping plan things for our wedding—it wasn't a coincidence. Me showing up late to the bar with the ring in my pocket, leaving you all those appointments to do together." He scratches a hand through his hair. "I've seen the way you two looked at each other for years, man. I tried to bring it up to both of you on more than one occasion, and neither of you wanted to hear it. I figured if I put the opportunity in front of you, you two might finally figure it out. Looks like that's exactly what happened."

"You fucking knew this whole time?" Holt must see the fury in my eyes because the smile drops off his face, and he backs up several steps. "This whole time I was grappling with my feelings, you were the mastermind in the shadows manipulating me?"

"No, it's not like that. I was trying to make you both see what I've seen for years. You're both too damn stubborn, and worried about how I might feel about it, so you shove it down deep, like you do with everything else. Just be fucking happy, man. I'm not here standing in your way. I never was. But I swear, if you don't go fix that sad fucking look I saw on her face—I know I'm small compared to you, but I will find a way to kick your ass."

I shove at his chest, writing kicking his ass on my mental to-do list for later, because I don't have time for that right now. I can't believe I was freaking out about this for no reason at all.

Chapter Forty-Five

MILES

I'm standing at Hannah's door after knocking, praying for an answer. But the longer I stand there, the more I lose hope.

I knock harder until I finally hear footsteps approaching, and I don't know how to describe it, but by the sound of the footsteps, I can tell it's Hannah's gait.

The steps stop and I wait on bated breath, waiting. Nothing.

"Honey, please open the door."

The lock clicks, and it's Hannah, alright. And her auburn locks are secured in one of those buns she loves to wear. But it's her eyes that grab my attention. They're bloodshot, small particles of her mascara dotting her under eyes like she's been crying for quite some time. I hate that I'm the one who did this.

"Hannah, I'm so sorry."

"You didn't show," she says, her voice breaking. "Why?"

"I know, and I can't imagine how you interpreted that. Can I talk to you?"

She bites her lip, nodding as she joins me outside. Not inviting me in the house isn't exactly the best sign, but hopefully explaining myself will give her proof that she's got nothing to worry about.

She leads us to the bench on the porch that overlooks the front yard, but gives us privacy from the road, thanks to a well-placed tree.

"I had every intention of being at breakfast. But I got back to my place and was completely blindsided by my mom standing at the top of my staircase. She was distraught," I say, trying to find the right words to explain it in a way that Hannah will understand without having to give away every single detail to the point that it makes me emotional.

I turn my hand face-up between us. "Can I hold your hand?" I ask without thinking, but thankfully she nods, placing her hand in mine.

I link our fingers together and squeeze, more for my own benefit than anything.

I take a deep breath, then continue, "It's his birthday today, and she takes it pretty hard. But I have a hard time consoling her when she's like this because she tends to take her pain out on me."

"Oh, Miles, if I had known—" she says, but I cut her off before she can make an unnecessary apology.

"There's no way you could have. I don't talk about him as much as I should. Besides, I've even been too preoccupied to realize it was coming up, which makes me feel even more terrible."

She leans into me, snuggling against my shoulder, and I wrap her in my arms, pulling her onto my lap.

"I'd like to tell you everything there is to know about him sometime, if you're willing to listen."

She pulls the back of my hand that's tangled in hers to her mouth, leaning her lips into it as she meets my gaze, and letting it linger, as if to say she's here for me without saying a word at all. Then, with tears in her eyes, she leans her forehead against mine. "I'd love to know every single thing that's made you the man you are today, including him."

"Thank you," I say. I look down at our hands and start playing with her fingers, putting off what I'm about to say. "We'll get there, but right now I just need you to know that whether my phone is dead, or I'm out of town, or busy at the bar, I'm all in with us. I may not always be able to be there in the moment, but from this moment on, I'm always going to be there for you. Because I'm so in love with you, there's no going back for me. You're my girl."

"Oh, thank fuck. I was so worried you'd changed your mind about us, Miles. I didn't know what the hell I was going to do, having to forget everything that's already happened between us."

She says it all with her face smashed against my own, like she's afraid of what will happen if she lets go of me.

I pull back and look her in the eyes. "I'm never going to change my mind about you, honey. I'm crazy about you, and every moment I get to spend with you, I'm just falling deeper in love with you."

"I love you, Miles. I have for a really long time, and in so many different ways. And although this way feels so new to me, I can already tell it's going to be my favorite."

"Mine too," I say, pulling her into me.

We come together, our kiss starting slow and soft. It's amazing I could be so in love with someone I'm still learning. But in the end, it is Hannah, someone I've cared about for years. Someone I'll care about for years to come. Years I'll spend getting to know the ins and outs of everything about her.

Just when our mouths are finding their own rhythm together, she pulls away abruptly. "I guess the only thing we have left to do is tell Holt."

"Oh," I say, suddenly remembering that detail I have yet to share. "I already did."

"What?" she yells, lightly smacking my chest. "Why didn't you tell me? What did he say?"

"He already knew."

She gasps like I just admitted her brother is a serial killer.

"This whole wedding planning thing? It was a ruse to bring us together and, as he said, *help us find each other.*" I say, using air quotes on that last part.

Hannah's jaw drops, as I assume mine would have if I'd talked to Holt under different circumstances than I did earlier.

"He knows I'm ready to kick his ass. Want to go do it together?"

She looks at my mouth, then back to my eyes. "I can think of something else I'd rather do first."

"Honey, slow down. We've got all the time in the world," I say as she drags me behind her into the house.

"Is it so bad that I want that time to start as soon as possible?" She asks, pushing me into her bedroom and closing the door in our wake.

"I suppose not," I say, lifting her chin to examine the streaks of mascara still under her eyes. I lift the hem of my shirt, hooking a thumb in it to wipe them away.

"Oh god, I bet I look like a mess."

I kiss her forehead. "My beautiful mess. Besides, I was the one who put those there. I'm sorry, honey."

She lifts to the tip of her toes, planting a kiss on my lips. "I forgive you, and I'm sorry I didn't trust that you had the best intentions."

"No need for apologies. You know that now, right?" She nods as her hands move to my waist, undoing my belt, then my jeans, shoving them both down my hips. While I'm trying to decide whether I should help or slow her down, she latches onto the hem of my shirt, pushing it up my chest, her fingernails leaving goosebumps in their wake. She's clearly got an agenda, so I'll let her take whatever she wants to. It's all hers, anyway.

I grab the hem of her threadbare tank top and she lifts her arms to let me pull it over her head. She shimmies out of her pants, revealing hot pink lace. She catches me staring and smirks, pulling me down for a kiss. Her tongue swipes across my mouth and I groan, opening to let her deepen the kiss. Just as my palms find her ass, she runs the heel of her hand down the hard length of me.

I groan at the friction, and it spurs her on as she reaches past my waistband, taking me in her fist, but lets go too soon.

She bends over her nightstand, coming up with a handful of condoms, and tosses them on the bed.

I barely sit before she's pushing against my chest. I lie down when I realize it's what she's looking for.

She slips her lace thong down her long legs and I'm transfixed by the show she's giving me, propping myself up on my elbows so I don't miss a moment.

She pulls at the hair tie holding her hair on the top of her head, and I watch it fall in waves, barely brushing her chest as it settles. I ball my hand in a fist, forcing myself back from reaching out.

"Tell me what you want, honey."

She fingers the waistband of my boxers, pulling down to free my erection, then says, "I want you. All of you."

She oughta know she already has it.

"Done. Now get over here."

She plants one knee on the bed next to my hip, swinging the other around until she's straddling me. My hands find her hips like they're magnetically attracted to the spot. She grabs a square from beside me on the mattress and rolls it on before settling herself over me.

Circling her hips, she's busy finding what she likes against the hard length of me. She's already soaked, coating me with her wetness, but I bring my thumb to the apex of her thighs, moving in a circular motion until she moans against the extra friction. She settles her hand on mine, showing me exactly how she wants it. When her hips start setting the pace, I slide a finger against her slick center, and slip it inside, forcing her thighs further apart with my other hand.

"You're so wet for me, Hannah."

She moans, swiveling her hips faster than before. I add another finger, working her clit as her whole body begins to tremble under my touch. She bucks her hips against my hand until she's savored every last second of her orgasm. The next thing I know, she's slumped against my chest, trying to catch her breath.

I run my fingers through her hair, the auburn tendrils splayed all across her freckled back. I run my hands across the constellations, loving the feel of her soft skin.

"Just need a second," she says, breathless.

"Take your time, honey," I say, trying to forget how hard I am underneath her, and just how good the brush of her tits feels against my bare chest with every heaving breath.

She sits up, reaching to kiss me on the mouth. It's more tongue and teeth than it is lips, and each time she nips at my bottom lip, it shoots a tingling sensation straight to my dick.

She grabs me in her fist, standing up on her knees. I lift her the rest of the way as she guides me inside her.

I lost count of how many times I was inside her last night.

Our bodies together like this still feels brand new to me, but it feels different from any of the other times I've had her. I'm not sure if it was finally telling her I love her, and hearing it in return. It could be finally having our relationship out in the open for those who matter. I can't quite pinpoint it, but it feels like more this time.

Hannah's hand combs through her hair, holding it out of her face as she rides me. She looks so fucking sexy like this.

I fist her hair with both hands, bracing her body with my

arms. She latches onto them, using the extra support to move more freely. The new freedom it allows changes the pressure of each thrust of my hips, and brings extra friction against her bundle of nerves.

She looks down at me, pure ecstasy in her expression as her eyes tell me everything I need to know. "I love you," I whisper.

She whimpers, like my admission only heightens her pleasure, her hips slamming into me with more force. "I love you too, Miles."

She moves her hands over mine, her fingertips caressing my knuckles, then trailing lower. "And these forearms don't suck either."

My hands flex in her hair, my arms rippling with the movement. Her eyes are glued to the spot.

"Oh, fuck" she says, her breaths coming shallow, hips jerking in random intervals, and I drive up into her harder until her entire body writhes with her release.

I flip us so Hannah is looking up at me, lying on her back.

She pulls my mouth down to hers, and with a few more thrusts, I find my release, too.

"Fuck," I say, breathing against her neck as I wait for my heart rate to come down. "You feel so good."

She smiles so big her eyes are merely slits. "We fit together so well. Who could've guessed?"

"I had a hunch," I say.

She laughs, and I can feel the rumble of it against my chest. She wraps her arms around me, locking them behind my neck as I bring my mouth to hers. Her kisses are slow and sensual, a reflection of the fact that we have all day—an entire lifetime—to enjoy each other.

Chapter Forty-Six

Hannah

After a week of preparation—and finding time in between to spend with Miles—the night of Serena and Holt's reception is finally here. I talked them into hiring a photography colleague of mine to take some photos of the night. They almost didn't, but finally listened. To have Miles' arms around me in a touchy-feely way, rather than a prom-pose way as we stand with the newlyweds for photos feels absolutely surreal, but also somehow so right.

We've been busy ever since this relationship came to fruition, so I'm excited about what comes after this night when we can finally slow down and enjoy life a little. But I'm not mad about the present circumstances—a romantic day full of love, Miles' secretive touches every chance he gets, or the stolen kisses between conversations with family and friends. I never expected it, but Miles isn't one to shy away from showing me affection, no matter who's around.

The other day we thought we were alone in my parent's living room. But Holt walked in when Miles' hand was sprawled across my ass and our tongues were fighting for dominance.

Ever the dramatic one, Holt made a gagging noise, and just to annoy him, Miles didn't stop until Holt yelled, "Okay, you two. I'm okay with this relationship, but I don't need to watch this."

He turned to him and said deadpan, "Then leave the room."

I've never seen Holt with such a powerful death glare before. It's a miracle that Miles is still with us here today.

But right now, Holt's too busy to pay attention to anything but his bride, as he should be. Her belly is still as flat as it always has been, but knowing they're expecting, I keep catching glimpses of him settling a hand over it, and Serena looking completely content, setting her hand on his too.

"You look so damn beautiful," Miles says in my ear, coming up behind me, wrapping an arm around my waist and kissing me on the cheek.

I turn in his arms, wrapping my own around his shoulders, and smile up at him. He's dressed in his unnatural colors of navy blue and white today, even though he tried to talk Serena and Holt into letting him wear his usual wardrobe. Serena was the one to give him a death glare on that one. He didn't even try to argue.

I like it. I've seen him in his element a million times, so it's kind of nice to see such a rugged man all tailored and proper.

"You do too, even though you hate your outfit," I say, leaning back to look him up and down.

"I don't know. Every time you look at me like that, I'm pretty sure I become a little more okay with this ridiculous getup they've got me wearing," he says, tugging at the neck of his collar that's still closed with a tie.

I set my hand on his to stop his fussing. "Only about an hour or so stands between you and a loosened tie and pushed up sleeves." Miles' forearms—I shiver at the thought of them. There's just something about them all out in the open like that.

"From the faraway look on your face, I'm sensing you think that's a good thing?"

I lean into him, unable to hide the smile his presence brings out in me. "A very good thing."

"You're such a horndog."

I smile, "Only for you." I feel his phone vibrate in his pocket between us. "How's the bar doing without you this weekend?" I think he's finally starting to get the hang of standing off to the side and letting someone else take the lead, although it's been easier said than done.

"Carolina's been great. I don't think there's really much I need to worry about anymore."

"Good, because I was hoping you wouldn't have to run off and put out fires later tonight. I need my dancing partner by my side."

"At your service, milady," he says, bowing toward me and making me laugh.

We've finished eating barbecue, and everyone's making their way toward one of those makeshift dance floors you can rent out. There's been music playing softly through dinner, but the DJ is now sitting at his booth playing more upbeat music at full volume to draw in the crowd as the sun lowers in the sky, burnishing the scene in gold.

Some of the dinner tables are strewn about the backyard, but Holt, Serena, the family, and closest friends were all upstairs at the tables and chairs on my father's pride and joy—the deck. It was amazing, no longer having to hide my feelings for Miles in front of the group of people I love most in the world. And all the beaming smiles aimed at us from all directions as we did mundane things like whisper in each other's ear were enough to deduce they're pretty happy for us too.

Even now, the easy way Miles holds my hand as we walk

through the backyard as he talks to Holt on the other side of him feels perfect. It's like he's trying to remind me he's right there with me, even if his attention is pointed elsewhere. I hope I never take this feeling for granted.

But Serena steals Holt away and onto the dance floor as the fast tempo morphs into their first dance, a heartfelt ballad about finding the one you always needed. We stand on the edge in the grass as Miles settles in behind me, watching the happy couple from his place with his chin on my shoulder. Seeing the love ooze from each of them as they sway brings tears to my eyes, and Miles must notice, because he kisses me on the temple, squeezing me closer around the middle.

When their moment is over, a Journey song my parents played enough during my childhood for me to know all the words starts to play and you can feel a rush go through the crowd as everyone starts to pile on the dance floor. To my surprise, Miles pulls me out there too and finds us a place close to Holt and Serena. As we start to sway, I turn to our other side and find Val and Brody snuggled together. Brody's singing every word in Val's ear, and although she's laying her head in the crook of his neck, you can still see her smile peeking through.

Miles' tie is nowhere to be found at this point in the evening, and his shirt is unbuttoned just low enough to see the curve of his collar bone. When he rolled his sleeves, I swear I stared at him like he was a stripper, teasing me by inching them up his forearms until they were in full view. I was so transfixed by his veins popping under the dusting of hair there that I didn't realize he'd caught me watching until he waved a hand in front of my face. My gaze moved to his face, where his dimples were barely visible under his beard.

Although he's still dressed in clothes he wouldn't usually wear, he looks more himself when he's not so buttoned up.

As we find the rhythm of the music with our arms and

hips, Miles kisses the crown of my head, then leans into my ear. "I love you."

I make eye contact with Holt over his shoulder in the same moment. He smiles at the sight of us, then whispers in Serena's ear, who looks at us. We both smile at each other, then I turn back to Miles. "I love you, too."

After the past several months of trying to hide my growing feelings for the guy holding me in his arms, this moment feels surreal. I truly felt that in pursuing Miles, I'd cause problems between two men who have been best friends for almost their entire lives. But Holt has been surprisingly cool about it all, despite the little jabs he gives.

The song ends, and we move differently, trying to match the new beat. As we begin to find it, Holt walks up beside us.

"Mind if I cut in?" He asks his best friend, who turns to me and smiles.

"Please do," he says, landing a quick kiss on my forehead before he walks off in the direction of Serena, who is freestyling it in the middle of a sea of people by herself. He twirls her, and they start dancing at a faster pace than the music calls for.

I turn to Holt, who's smiling at his best friend and his wife, acting like fools. Then he grabs my hand, moving the other high up on the small of my back. Instead of putting my hands around the back of his neck, I squeeze him in a hug.

"I'm so happy for you."

He wraps me in a hug, and when we both pull back, he smiles down at me. "I'm happy for you, too," he says.

A twinge of nervousness spikes through my belly. This is the first time he's brought up the elephant in the room since Miles informed me that he knew about us.

We've seen each other plenty the past week, but there was never enough down time for an actual conversation. I guess it's happening now.

"Are you?" I ask with a grimace.

He grasps my shoulders, leaning into his answer. "Of course I am, Hannah. I've never wanted anything more than to see you happy. And I want that for Miles, too. If it just so happens that two of the most important people in my life make each other happy, then I'm happy too."

"I'm sorry we hid it from you at first. I thought the timing was terrible. We tried to keep things platonic, but—"

He cuts me off by palming my face like we're five and eight all over again and I'm the annoying little sister. "Yeah, yeah. I get it. One thing I ask is to never know the details. Please and thank you."

I laugh out loud at that. "I definitely wasn't going to give you any, I promise."

"Did you two realize you were being set up that whole time?"

"Yeah, and why was that?"

Holt looks away, chuckling. "As much as you've tried to hide it all these years, I wasn't blind to the way you always felt about him. Back then, I wrote it off as a crush, but when you started dating—and let's be honest, striking out in love in your early twenties—I just wished there was someone who would treat you right for once. And I know it's not my place to tell you who you should be with, but it became clear I was the one standing in your way." He looks out into the crowd of people around us, then turns his gaze back to me. "Because that's what you deserve, Hannah. To be treated right by someone who actually understands you. And I know Miles does both of those things. It was the night of your housewarming party when I first realized it. All my attention was on Serena, but I heard you laughing. I looked up to find you and Miles with your heads bent together. You had your head thrown back, laughing the way you tend to do, but what really got me was the smile on Miles' face. We both know he doesn't do that often, so it was my first hint that he was as taken with you as you were with him."

I think back on that night, and how I felt about all the things Holt is talking about, and how scared I was to find him at my door when I hadn't invited him—thanks, Val. That was the night I decided to pull back from Miles.

"Then as soon as I noticed it, it seemed like you were never around anymore if Miles was there. I kept trying to find ways for the two of you to see each other, but you'd ask who was going to be there, and didn't show up anytime I mentioned Miles. For a while, I was convinced you had a boyfriend you didn't want us to know about."

I turn and find Miles and Serena laughing as they bounce around the dance floor, making everyone in their wake laugh at their antics.

"Do you remember that night Val and Brody brought me home from my disaster of a date?"

Holt's face drops, "Of course I do, how could I forget?" he asks, because I had some choice words for him the next day after he wouldn't let it go when I asked him to stop asking for details about my date from hell. In his defense, he was margarita drunk and clueless about how uncomfortable I was.

"After that night, I knew I needed to take a break from dating. I was still in that phase when I realized there was a chance that Miles might be interested in me. There are still days I wonder if I'm going to ruin everything by moving too quickly."

"Well, for the record, you were never the problem. None of those people were good for you. You and Miles are kindred spirits. That's the difference."

"Thanks, Holt. That means a lot."

He stops dancing and hugs me. Holt's hugs have always been the type that make me feel so cared for, bur this one is special. It's a confirmation that things between us will be okay, despite my fear that they wouldn't be once he knew the truth.

"Now I'm going to go get my bride away from my best friend. Love you, sis."

"Love you too, Holt."

I'm practically dead on my feet at the end of the night, but I'm still barefoot out on the dance floor with Miles. He's been the perfect boyfriend today. But the best part? He's still been a good friend to my brother. That's one thing I made him promise me. I didn't want him to pull away from his friendship with my brother to be with me. There were several times tonight when I went off to dance with Serena, Val, and the girls, and we came back minutes later to find them jabbering away just like they always have.

Miles softly sings along with the song that's playing over the backyard speakers about thanking God he's mine. Every single lyric he murmurs in my ear rings true to our story thus far, sending goosebumps up my arms despite the thick, humid night air.

"I love you," he says into my hair when the song ends. I'm still getting used to hearing declarations like this out of the mouth of the one person I've admired for years. I look up into his eyes, dark but twinkling, thanks to the white lights hanging overhead.

"I love you, too. And I can't believe you're mine," I say, extending onto my tiptoes to kiss him, the rest of the world disappearing for a moment in time.

Epilogue

NINE MONTHS LATER

HANNAH

"You about ready?" Miles calls from the kitchen as I put the finishing touches on my makeup in the mirror of his bathroom.

I've made this place my second home in the past several months since our relationship became official.

"I'm on my way!" I yell as soon as I've blotted my lipstick in the mirror, then run out of the bathroom.

I slow to a stop when I approach Miles. He takes my hand and spins me around. "You look beautiful, honey," he says, finishing the spin with a quick kiss on my lips. "Ready?"

"Yep!" I say, pushing him toward the door. "Are you excited?" I ask, bouncing my way down the steps, unable to hide my excitement.

When Miles reaches the bottom, he waits for me, holding out his hand. We walk to the back door of the bar together.

"I am excited. A little nervous, though. I'm hoping everything goes off without a hitch."

I pat his butt and lean into his side. "Well, you've got a whole team of us behind you to help with any disasters. It might take some time to iron everything out, but just remember—people are here to have fun and to get their drink on. As long as we can check both boxes, we'll be fine."

"I'm glad one of us has all the confidence in the world," he says, holding the back door of the bar open for me. I land a kiss on his cheek as I walk under his arm down the hallway. A buzz of excitement is rattling through my chest when I hear all the chatter happening in the main room.

It's a packed house tonight, and I'm so damn proud. When I make it to the doorway, I stop on a dime, my jaw dropping as I look around. I see plenty of people I know, and even some I don't, taking up all the tables in the place.

I turn back to Miles, who's still slowly creeping his way toward the doorway like he's scared of what he'll see. The moment he reaches the threshold, his eyes grow wider as his head swivels in all directions.

He's the perfect picture of disbelief. He's been putting in the work, hoping for this kind of turnout these past several months, and it's finally happening.

I point through the front windows, "Look, people are out there taking photos in front of the new mural!" One of Miles' old classmates painted an Ireland-inspired mural outside a few weeks ago and people have been loving it.

He smiles big enough for his dimples to pop through the layer of scruff on his cheeks and steps up behind me, wrapping his arms around my middle. "You know I owe a lot of this to you, right?"

I shake my head. "No, Miles. This was all you. I just put some ideas in your head. But you and your employees did all the work. I'm so freaking proud of you."

"Hey, lovebirds! Get your cute butts over here!" Ella yells. We both turn to find her sitting at a booth with the rest of our friends, decked out in their hunter green *O'Harrow's* t-shirts. They're ready to kick ass on the first ever trivia night at *O'Harrow's Irish Pub*.

As we walk over, I notice everyone huddled around Val. My mouth drops open, turning to Brody, who is already looking at me with a huge smile on his face.

"Ohmigod," I say, practically ripping Miles' arm off as I pull him up to our table of friends and dive toward the middle, where Val has a very shiny piece of jewelry glittering on a very important finger.

"You're engaged!" I shriek with no chill whatsoever. "Holy shit, my best friend's engaged!" I yell, everyone near us cheering at that news.

Two weeks ago, I accompanied Brody to his appointment at a local jeweler, so I knew this was coming. But that doesn't change the fact that I'm absolutely freaking out right now. I finally pull everyone else out of the way and tackle my best friend. The only sound I hear is her muffled laughter against my ear. "Congrats, bestie."

When I get back to Miles, he pulls me in for a kiss.

"See? I told you they were in love, Chuck."

I turn to find Chuck and Freddie sitting at the bar, smiling like they're up to no good.

"Yeah, Chuck. I suppose we are."

Miles

"Is this where you kill me?" Hannah jokes as I flip on my blinker and slow down so I don't miss the gravel driveway. I turn down it and drive slowly, rolling down my window as Hannah does the same in the passenger's seat. It's just warm enough today to sense that summer is close, but now that the sun is down, it's a breezy sixty degrees. The perfect night for a fire, which is something I hope to do plenty of here someday, but right now I've got something else in mind.

"Not even close, honey."

Hannah was at my side all day, rubbing my back because she knew I was nervous. What's funny is, she thought I'd been nervous about the first trivia night at the bar. Don't get me wrong, I was, but this is the main event.

I reach the end of the gravel, a grove of trees surrounding us, save for a small shed off to the east.

"Okay, seriously. Where are we?" I turn to find Hannah looking back at the road like she's afraid someone will catch us out here.

"Stay there and I'll be around to show you the way."

I pull my handy headlamp from the side compartment in my door and click it on as I jump out into the grass.

I round the truck and open Hannah's door.

She immediately wraps her legs around me and pulls me in close as I lean against the truck. I click my headlamp off so I don't blind her.

"You're the only man who can make one of those things look sexy," she says, tapping the lens of my light.

I pull out the extra one I stashed in her door and hold it up. "And lucky for me, you're the only woman who can do the same."

She slumps against me at my hinting she needs to wear it.

"I promise it'll be worth it."

She sighs and puts it on as I lift her out of the truck and onto her feet.

"Are you sure we won't get into trouble for being out here?" She asks as we both click our lights on.

I chuckle, lacing my fingers with hers. "Positive. Now come on."

I pull us toward the markers I spent most of my morning staking out the yard with.

"What's this?" Hannah asks as we step inside the barrier.

"So many questions."

"I only ask so many questions because if I don't, you won't even talk."

I roll my eyes at her reasoning. "Okay, stop here," I say,

pulling on Hannah's arm until she's standing in front of me, encircled by my arms.

"Can you imagine it?"

"Imagine what?"

"This will be our foyer someday."

She turns in my arms, catching my cheeks in her hands. "What?"

I point my lamp up so I don't blind her, meeting her eyes.

"You see those stakes?" I ask, pointing all around us.

"Yes," she says breathlessly.

"That's the perimeter of our house. That is, if you'll live out here with me."

"Of course I will," she says and now I can see the tears collecting just above her lower lashes, ready to spill. "You really want to live with me?"

"Is that really a question? We're already together all the time. I want to make grilled cheese with you, and I want to watch you over your shoulder as you work magic on the photos you take. I want to bitch about the pub with you, and run all my ideas by you. I want to visit Stars Hollow for forty-four minutes every night while you scream at the TV about how much you hate Dean. I want to kiss you, and make love to you, and I want to fill every nook and cranny of our closets with things we own together.

"I love you, and I want to build a life with you, Hannah. And now that Val's engaged, and that tiny space above the bar is too small for the two of us, I'm ready to put this piece of land my grandpa left me to good use. What do you say?"

She jumps into my arms and right before she kisses me, she says, "Yes."

Acknowledgments

It feels like just yesterday that I was writing the acknowledgments for my first book, and here we are on book number two? What?!

First and foremost I'd like to thank my husband and dog for dealing with me while I stared at my computer for what felt like two months straight. I'm sorry about the missed snuggles and belly rubs.

Thank you to my family for all your support of my writing career. Whether you're in my immediate family, or extended. Your love has been felt since becoming an author. I did not expect it, but I appreciate it nonetheless.

Thank you to everyone who sent me beautiful messages after reading *Coffee & the Contingency Plan*. It's because of you that we even made it to book number two. Becoming an author is scary, and doing so with anxiety is even worse. Thank you for reading my words.

Thank you to my amazing beta readers. Your feedback elevated this story to completely new heights that I didn't even know were possible. And because of you, I now know it's a charley horse, not a Charlie horse *face palm*. Alaina, Kelsey, Paige, and Tori—THANK YOU for reading my words when they were very, very rough. You're all the best.

To my other early readers, Janni, Natalia, Kristen, and Vanesa, you helped more than you realize. Thank you so much.

To Sam (Ink and Laurel), my cover artist. You took the idea straight from my head and added even more detail than I thought possible. You're an amazing person, and so talented. I'm blessed to work with you. Thank you for everything.

To Kristen, my editor, thank you so much for helping tighten up my manuscript your help was greatly appreciated. And thank you to all the love you give to all of us indie authors. I think I speak for us all when I say we appreciate all the support you give. Thank you!

And, of course, I can't end these acknowledgements without mentioning all the beautiful friends I've made on my author journey. I anticipate the day I finally get to meet you all. But a special thanks to: Miranda Valentine, Alaina Rose, Kelsey Schulz, Celia Ochoa, K.H. Anastasia, Holly Whitworth, Sarah Estep, Katie Gowritely, Taylor Lynn, Maria Patrick, Anna P, and Heather Garvin. In some way, shape, or form, you kept me going while writing this book, and I am so grateful for your insight and friendship!

About the Author

Jessica Costello is a creative-minded adventure enthusiast who enjoys writing love stories that are sweet, mixed with heat and humor. She's living her own rom-com with her husband and their Mini Aussie in the Midwest.